Re-Make / Re-Model

I tried but I could not find a way

Looking back all I did was look away

Next time is the best we all know

But if there is no next time where to go?

She's the sweetest queen I've ever seen (CPL593H)

See here she comes, see what I mean? (CPL593H)

I could talk, talk, talk, talk myself to death

But I believe I would only waste my breath

Ooh show me

The Boggabilla Aboriginal Medical Clinic was somewhere between delightfully rustic and somewhat rundown, but it was the key to indigenous health in that town of several hundred. The waiting room had two old and grubby brown, floral couches donated many years past, posters on a large noticeboard covering everything from children's vaccinations to Covid-19, and a desk, chair, and the printer / fax on a stand for receptionist, Asha Reid. Auntie Margaret left the nurse's room to stop in front of Asha's desk.

"Nurse Janet told me you're leaving us," Auntie said.

"It's time to return to my kin," Asha said.

"We're going to miss you."

"I'm going to miss you, Auntie."

"Goodbye Asha."

"Goodbye Auntie."

Auntie Margaret limped out the door where Janet turned the sign from open to closed.

"That's it for you," Janet said. "Thanks for everything."

Just then Keith, the doctor and Janet's husband, came from the consulting room.

"Let's go," he said.

They headed into a late October evening, humid but less intense than daytime.

"Hi Asha!" a familiar voice called.

"Hello Billy," Asha responded.

"Can I ask you out?"

"You can ask me but my answer's the same."

"No?"

"That's right Billy."

"I'll ask again tomorrow. See you Asha."

"See you Billy."

He walked away while grinning brightly. Asha had to admire Billy's perpetual brightness and not letting things get him down. It was a strength, not only of Billy but many of the indigenous men in Boggabilla, and also a weakness. There were many times in life when you had to get serious or be left behind. They reached the 'T' intersection of the Newell Highway next to the Crooked Knee Hotel and stopped.

"You've been great, Asha," Janet said. "Having an indigenous receptionist has been a blessing. You've been helpful with our clients, especially when we had to deal with sorry business."

Asha was pleased she could help in different ways, and really she had mixed feelings. "I've enjoyed working here this past year. If I was settled I would stay but that hasn't worked out for me."

"I know. How are you getting home?"

"The bus to Inverell leaves early on Monday morning; then I catch another bus to Grafton, and then another bus to Sydney. There I stay overnight to catch the train to Cootamundra early the next morning. I'll stay at the hostel across from Central Station like I did on the way here."

"That's a journey and a half!" Keith exclaimed.

Asha grinned. "My time here after high school has been a good experience in many ways."

"Good luck Asha," Janet offered with a hug.

"Yes, good luck," Keith also offered.

"Good luck to you both," Asha said. It was fantastic for a white doctor and a white nurse to be the backbone of the clinic. Asha went into the hotel dining room, cool and dark after outside, to buy a soda water from the bar. There she put her glass on a table before ordering a battered barramundi, which was the least over-filling on their menu, to sit and wait.

"Hi Asha,"

John, another indigenous guy who wanted to date her.

"Can I share your table?" he asked.

That wouldn't do any harm. "If you want to," Asha said. "Do you know I'm going home on Monday?"

"Home, home?"

"Home to my kin."

"Yeah, alright."

A few indigenous guys had shown an interest, mostly older than Asha now aged 18, but there was something wrong with Boggabilla and it flowed through the people who lived there. They were born in it, they were raised in it, and they couldn't get away from it. A few white guys had talked with Asha but there was something wrong with them, too. When the evening and weekend pastime was doing laps of the town, endlessly driving around and around in their utes; that showed something was wrong. Beyond that, she didn't trust those white guys with their Holden utes with lights, bull bars and custom paint jobs, jeans and cowboy hats too. Asha knew they wanted something but only that one thing, and while some local indigenous girls were naive enough to fall for sweet talk and flash cars, Asha wasn't like that. Indigenous guys were less likely to have jobs, where the combination of fortnightly welfare payments with nothing to do was – destructive. Even though indigenous guys were more genuine, Boggabilla flowed through their veins. Asha suspected, no knew, that most remote towns and settlements in Australia were the same. Her barramundi arrived.

"You can have some of my chips, John," Asha said.

"Thanks Asha, you're the best."

Asha burst out laughing at his sincerity. "Sorry," as she bit her lip to smother her smile. The fish was good, the chips were great but the salad was dreadful. She finished her fish; she guessed that was healthy enough, while John ate half her chips so that helped. The salad: a lettuce leaf, a sliced tomato and a sliced onion, Asha ate that too. She put her knife and fork down.

"That's it John, now I have to go home."

"I can walk with you for protection," he said seriously.

"I'm safe this early in the evening. What are you doing for work these days?"

"Nothing."

There was no shame in that because there was nothing to do. Asha stood.

"Goodbye John," she said.

"Bye Asha."

Asha's home was only five minutes away, being a furnished one-bedroom flat in cream-painted fibro cement sheeting, basic but practical. Better that it had bars on each window and three deadlocks on the door, such things were essential in Boggabilla at night. As always Asha turned the airconditioner on; even though noisy it was essential too. But what to do? Facebook to post her last day of work experiences, followed by television and an early night. Asha lay on the couch away from the cold draft of the airconditioner with her smartphone in her hand.

* * *

Asha seemed like in a dream; the strangest dream. Her dream was vivid though. Slowly the mist parted – Asha realised that screaming, shouting and swearing wasn't a dream. She sat up to peel away the curtain beside her bed where, bathed in eerie, orange light, two indigenous men were pushing and dragging an indigenous woman along the footpath. Asha watched for a moment as the woman twisted and bucked until one man shoved the woman hard enough to fall. Asha reached for her smartphone, entered the pin which seemingly took forever, and dialled 000.

Two rings. "Police, fire or ambulance?" a female asked.
"Police."
A few more rings.
"Police emergency," another female voice announced.
"Two men are attacking a woman outside my flat."
"Which address?"

"Sixty-five McIntyre Lane, Boggabilla, New South Wales."

"A unit will be despatched. Is the incident continuing?"

They'd gone back to dragging her again. "You have to be quick."

"Units are responding to a major disturbance in town."

That would be right. Asha ended the call before realising she couldn't just watch this woman being dragged away to some dreadful fate. No, Asha knew this woman's fate. Asha put her smartphone down to hear her bundle of keys rattle. That might help. Asha grabbed those keys, unlocked the deadlocks on her door, and ran while slipping the key ring over her index finger to reach the two men standing either side of the woman again prone on the ground.

"You two, get out of here!" Asha warned. "Police are coming so get out!"

"You're a pretty girl," one leered.

"Keep away from me."

He grabbed for Asha who swung at him, just clipping his face.

"Fuck!" he exclaimed as blood oozed from a gash on his cheek.

"I told you to keep away."

"Fuck you!" as he grabbed for Asha again, who swung at his bare arms and felt her keys cut through his flesh.

"Fuck her," the other said as he pulled at Asha's left arm, just as she swung at his face. He stumbled as if drunk and fell to the ground.

"I'm warning you!" Asha threatened.

"Let 'em go," the first guy said.

"Yeah, alright," the other said as he got to his feet.

They strolled away as if nothing had happened. Asha knelt by the woman, a bit fat though not that old, maybe late-twenties or early thirties.

"How are you?" Asha asked.

"My head hurts."

"Can you stand?"

Slowly, unsteadily she got to her feet. Asha recognised the signs; she didn't smell of drink so she must have been into drugs. Asha put her arms around this woman.

"My home is just over here. Let's get you inside and cleaned up."

They staggered along the path.

"My name's Asha."

"I'm Sue. Thanks for helping me."

"I called the police...."

"They never come," Sue interrupted.

Asha knew that. *What was one more rape?*

Asha led Sue into her flat, and guided Sue to sit on the bed before deadlocking her door. Asha half-filled the basin in the bathroom with warm water, grabbed the facecloth, dampened it before using it to wipe dirt and grime from Sue's face and arms; on that balmy night Sue wore a tie-dyed dark and light blue t-shirt over baggy, black shorts and brown sandals. Asha then rinsed to wipe Sue's legs before throwing the facecloth into her laundry basket.

"You're not from here, are you?" Sue asked.

Asha returned to the bedroom. "I'm from the south," she said.

"You must think terrible things about us," Sue said while looking up to Asha standing.

"We were invaded, our land was taken from us, and there are things that can be done to help us but they aren't being done."

"Yeah, okay."

"Do you know those men?" Asha asked.

"Yeah, I know them. They know my old man's doing time and they came around with some weed. I told them a few joints and nothing more but they got other ideas. When Ben grabbed for me I ran, and I got a long way before they caught me, then you came along."

"Do you have children?"

"They're with my parents. Better that than taken by the state."

"Have you been busted?" Asha asked.

"Can you guess what for?"

"Weed."

Big smile.

Asha picked up her smartphone to see it was two-seven in the morning. Police hadn't shown up either.

"Will those guys wait at your place?" Asha asked.

"Yeah, they might. Weed makes you horny, you know."

"You should have thought of that."

"I know. Like I said, you must think terrible things about us."

"I don't." Asha thought. "Do you want to spend the night here, Sue?"

"I couldn't."

"I'll sleep better knowing you're safe."

"I suppose you will. Alright, I'll sleep on the floor."

"Don't be silly, there's room in this big bed. I'm used to sharing with cousins in single beds."

"Like we've all done."

"It's late so we should sleep now. Make yourself comfortable."

Sue took off her sandals, t-shirt and shorts, and her bra. Asha slipped into her bed next to the wall; Sue got in to lie as far away as she could get.

"Sleep well Sue."

"You too Asha."

Still the police hadn't come.

Overreach

by

Mark Morey

All rights reserved

Mark Morey

http://markmorey.blogspot.com

978-0-6487869-9-3

Published In Australia

May 2021

Cover: Canberra at night looking across Lake Burley Griffin towards Parliament House

Other Works by Mark Morey

The Red Sun will Come - June 2012

Souls in Darkness - August 2012

The Governess and the Stalker - July 2014

Maidens in the Night - September 2014

One Hundred Days - September 2015

The Last Great Race – April 2016

The Adulterous Bride – October 2016

No Darkness – March 2017

In Our Memories – November 2017

Blood Never Sleeps – March 2018

Ketsumeidan – October 2018

Yuejin – Aim High! – July 2019

Wenge – Destroy The Old! – July 2019

Ice – February 2020

Across the Border – July 2020

Burrangong Creek – January 2021

- Akubra hat – a broad-brimmed hat often worn in rural parts of Australia, made from the felt of rabbit fur.

- Australia (The Commonwealth of Australia). Founded on 1 January, 1901, after referendums in each colony of Australia saw a majority vote in favour of the proposed Australian constitution. After federation, each former colony became a state within the Commonwealth of Australia, retaining control of day to day government activities such as transport, healthcare, education, police and law and order. The sixth-largest country in the world, Australia is the oldest, flattest and driest inhabited continent, with the least fertile soils. This dryness and lack of soil fertility is why Australia has a population of only 26 million, with most of this population concentrated within a well-watered and fertile strip of land between the Great Dividing Range and the sea. Inland Australia is dry, flat and magnificently, endlessly spacious.

- Australian Federal Police (AFP). The law enforcement agency of the Commonwealth of Australia, responsible for trans-national policing, protection for commonwealth government facilities, and also providing day-to-day policing for the city of Canberra.

- Australian Security and Intelligence Organisation (ASIO) – Australia's national security agency responsible for the protection of the nation from espionage, sabotage, acts of foreign interference, politically motivated violence, attacks on the Australian defence system, and terrorism. ASIO is broadly comparable to the British Security Service (MI5).

- Canberra. Founded in 1913 as the seat of government of the Commonwealth of Australia, Canberra is a planned city with a population of 426,704 (2019), and is the wealthiest city in Australia with a median adult income of A$52,532 (2016). Canberra is located within the

Australian Capital Territory occupying an area of land partitioned from the state of New South Wales.

- Centrelink – the Australian Commonwealth Government social security agency

- Closing The Gap – an agreement between Commonwealth and State and Territory Governments of Australia to reduce disadvantage among Aboriginal and Torres Strait Islander people with respect to life expectancy, child mortality, access to early childhood education, educational achievement, and employment outcomes. After 11 years, most of the 16 targeted achievements of Closing the Gap aren't on track.

- Cootamundra. Originally settled in 1861 and located in the South-West Slopes region of New South Wales, Cootamundra has a population of 6,782 (2016), and is relatively poor with a median adult income of A$28,288 (2016). By car or bus, Cootamundra is 164 kilometres west of Canberra (not far by Australian standards), and 90 kilometres north-east of Wagga Wagga.

- Meth – methamphetamine

- New South Wales. The colony of New South Wales was first settled in 1788 as a convict settlement on Sydney Cove, later to become the state of New South Wales within the Commonwealth of Australia. New South Wales extends from a relatively narrow strip of fertile and well-watered land on the coastal side of the Great Dividing Range, to fertile but less well-watered agricultural land west of this mountain range, including the South-West Slopes region in the western foothills of the Great Dividing Range. Further west in New South Wales the quality of soil deteriorates to semi-desert, and to desert in the far west. Rainfall is variable in inland New South Wales with drought never far away. Water is a precious commodity in most of inland Australia, and in most of inland New South Wales. As result farms are large, while inland towns and cities are small and sparsely spread. The New South Wales school year runs from late summer to early the next summer (late January to early December).

- Ute – utility (cab and tray vehicle)

- Young. Originally settled in 1861 and located in the South-West Slopes region of New South Wales, Young has a population of 7,170 (2016), and has a median adult income of A$34,528 (2016).

- Wagga Wagga - means 'dancing and celebration' in the Wiradjuri language. Wagga Wagga is commonly known as 'Wagga'. A relatively prosperous inland city in the Riverina region of New South Wales, with a population of 56,442.

- Weed – cannabis

Chapter One

Luke waited by the staircase of the Parliament House carpark, discreetly observing. It was quiet that Sunday morning due to Covid-19 ticketing restrictions.

"Luke Monk?" a male voice asked.

Luke spun around. "John Connell?'

"Yeah mate."

"Pleased to meet you," but they couldn't shake hands.

"Let's go inside and I'll show you around."

Luke climbed the staircase beside the well-dressed John Connell, who on weekdays worked in Parliament House Information Technology. John had the same objectives as Luke and the rest of his team, just arrived in Canberra.

"Luke," John said. "The only ways into Parliament House are the loading bay further along the carpark, and where we're about to enter. Visitors and hand luggage are screened at both entries, like at an airport."

They reached the top and beautiful views across the lake towards Canberra city centre in one direction, and across the lake to the War Memorial in the other direction. At reinforced glass doors they showed tickets downloaded to smartphones to a security guard, before placing personal items in trays to be screened while they passed through a metal detector. That level of screening made an assassination attempt quite difficult. Once reunited with smartphones and keys, they headed off.

"When parliament is sitting and the Prime Minister is on the premises, visitors aren't allowed into Parliament House because of the Covid-19 risk," John said. "I could get you press passes but there are other issues, like the security screening we just went through."

"How can you get things like press passes?" Luke asked quietly.

"The previous Liberal-National government imposed budget cuts and headcount targets. Because of reducing headcount targets they've hired more contractors like me, while because of budget cuts, security assessments are quite basic these days. As long as you don't have a criminal conviction, you're fine."

Luke understood as they passed a gallery of paintings of past Prime Ministers. Inside Parliament House was amazing: spacious, light, bright and looking brand new. Unmarked green-painted walls, parquetry floors so highly polished they were like mirrors, lush light grey carpet away from areas with foot traffic; simply incredible luxury. Surely the most beautiful and luxurious parliament house in the world, and perhaps the most beautiful and luxurious building in Australia. John climbed a staircase with Luke beside, to walk along a glass-walled gallery.

"This is the entry to the House of Representatives," John said. "The public gallery is just through here."

They passed a security guard at a desk to enter the light, bright and spacious chamber in pale green, lit by natural light flooding from big windows close to the tall ceiling. It didn't need artificial lights and indeed lights weren't turned on.

"Green represents the House of Commons in England, while this pale shade of green mirrors the colour of Australian gum tree leaves."

John continued to the front where they looked down to floor of the House of Representatives.

"All entry doors have security guards, while even though visitors aren't allowed when parliament is sitting, press and staffers use these galleries. On the left of the long table are government benches, on the right is the opposition, and at the rear beneath us are independents. The Prime Minister sits at the far end of the left front bench."

Luke looked down to that bench. "We'd never get to her," he said.

"You can't get a firearm or an explosive into the building, and even if you could, getting to the Prime Minister will be difficult."

"What about where the Prime Minister lives?"

"Come with me for a drive, like I promised."

Back to the carpark where Luke climbed into the front passenger seat of a red Mazda 3. Soon they were on their way around the circles and roundabouts of Canberra's planned road system. For visitors, Canberra was extremely difficult to navigate, but for a local like John it looked too easy. They merged from a circular one-way road onto a six-lane arterial road with a broad, centre median.

"The Prime Minister's lodge is on the left where the police car is parked," John said as they zoomed past.

Luke contemplated the car, two officers, and two and a half metre tall, beige-coloured brick or concrete walls with razor wire on top.

"We'd never get in there," he said.

"There's a security detachment inside and CCTV," John said. "Even if you got inside you wouldn't get very far."

"How does the Prime Minister get from there to Parliament House?"

"By car."

"With her security guards," Luke commented.

"Yes."

"Let's go to Hawker."

John took an exit to the left, it was an arterial road like a freeway, and then roads and roads in all directions, to eventually emerge in familiar territory. John parked his Mazda near the Airbnb. Soon they were climbing stairs for

Luke to unlock the door of their flat. Alice was in the kitchen where she turned the stove and rangehood off.

"Alice," Luke said. "This is John."

"Hello John."

"Hi Alice."

The other two guys stood: one taller and one a bit short.

Mike and Jake, this is John.

Greetings were exchanged.

"Please sit," Luke offered.

There was room for three on the burgundy-coloured, leather couch while Luke and Alice sat on the matching burgundy leather armchairs.

"We'll share a little bit about our pasts, but no specific details. I'm Luke Monk and I'm 47 from Sydney, where I was laid off after Covid-19. Shortly after that we had a change of government and a female, Muslim Prime Minister. Female is bad enough but a Muslim of Pakistani descent isn't acceptable. Alice?"

"I'm Alice Monk and I'm 45 from Sydney. Like Luke I was laid off after Covid-19. That was a bonus because I can help with what needs to be done about Prime Minister Yaseera Devi. After that, regardless of how our economy goes, I'm going to be a stay at home wife. I'm reclaiming my femininity, which isn't possible with full-time work and not enough time for my husband."

"Alice is a Tradwife now," Luke said, to nods of approval. "Men can only be masculine when women are feminine."

"Agreed," Alice said.

"John?"

"My name's John Connell, I'm 24, I live here in Canberra, and I have a girlfriend where she thinks we've got more than we really have. I work in Parliament House Information Technology where I can help you all with this cause."

"Next?" Luke asked their new arrivals. Both wore dark t-shirts, jeans and brown, ankle-high boots. Mike was in fine shape but Jake was a bit too slim.

"I'm Mike Thomas, 24 from Sydney, and I'm a qualified mechanic, only the dealership was taken over by an Indian who put his brother-in-law in charge of the workshop. After that I was stood down because of Covid-19. I have a partner in Sydney."

"Is your partner a Tradwife?" Alice asked.

"That's not her thing."

"I understand."

"My name's Jake Tanner, I'm 21 from Sydney where I work as a food delivery driver, which is the best job I can get. We have a few issues in Australia, including women taking our jobs and migrants taking our jobs too. Now we have the Muslim offspring of migrants running our country." A pause. "Is it alright for us to stay here?" Jake asked.

"I hope you don't mind single beds in the second bedroom for as long as this takes."

"That's fine," Jake said.

"No problem," Mike said.

"Don't worry, I'll look after my three men," Alice said. "Cooking, washing and so on."

Luke was glad Alice clarified that.

"John," Luke said. "Do you have any ideas?"

"I'll access the Prime Minister's diary and let you know when she's out and away from Parliament House security. With advance knowledge of her appointments, we can plan something."

"That's amazing!" Alice exclaimed.

"Be patient, and when I get in touch, be ready to act." John stood. "I need to go."

"Is your girlfriend expecting you?" Alice asked.

"Yeah, she is. Like I said, she thinks we've got more than we've really got. I just toss her a few bones every now and then."

"You could try a collar and a chain!"

John laughed. "I'll try that one day. See ya."

He headed out. Alice returned to the kitchen while Luke settled down to relax. Soon enough their mission would play out.

Chapter Two

As his coffee machine hissed and bubbled in the background, Matt went to his tablet where he had an email from Gemini Modelling Agency.

'Thank you for your request. We have attached portfolios of three models which we are sure will meet your requirements.'

The first was Sophie Weaver: date of birth March 17, 2003, age 17. Natural blonde hair, blue-grey eyes, height 175cm, bust 86cm, waist 64cm hips 89cm, bra size B, dress size 8. Second-generation Australian from Swedish ancestry, living in Young. Matt scrolled her portfolio shots where she had a flawless fair complexion, waist-length blonde hair, gorgeous light blue eyes and a captivating smile. Pictures: an evening dress, jeans and a blouse, a brief bikini, and tiny denim shorts with a halter top. Tall, slender, pretty, leggy, well-proportioned. Definitely.

Next was Asha Reid: date of birth October 10, 2002, age 18. Black hair, brown eyes, height 175cm, bust 86cm, waist 64cm hips 89cm, bra size B dress size 8. Wiradjuri living in Cootamundra. Matt frowned as he went back to Sophie Weaver to find they were identically-sized to the centimetre. Matt scrolled Asha's portfolio shots, unusual name, where she had thick black hair to about her shoulder blades, a lovely coffee-coloured complexion, dark eyes, full lips curled in the centre a lot like Kate Moss, delightful. First Nations people in New South Wales were mixed-race, but Asha with her black hair and darker complexion looked more indigenous than many. Pictures of Asha in an evening dress, slacks and a blouse, a mini skirt and a different blouse, a brief bikini, and jeans and a t-shirt. Like Sophie Weaver she shone from casual to dress-up, but with those proportions she would. Asha Reid: more than definitely for his shoot.

The last was a white girl, Olive Cooper from Wagga Wagga, aged 20. Nothing special and in fact a bit plain.

'Thank you for these models and I'll use Sophie Weaver and Asha Reid. I'll contact them now, regards, Matt Taylor.' Send.

Now Matt needed another model, either from asking Sophie and Asha or using a local girl shot separately. Matt rang Sophie, who answered "hello" in a sweet voice.

"Hi Sophie. My name's Matt Taylor. Gemini Modelling Agency put me onto you for a photo shoot for a bikini calendar featuring Australian country girls in the Australian bush, probably on Friday. Are you interested?"

"I'm interested."

Matt wondered. "Seeing as you're in Young and my other model is near there, do you know somewhere we can shoot?"

"Koorawatha Falls just north of Young is a bush reserve with a lake and a waterfall."

"That sounds good. Do you have friends who might be interested in modelling for me? Remember this is a bikini shoot for a calendar."

Silence for a moment. "There's one, Emma Edwards. I'll get Emma to text you some pictures but I know she's great in a bikini."

"Is Emma your age?"

"Emma's 20."

"You know the award rate: 507 65 for the day."

"I'll let Emma know. Is there a demand for bikini calendars these days?"

"Garages and sheds are always brightened by beautiful young women in bikinis."

"I know a garage like that!" Sophie exclaimed.

"Do you have bikinis?"

"I've got a few bikinis."

"Can you bring them, and I'll bring bikinis in your size too. Pack lunch and a drink and bring that." Matt thought through his plans where the day before would be ideal. "I'll stay overnight in Young or nearby. We'll start the shoot at 10 in the morning at Koorawatha Falls and it'll take most of Friday."

"I'll be there, and if you pick Emma she'll drive me." A pause. "You want Australian country girls but really we're immigrants, even Emma whose family has been here for many generations."

Matt smiled to himself. "Yeah, I know. My next call is an indigenous model."

"Cool!"

"I'll see you on Friday, Sophie."

"See you."

Matt hung up. Next call, and again a sweet "hello."

"Hi Asha. My name's Matt Taylor. Gemini Modelling Agency put me onto you for a photo shoot for a bikini calendar featuring Australian country girls in the Australian bush, all day Friday just north of Young. Are you interested?"

"Yes Matt, I'm interested in your bikini calendar shoot."

"Do you have friends who might be interested in bikini modelling?"

"I know what it takes to be a model and I don't have family or friends who would be right."

"That's fine; I have two other models, and three's enough for the concept I have in mind. Can you get to Koorawatha Falls just north of Young?"

"Someone from my family can give me a lift."

"I'll be staying overnight so I can drive you."

"That's great, Matt. I'll text you my address."

"Do you have bikinis?"

"I've got two bikinis."

"Can you bring your bikinis and I'll bring some in your size too. Pack lunch and something to drink, and I'll pick you up at nine in the morning on Friday."

"I'll see you on Friday."

"See you Asha," and Matt hung up.

Sophie and Asha, although young, handled that with maturity. If they could transform their maturity into this shoot, Matt was sure this would work. Just then his smartphone 'tinged' with a message which was Asha's address. Not long after he got three pictures from Emma Edwards in a black bikini, and proper pictures not blurry selfies. Beautiful, a full figure but not a gram of excess weight; a real bikini model.

Matt composed a text response: *'thanks Emma you're perfect i would like you to model for me do you have bikinis and whats your size'* Send.*

'lots of bikinis and im size 10'

'bring your bikinis and i'll bring bikinis too bring lunch and drink for friday at 10 at koorawatha falls' Send.

Moments later from Emma: *'kk'*.

Young millenials.

Chapter Three

Luke emerged from their bedroom, freshly showered and shaved. The dining table was set with knives, forks, teaspoons, coffee mugs, a sugar bowl and a plastic bottle of milk, while Alice was in the kitchen with the rangehood rumbling.

"Hi guys," Luke greeted Mike and Jake at the table waiting.

"Hi Luke," they echoed.

"When Alice said she was looking after her three men," Jake said. "She wasn't joking."

"What are you cooking for breakfast?" Luke asked Alice.

"You'll find out soon enough. Take a seat."

Alice filed their coffee mugs from the percolator jug before bringing two plates and two more plates. With milk and sugar in his coffee and freshly-cooked scrambled eggs on toast, it was a great way to start the day.

"This is nice, Alice," Jake said.

"I promised I would look after my three men."

"Weather outside looks miserable," Mike said.

Spring weather: late-November warm but cloudy with drizzle. Luke wondered.

"After this we'll talk about things," he said.

"Alright."

When Luke finished, Alice cleared the table. The Airbnb had a dishwasher so soon they were in the living room, Mike and Jake on the leather couch with Luke and Alice opposite in the two armchairs.

"Alice, when did you decide to become a Tradwife?" Mike asked.

"I've always looked after Luke, as much as time allowed when I was working. Giving up work was the next step from that. What about your partner, Mike?"

"With Covid-19 and me out of work, she's supporting us. She's alright I suppose. Nags a bit."

"In what way?"

"Well, the lawnmower's a bit worn and stubborn so I have to cut the grass. But instead of asking me, I get told the grass is too long. Or if a tap is dripping and I have the tools to fix it, instead of being asked, I get told that tap has been dripping for weeks. For fuck's sake it might be in the laundry and I didn't know!" He looked to Alice. "That makes me angry sometimes."

"I'm not surprised you get angry," Alice said.

"What do you think of domestic violence?"

"I think women bring violence on themselves."

"Agreed."

"How's your partner in other ways?" Alice asked.

"She says no a few too many times."

Alice tilted her head while she looked at Mike. "Women go into relationships eyes open, where sex is part of what they're getting into. To refuse sex is not what relationships are about."

"Do you believe in men raping their wives?"

"There can't be rape when sex is an expectation."

"Agreed again. Luke, has Alice always been like this?"

"If you're asking has Alice ever refused me, the answer is never outright. Sometimes if it hasn't been possible at a moment; as soon as possible is promised."

"That won't be an issue now," Alice said.

"That's right," Luke agreed.

"Life's too busy when you're both working full-time," Mike said.

"In time you'll look back and wish you'd done things differently," Luke said.

Mike nodded his head. "Once this pandemic is over, we need to reset our relationship or I need to reset my life."

"Don't be too hasty," Jake said.

"Why?"

"My experience is women have checklists. Tall enough, check, well-dressed, check, your own home, check, decent car, check, earns enough, check, enough money in the bank, check. If you don't meet every single item on their checklist you don't have a chance."

"Then they sit at home, alone, wondering where all the good men have gone."

"Check."

Luke realised what that was about. "You're an incel?" he asked Jake.

"Check."

"I'm sorry to hear that," Alice said.

"Did you have a checklist?" Jake asked Alice.

"No. We both migrated in our early teens, you can hear our accents, and Luke was a kindred spirit. Once I got to know Luke I knew he would be good for me. That was my checklist."

"We were young and I didn't have anything," Luke said.

"We had each other."

Mike looked to Jake. "Your problem is women working, taking all the good jobs, and then not interested in you because you can't get a good job."

Jake laughed. "Yeah, you're right. Migrants too, like our Paki Prime Minister."

"Migrants flooding our cities," Mike said. "I went for a drive to the city centre yesterday, and compared to Sydney! Fuck! Everything in Sydney is clogged to a standstill because of migrants flooding the place. Without migrants, Sydney would be like here."

"Canberra without congestion is a pleasure to drive around," Luke said.

"In Canberra I haven't seen the enclaves of Vietnamese here, Chinese there, Koreans in this place, Lebanese in that place, like in Sydney."

"Migrants are much less here than in Sydney," Alice said. "I'm a migrant myself, but Anglo-Irish like real Australians. Over the past ten years, more and more, I feel like I don't belong. This isn't the Australia I came to 31 years ago."

"What about us who've been here for generations?" Mike asked.

"I know. The problem is if I went to England, I wouldn't belong there!"

"Really?"

"That's the reason my parents moved here."

Mike shook his head in seeming disbelief.

"Do you want another coffee?" Alice asked.

"Yes please Alice," Luke said.

Alice filled four mugs from the percolator, to place a tray which also had milk, sugar and teaspoons. They helped themselves.

"I'm sorry to hear about your situation," Luke said to Jake.

"Yeah. I passed Year 12 while doing part-time food delivery for spending money. Then I went to the University of Western Sydney and did a degree in marketing, for all the good that did me."

"You've got a degree and do food deliveries?" Luke asked to make sure he heard right.

"A degree's worth nothing these days. I'm not totally celibate, but I don't earn much so I've got to watch what I spend."

"Women sell it but they won't share it," Luke said.

"That's wrong," Alice said.

"Because of feminism, many things have gone wrong," Jake said. "Be careful with your partner," Jake said to Mike. "She might nag and she might refuse, but that's better than being an incel."

"I'm really sorry to hear that, mate."

"Don't worry; I'll finish that Paki Prime Minister off. That won't change where I am but it'll make me feel better." He half-smiled.

On that note with everything quiet, Luke remembered Alice's comment about looking after her three men, before she clarified what she meant. But what if Alice hadn't said that? What if her wifely role was to look after their team in all ways, especially Jake who needed looking after. Although 45, Alice was better looking than many girls half her age. Not tall which made her more feminine, slim; a genuine Australian size 8, fair skin with a few cute freckles on her nose, and shoulder-length natural burgundy-red hair contrasting against her hazel eyes. Alice was an English rose who looked after herself. For sure the young guys would be more than happy with her; while Luke was certain if he told Alice she would do it. It would be fun to watch, fun to be watched, fun for Alice, fun for everyone. Luke drew a deep breath: ***do it!***

Luke leaned close to Alice "Do you want to go to our room?" he whispered.

"Sure."

"We're just taking a break guys," Luke said.

Luke and Alice left for their bedroom where Luke closed the door. Already Alice was unbuttoning her blouse before Luke put his hand on her hands.

"What do you think of Mike and Jake?" Luke asked.

"They're alright," Alice said. "I'm sorry about Jake though."

"Do you like them?"

"They're alright."

Luke rubbed Alice's soft cheek with his forefinger. "You're sexy," he murmured.

Alice smiled brightly. "To you I'm sexy. Really, I'm a middle-aged mother of two."

"You're sexier than women half your age. You're sexy enough to arouse Mike and Jake."

"Ah, you want me to fuck them. My answer's no, Luke."

"No because you don't want to or no because you're naughty?"

Alice stood pigeon-toed with her head down and her finger in her mouth. "No because I'm naughty."

"You know what I do to naughty Alice?"

"Alice knows."

"Take off your clothes."

Luke watched Alice sit on the bed to take off her white sandshoes, then her blue blouse, her blue yoga slacks, her blue lace bra and her blue lace panties. He sat on the edge of the bed.

"Lie across my knee," he ordered.

Alice did, presenting her gorgeous bum. Luke rubbed it gently.

"It's not too late," he said.

"I'm a naughty girl."

"How many times should I hit a naughty girl?"

"You should hit a naughty girl six times."

Luke used the flat of his hand, slap, slap, slap, slap, slap, slap, slap, slap, slap, slap. Ten times, as a naughty girl deserved. He gently rubbed her red bottom.

"Get up now, and lie on your back on the bed."

She did while Luke went to the bottom drawer of the cabinet beside his side of the bed. He quickly found what he wanted and turned it to medium fast. Then he spread Alice's legs to ease the vibrating Ben Wa ball inside her. He put his hand on trimmed black hair between Alice's legs, to feel and hear the buzzing inside her.

"Now you can dress," Luke said calmly.

Alice pulled on her panties and her bra, and fastened it.

"That's all," Luke ordered. "I believe there's a tray with dirty mugs on the coffee table."

"Alice has been very naughty this morning."

Luke followed Alice into the living room where the look on Mike's face, and especially on Jakes face, were priceless. Luke sat in the armchair while Alice carried the tray to stack the dishwasher, and then gingerly crept across the room, her face really flushed, to sit in the other chair.

"What's that noise?" Jake asked.

"I've been naughty," Alice said with her head hanging, to which Mike burst out laughing.

"Really?" he asked.

Alice nodded her head.

"I love it!" Mike exclaimed. "How long for?"

"Until Luke gives me permission."

"When will that be?"

"After lunch at least," Luke said.

Alice nodded her head while Mike beamed brightly. Making lunch in her underwear, eating lunch too, while being vibrated inside – cruelty in pleasure.

Chapter Four

The car's GPS, an Australian-accented female voice, guided Matt to 30 Sutton Street, Cootamundra a few minutes before nine. White, aluminium-clad with a red-painted, corrugated iron roof, and a full-width veranda overlooking a lush, green lawn with two small trees in enclosures formed by timber sleepers. Just as Matt climbed from his car the front door of the house opened for Asha to sprint across the veranda, down three steps and along a concrete path. There she stopped, delicious in tight jeans and a blue short-sleeved cotton blouse, cradling a backpack.

"Hi Asha, I'm Matt."

"Hello Matt."

Matt touched the pad before pulling the tailgate to allow Asha to stow her backpack. He wrenched the heavy tailgate closed.

"You have a sports car," Asha said.

"It's not really. Climb in."

She did as Matt got in to reprogram the GPS for Koorawatha. When the Australian-accented female voice prompted him to go, he did, then scrolled to music. That would pass the time for the calculated one hour, 16 minute drive, but which would take less than that.

"This is a nice car," Asha said.

"It's just a Hyundai."

"I think this is a nice car. It's a lovely day today. Sunny, hot but not too hot, and a little bit of a breeze."

"It's a good day for photography. Now that it's almost December, do you think we'll ever forget the year 2020?"

"Never! First terrible fires and now a pandemic. The only good thing is we weren't harmed by that too much."

"I'd lost faith in our politicians but somehow they did all the right things and we weren't harmed by Covid-19 that much. I've been shooting this calendar every year for I don't know how long, but this year's shoot might sell more in other countries given they can't do what we can do."

"They can't do simple things like go for a drive to shoot pictures."

"Yeah."

"I'm looking forward to today. What's that music?"

"It's Roxy Music; my father likes it and I like it too. It's old but good."

"I've never heard anything like it. What's CPL593H?"

"It's a British car registration number."

"Oh I get it! I thought it was a love song but he's singing about his car!"

"It's about a girl he's too shy to ask out for a date. Bryan Ferry saw a beautiful girl in a car with that registration."

Asha laughed. "I understand. The piano at the end was really off."

"That's deliberate."

"I guessed that."

They left Cootamundra where Matt accelerated to about 110 and flicked the cruise control switch. At that time on a Friday morning the Olympic Way was virtually empty all the way to Young, which was a lovely drive.

"I'm happy and even a bit surprised to be modelling after signing only last week," Asha said, as they slowed for that big town almost a city.

"I want to show Australian country girls, but the real Australians are First Nations like you."

Silence for a moment. "That's not often said."

"Whites took your country by declaring it uninhabited, which was wrong. I'm aware that if we right that past wrong, we'll solve some pain in the process."

Again silence for a moment. "Some suffer more pain than others, but any pain solved will make a difference."

Driving through Young was quiet too, as was the 43 kilometres further to Koorawatha. As he slowed for the sleepy village, Matt cancelled navigation when he saw a faded, green sign pointing left to Koorawatha Falls, five. Like the day before he turned onto that well-graded, dry, dirt road lined by gum trees with paddocks of already browning grass stretching far into the distance. This was sheep or cattle country.

"This is the real Australia," Matt said.

"This was our country," Asha said.

"I know. We need a treaty."

"We need many things including a treaty, which will right a past wrong. More importantly for the future, we need an Indigenous Voice to Parliament."

"I feel more positive about the Voice to Parliament, and a treaty too. This government has only been in power for a few weeks. Give them time."

"Do you know how that happened?" Asha asked.

"Two ministers of the previous government were charged by the Australian Federal Police, one for corruption relating to the sale of water that didn't exist, and the other for corruption relating to the purchase of land at ten times its value. An independent member of parliament moved a motion of no-confidence against the government, which was supported by the Labor opposition, other independent members of parliament, and by a group of five from the government who crossed the floor and have since declared themselves independent. Under our constitution when a government loses a motion of no-confidence, the Governor-General has the power to dismiss the Prime Minister's commission and appoint a replacement Prime Minister in their place, which he exercised in this instance by appointing the leader of the opposition, Yaseera Devi. Prime Minister

Devi then called a double-dissolution election with a four-week campaign, where Labor won enough seats to form government with agreement from several independents to support Labor on no-confidence motions and money bills."

"I'm not sure I understand but now we have a new government, and our second female and our first Islamic Prime Minister."

"What do you think about that, Asha?"

"It's good to have a woman leading our nation in these uncertain times, and there's no harm in having a Prime Minister from a minority group."

At the sign Matt took the track on the left, and track it was too. Like yesterday he drove slowly given the lack of ground clearance of his car, across a narrow timber bridge, past boulders, but it was lovely country. Sophie Weaver picked a great spot. Around a curve was an old, white Toyota with Sophie and Emma recognisable from their pictures. Matt tilted the sunroof to reduce heat build-up and parked. He got out with Asha to be in a quiet reserve of gum trees offering dappled shade, a few wattles with thicker foliage, and a waterfall with a narrow cascade into a decent-sized lake behind a stone weir. Short, green grass under the many trees with slate near the weir. The two girls approached. From yesterday Matt had his shots written in his notebook, although he had them in his head so he rarely referred to what he wrote down.

"Hi Sophie and Emma. I'm Matt and this is Asha."

"Hi," they greeted in unison.

"What do you think?" Sophie asked.

"This is great. Now we need to get ready for this shoot. No stilettos or shoes, just bikinis."

"No problem."

"Where do we dress?" Asha asked as she took her backpack out of Matt's Veloster.

"Hide behind trees and I'll look the other way."

They headed off while Matt grabbed his camera bag, but given the shaded light he wouldn't need more than his digital SLR and a medium-length lens. By the time he'd screwed the lens in place he sensed company. He looked up to spot Emma in the same black bikini as the pictures she texted, Sophie in brief blue and Asha in brief red. Just right, especially Emma who was even more attractive than in her pictures. Not quite but almost model-tall, and busty with a gorgeous bottom and just a gorgeous figure.

"That's great girls, you're all beautiful!"

"Do you want makeup or anything?" Emma asked.

"I want natural, beautiful, Australian country girls."

Emma nodded her head slowly. "I understand," she said.

Matt's first shot used a victim from a past storm which offered a great backdrop.

"Now we'll start," Matt said. "Asha, please sit on that fallen tree just in front of the branch sticking up, leaning back against that branch. Gaze into the distance, pensively."

Asha did and it was good. Matt took a couple of shots.

"Lift your left leg up and wrap your arms around your knee."

She did and that was better.

"Good Asha, good."

A couple more.

"Great Asha; that's it."

Matt's next shot was more suggestive which suited Sophie more.

"Sophie, please sit on the stone weir next to where water's running over the edge, with your hands flat on the weir and your legs hanging down. Perfect."

Matt scrambled down the bank to be level with Sophie's feet.

"Spread your legs and look down at me. Spread more, good. Look to the camera like you're showing off to it. Not empty like that; more like you want to seduce the camera. Love the camera like you love your boyfriend. Yes, just like that."

Matt took a couple of shots where Sophie had the right look.

"Great Sophie."

A couple more.

"That's it," Matt said.

Matt climbed the bank to have Sophie intercept him.

"Can I see?" she asked.

Matt turned his camera over and pressed the button. He scrolled backwards one at a time.

"Cool!" Sophie exclaimed. "I've never seen bikini pictures like that before."

"Can I see mine?" Asha asked.

Matt scrolled through her shots.

"Nice."

"You two get changed by the cars. Now Emma," and Matt had kept his third for Emma, given she looked older and it suited her. "I'll get something from my car for you."

Matt turned around and took a few steps to be confronted with Asha topless and Sophie still naked.

"Hey!" Sophie exclaimed as Matt spun around.

"Sorry," he apologised.

"We're ready now."

Sophie now wore a golden-yellow bikini as brief as her blue one, while Asha was in black. Matt grabbed the Akubra hat from the back seat to return to Emma.

"Try this but tilt it backwards so it doesn't shade your face."

She did and it fitted well.

"Please lean with both hands on top of that fence post, and gaze across these paddocks as if you're gazing towards a boyfriend who's left you."

"Do you want me to loosen my ponytail?"

"You can leave your ponytail as it is."

Emma posed as Matt climbed through fence wires to enter the paddock. There he took a few shots.

"Perfect Emma."

"That's classy," she said.

"Now you can change and I promise not to sneak up on you."

Emma changed into blue.

"Emma, please sit on the thicker part of that fallen tree with your legs spread a bit. Sophie, sit on the ground between Emma's legs, cross-legged looking up at her. Emma, look down at Sophie."

That wasn't right.

"Emma, can you loosen your ponytail?"

Emma did, with her dark brown hair falling below her shoulder blades. She tossed the elastic ring to Matt who stuffed it in his pocket.

"Now, look into each other eyes with love. Great."

Matt ran a few shots.

"Great, thanks girls. Asha, your turn. Wade into the lake until the water is near your knees."

She did.

"Spread your hands out like this," as Matt spread his arms out with his palms parallel to the ground.

She did, with her hands parallel to and close to the water of the lake.

"Look at me mischievously. Like when you were a girl and did the wrong thing." Fantastic! "Great Asha; turn around slowly." Matt said as he took a few shots. "Superb, really superb." More shots. "That's it."

"Now, everyone please change. Asha, in the box in the boot of my car is a white bikini in your size."

After changing they came to Matt, with Emma in dark red, Sophie in brief black, and Asha gorgeous in white contrasting against her darker skin.

"Asha, please stand in front of that big tree with your legs partly spread."

Matt sat cross-legged in front of her, where the ground fell away so he was quite low.

"With your hands on your hips, look down at me like you're the beautiful woman you know you are. Show the camera you're really sexy. Sexy girl, yes, good."

She did, perfect. She was a natural as Matt took several shots.

"Thanks Asha."

"Can I see?" she asked.

Matt turned his camera over where they all gathered around.

"You're gorgeous!" Sophie exclaimed.

"They're nice pictures," Asha said. "Is modelling like this?"

"Bikini shoots are like this," Matt said. "Are you comfortable?"

"I'm comfortable."

"Good. Sophie, please sit on that rock with your legs spread."

Sophie did, and without prompting she looked sexy to the camera as Matt took a few shots.

"Great Sophie."   Now Emma who had a great figure for this type of work. "Emma, please face that tree with your hand on your hip while looking over your shoulder at me."

She posed but that wasn't right.

"Smile and spread your legs a bit."

Emma posed that way before Matt took several shots. Standing like that highlighted Emma's lovely legs and great arse, and more of her of course.

"Thanks Emma."

"Can I see those?" Emma asked.

Matt turned his camera over and pressed the button. He scrolled backwards.

"That's hot," Emma said.

They were.

"What is it?" Asha asked.

Matt scrolled Emma's shots forward.

"How do you get these ideas?" Asha asked

"I don't believe in God but I do believe that woman is God's most beautiful creation. This makes my job easy. Also, I came here yesterday and planned this."

Asha nodded her head thoughtfully.

"You're Buddhist, Emma," Matt said.

"You've seen my tattoo."

She had an infinite knot tattoo on the back of her neck. Discreet and tasteful. "I hope one of my shots shows it," Matt said.

"Where's your tattoo?" Asha asked.

Emma gathered her hair forward. "There."

"That's lovely. What does it mean?"

"It symbolises the infinity of life: birth, death, wisdom, compassion."

"Cool."

Matt's next was three together. "Girls, can you all change into black?"

"More changing!" Sophie exclaimed and laughed.

"They're only bikinis."

"I know."

They changed, which didn't take long while Matt waited.

"Stand on the bank of the lake in front of the waterfall, close to each other with your right hands on your hips and your legs spread a bit. Emma on the left, then Sophie then Asha. Closer with your ankles in front of each other's legs. Hook your left thumbs into your bikini bottoms and pull them down a bit, but not enough to show anything. A bit more Emma. Perfect. Smile at the camera."

Matt ran off some shots.

"Asha, can you pull your bikini a bit lower?" She did. "Great, and don't forget to smile."

More shots before Matt lowered his camera and checked the time on his watch. "It's after midday so we'll break for lunch."

"Do you have egg sandwiches?" Emma asked Sophie before laughing.

"Yes I do and cordial too."

Together they went to Emma's old car while Matt and Asha grabbed backpacks from his car.

"Mum made sandwiches but I don't know if they're egg," Asha said as they walked towards the big tree. There in the shade of that tree they sat in a circle.

"Matt and Asha, do you want lemon cordial?" Sophie asked. "I have plastic cups."

"Yes please," Asha said.

Matt reached into his backpack for his thermos. "I wouldn't make it through the day without this coffee!"

"You'll regret that," Sophie said. "You'll be looking for a tree sooner rather than later."

Asha opened her plastic box. "I have scrambled egg!" she exclaimed.

"So do we."

Sophie filled three blue plastic cups with cordial to share around while Matt started on the salad roll he bought earlier that day, and sipped his coffee too. It was a lovely spot with friendly company. Country girls were salt of the earth.

"Alright everyone," Asha said. "Tell me about yourselves. Sophie first."

"My name's Sophie, I'm 17, I grew up in Wagga but this past year I've been living in Young, and I've just finished my Year 12 exams. Next year my boyfriend and I will be moving to Wagga to study medical administration, and I took up modelling to earn spending money while I study."

"How did you get the idea to model?"

"I know models are tall and slim and I'm like that. My mother's the same so maybe it's in our genes, but whatever it is, this is how I am. I have school friends in Wagga, school friends here in Young, and I have my boyfriends friends like Emma. I live at home with my Mum and her partner, and with my boyfriend, but we'll be moving to live with my grandparents in Wagga."

"Emma?" Asha asked.

"My name's Emma and I'm 20. I have a business in Young and I'm a friend of Sophie's boyfriend, and a friend of Sophie. Matt needed an extra model and Sophie asked me. I've enjoyed today so if more opportunities come along, I'd like to do this again."

"Now my turn. "I'm Asha and I'm 18 years old, I'm Wiradjuri and I live in Cootamundra. I passed Year 12 last year and then spent a year away. When I got back I discovered modelling on the internet. This is my first time modelling and I've loved it! My ambition is to be the next Samantha Harris. If I need to move to Sydney to do that, I will."

"You want to be a professional model," Sophie said. "You have the look for it."

"You have the look, Sophie. You could be professional."

"I don't like Sydney, but if the economy doesn't improve I might go further with modelling." Sophie sipped some cordial. "You really want to be a model?"

"It's a career that can pay well, and it's a way of showing Australia and the world that I'm First Nations and as good as anyone."

"Good for you."

Matt was quite startled. *Eighteen and so together!* Proud of her ancestry was a serious understatement.

"Asha," Emma said. "You're beautiful and I hope you go far, especially for your people."

"Agreed," Sophie said.

Again an understatement. Matt then realised he'd finished his coffee and Sophie was right, of course.

"Now I need to find a tree," he announced, to which Sophie laughed.

Matt headed off while Asha felt unusual: butterflies in her stomach, her body tingling, her nipples sparkling, and her pussy aching even. She'd felt like that for most of the day and guessed it was the arousal of posing sexy in bikinis.

"Are you alright, Asha?" Emma asked.

"I'm fine." Asha looked around but Matt wasn't in sight. "I feel aroused, actually."

"That's because of Matt," Sophie said.

"Pardon?"

"I sense something between you two."

"But he's old," Asha blurted out without thinking. Matt was old but he was handsome and nice. Really nice.

"Matt seems mid to late-twenties; that's not old," Sophie said. "My mother's partner is 15 years older than my mother and they're too much in love. Women mature faster than men so you and Matt fit. Do you feel horny?"

"Yeah and other things. Fluttery inside and sparkling everywhere."

"I won't say that's love but definitely that's lust. Don't push Matt away just because of your age difference."

"Sophie's right," Emma said. "Older men are better for sure. It's your choice, but if I felt something I would go with it. I wouldn't want to look back later and regret I didn't."

"Do you have regrets?"

"I've not met that man yet."

"I felt that way once and he's my boyfriend now," Sophie said. "I still feel it, but calmer. It's mellow now but still great. I'm not an expert but love and lust aren't that far apart. Love is more here," as she touched her head, "and here," as she touched her heart.

"Love without lust seems kind-of empty," Emma said.

"It does," Sophie agreed.

"We've got the rest of the day here and Matt's driving me home," Asha said. "I'll think about it."

Matt was really nice and handsome too. Tall, lean but not thin, big pale blue eyes, and light brown hair a shade or two darker than Sophie's blonde. Serious but not serious, fun actually, and nice. Really nice and respectful too; that was important. But Asha didn't know how to take things further even if she wanted to.

Matt returned. "Girls," he said, "if you need to go, go now, and I'll look the other way."

"Do we change bikinis?" Asha asked.

"Yes please. I have a green and gold bikini in the car for you, Asha."

"Alright."

As they changed, Matt thought they were salt of the earth for sure. Sophie was bright and vivacious, beautiful, and had a live-in boyfriend at age 17! Emma was charming, while Asha was gorgeous and totally together. Matt thought either Sophie or Asha could do the upcoming Canberra shoot, except Asha being First Nations would make a subtle, political statement which would benefit her people. Also, Asha had the desire to be professional which Sophie didn't have, where the Canberra shoot would help with Asha's career. There was another issue playing for quite some years which gave Asha an advantage over Sophie when it came to being professional. Matt decided to see how the rest of the shoot played out before asking Asha if she was interested. By then Asha, Emma and Sophie returned.

"Emma, please lie face down on the slate beside the lake and lift your bottom up a bit, and lift your head up to look at me. Sexy smile."

Emma did that while Matt walked around her in a circle taking shots of her. Given her figure one or more of those would work. Matt returned to be front-on to Emma.

"Half-smile for me. Sort-of sexy smirk." Perfect! "Great Emma, thanks."

Next Asha. "Asha, please stand on the slate with your back to the lake. Hand behind your head, one leg forward." Not quite what Matt wanted. "Hook your thumb on your bikini bottom and pull it down without showing."

That was what Matt wanted.

"Great Asha. "Look sexy right into the camera. Make love to the camera. You're a sexy girl."

She did; beautiful!

"That's great Asha."

In the background the only noises were the warbling of magpies, the gentle rustle of a light breeze, and Emma and Sophie talking quietly together. Clearly they were close friends. As he took his shots of Asha, Matt wondered if he could use their friendship for something special. He lowered his camera before turning to face Emma and Sophie; Sophie's eyebrows raised.

"Alright girls," Matt said. "Do you want to do some posed topless shots?"

"You said this was a bikini shoot," Emma said. "No, posed; I understand. Yeah. Sophie?"

"Sure," Sophie agreed.

"Girls, do you mind kissing?" Matt asked.

"Kissing each other?" Emma asked.

"Pressed close, arms crossed."

Emma smiled. "Yeah, alright," she said slowly.

"No," Sophie said firmly. "Asha, do you want to kiss me?"

Asha laughed.

"Seriously! Black and white; it's powerful."

Sophie was right; that was symbolically powerful.

"Yes, I'll kiss you Sophie," Asha agreed.

Matt wondered if he was pushing things. "Are you sure?" he asked.

"Yes, I'm sure."

In a flash Asha removed her bikini top revealing her firm, round breasts. Sophie removed her bikini top before casually closing on Matt. Sophie had attractive breasts, firm and nicely-shaped too.

"Where do you want us?" Sophie asked.

"With the big tree in the background."

Sophie took Asha's hand to lead her to the tree, to face each other.

"Close together, arms crossed," Matt instructed as he raised the camera to squint through the viewfinder at the two girls already kissing, arm in arm. Sophie was right; dark and fair was more than beautiful, it was powerful. Matt ran off shot after shot as arm in arm became groping, Asha squeezing Sophie's bottom while Sophie grabbed at Asha's thick shock of black hair. Matt crossed from right to left as still they kissed, no tongue just kissed, with Matt sensing their near-desperation: Sophie with both hands in Asha's hair and Asha holding Sophie's neck, before Sophie hugged Asha tight and Asha held Sophie's head; hands tangled in long, blonde hair. Matt had never seen a kiss so delicious. Eventually Sophie grabbed Asha's arms to ease her away.

"Fuck yeah!" Sophie exclaimed. "That was awesome! Did you get your pictures?" she asked.

Matt didn't know how many, 20 or 30. "I got plenty," he said. "If I could do a calendar of just you two kissing, I would."

"Ha! Asha?"

"That felt nice," she said quietly.

"That felt nice for me but it's more. We can't unravel the past, it's too far gone, but we can say now we're white and indigenous together."

"We're symbolic reconciliation."

"I've had indigenous friends," Sophie said. "Not here in Young for some reason, but in Wagga. If whites didn't like me having indigenous friends that was their problem, not mine. If we all do this, make an effort, we'll get somewhere."

Asha tilted her head. "Some whites treat us badly and I think we become defensive. Perhaps we become frightened. Whatever it is, friendship becomes difficult."

"That might be the problem here," Sophie said. "Emma?" she asked.

"There's a divide," Emma said. "If these pictures can chip away at that divide, that's good."

"That was my first kiss!" Asha proudly announced.

"Really?" Sophie exclaimed.

"It was good – great," she repeated.

Sophie turned to face Matt. "What now?"

After that, Matt decided not to bother with his last planned shot. "I've got enough now, so that's it. Thank you all."

"Now we can swim!"

"You can swim but I don't have swimmers."

"Rule here is no swimmers!"

"She's right," Emma said as she removed her bikini revealing her delightfully voluptuous form. Sophie removed her bikini bottom.

"You're blonde!" Asha exclaimed.

Matt glanced between Sophie's legs and Asha was right – trimmed, natural blonde.

"Black, blonde, dark, fair; doesn't matter," Sophie said. "What matters is here," as she put her hand over her heart. "Last one in!" as she raced to the water, followed by Emma and Asha. Matt watched them.

"Come on Matt!" Sophie exclaimed. "We do this with guys all the time."

"We do," Emma said.

Matt put his camera beside his bag before removing his shoes and everything else. He waded into delightfully warm water, muddy but refreshing, to be hit by a torrent followed by laughter. He turned to face Asha before doing the same to her. In no time they were both drenched and Asha had her hands in the air.

"Alright, alright," she said with a bright smile. "You win."

Matt slowly swum across the lake before turning to float on his back. Soon they were all floating on their backs.

"Our people used to live like this," Asha said. "It's a pity there's so much hate. Hate from some, mistrust from others."

"Mistrust; that's a good word," Emma said. "I'm not racist, never have been, but mistrust is what divides us here in Young."

"On our side there are some who hate," Asha said.

"That's not unexpected."

"Not unexpected but hate just creates more hate, and for the rest of us a bit of fear." Asha turned her head to catch Matt's eyes. "I hope our picture causes just one, or a few, to realise there's more that unites us than divides us."

"I hope it does," Matt said while thinking that was a mature comment from a young woman who no doubt had been racially taunted more than a few times.

"I know it'll be a while before this calendar comes out, but I will have to explain this to my boyfriend," Sophie said.

Sophie was right. "Will that be alright?" Matt asked.

"I'll tell him it was just a picture for a calendar, but really that was an awesome kiss!"

"What about your family?" Asha asked.

"Mum knows me so she won't be surprised. What about you?"

"I'll tell my family we took a special picture for reconciliation, but I won't tell them how good it was. We studied art in high school; this is like art."

"Photography is a form of art," Matt said. "In your case, thanks to Sophie, we're using a picture to tell a bigger story."

"I wish we could be like this all of the time," Asha said.

"Love beats hate every time," Matt said.

"That's right."

Matt now wondered how to frame this. "All of you, you've been great today. You're all beautiful but modelling is more than beauty. Asha, I want to use you for another shoot. As you know there's a demand for indigenous models but only a few have made it. You could be part of the next generation."

"Thank you Matt."

"Sophie, I know you want to do more modelling."

"I have plans to model while I study," Sophie said, "but after hearing Asha my study plans might be secondary to modelling. Do you think I have a chance?"

"You're naturally beautiful, you have a great figure, and you were great today. You could go further but opportunities from Wagga will be limited."

"I understand. I'll talk with my boyfriend."

"In the meantime I'll see what I can do for you. Emma; if something comes up, you're available?"

"I have my business," Emma said, "but if you want me I can make time."

"Asha, I have a shoot to do in Canberra," Matt said. "You'd be perfect."

"Bikinis, topless, kissing?" Asha asked with a bright smile.

"It's a sophisticated shoot with fashionable dresses, blouses, slacks, makeup, hair styling and all that."

"That will be good experience for my career."

"Yes it will be."

Asha and Sophie had figures that worked for bikini shoots, and were tall and slender for high fashion. They could wear anything or nothing and the camera loved them both. Emma was gorgeous and her figure was ideal for a bikini, less so for fashion, but if ever he had another bikini shoot she would be first on his list. A kookaburra called which sent a shiver up Matt's spine. Asha was right; he wished he could be like this all of the time. Floating in the lake that afternoon, he was the thorn amongst three roses.

"Race across the lake!" Sophie announced. "There and back twice."

"I'll give you a head start," Matt offered.

"I should give you a head start!"

That was 'no'. Sophie stood; they all stood.

"On my mark, go!"

They thrashed across the muddy water, there and back, there and back. Sophie first, then Matt, Asha and Emma.

"Beat you!" Sophie proudly announced.

"Don't worry," Emma said, "Sophie usually wins." Emma looked around. "We should head home soon."

"We don't have towels so how do we dry?" Asha asked.

"Lie on the bank under that tree for protection from the sun. The warmth will dry us."

They climbed out of the lake to lay on grass face-down, side-by-side: Emma, Sophie, Matt, and Asha to Matt's right.

"I've just gotten back from being away for a year," Asha said. "I worked in a clinic in Boggabilla to help my people. It was – difficult. Every evening was like a war: drinking, fights, women and children fleeing their homes, rapes too. Each morning was like after a war: smashed glass, fires still smoking, rubbish, quiet. The problem is there's nothing to do except drink, take drugs, or sniff petrol or glue. This is why we have all these gaps to close. Health, education; why would you get an education when there's nothing to do? Violence, arrests, shortened life spans. I wish I had an answer."

Matt realised Asha had the answer. "We need to give these communities something to do."

"That's easier said than done. They've been surviving on welfare, drinking and drugs for decades."

"Alright, we start with the young there. Set up businesses, train them; give them pride for each and every day. I don't know what businesses but I know we can't foist a solution on communities. That's bound to fail."

"Get women there involved," Asha said. "Women play a bigger part in our culture than in your culture."

"Really?" Emma asked.

"Yes."

"I like that. Why don't they move to where there are jobs?"

"First Nations people have an affinity to the land," Sophie said. "Asha can explain it."

"We're part of nature and nature's part of us," Asha said. "This is told through The Dreaming, which is when the creatures of nature formed our society. The creatures made all natural things and put them in special places, and in many cases the great creatures changed themselves into sites where their spirits stayed. So I'm this land and this land is me, and this land is my reason for existence."

"Is that it?" Emma asked.

"There's more. Our laws were made by the creation ancestors. Great creatures made the laws of life, where the plants and animals who obeyed those laws were made into people. The plants and animals who didn't obey those laws were made into rocks and stone, which is how hills and mountains were formed. When they were done, the spirits of our creation ancestors rested in sacred sites. My clan has a sacred site, and we have a creature by which we identify ourselves. The creature of my clan is the wallaby which means I'm descended from the Great Wallaby, as are members of my clan. I'm bound to protect all wallabies, and I can't marry or have a relationship with another wallaby. I also have my dream creature, the eagle. So my spirit's linked to the Great Eagle of the Dreaming."

"What's a clan?"

"Family in your world is kin in my world, which covers parents, grandparents, brothers, sisters, aunties, uncles and cousins, although we call all elders auntie and uncle out of respect. Now, my clan is my group of kin connected by blood. Each clan had an area of land within the Wiradjuri Nation. Can you guess the name of my clan?"

That was obvious. "Cootamundra," Matt said.

"Good guess," Asha said with a bright smile.

"Amazing!" Emma gasped. "So if people move from remote towns to where there's work, they move from the land that's them and they move from their sacred sites."

"Yes. But the bigger problem is they're poorly educated, welfare-dependant and drug-addicted."

"You didn't learn about The Dreaming at school?" Sophie asked.

"No, I didn't," Emma said. "Obviously you learned this at school in Wagga?"

"Yes I did."

"Asha," Emma said. "You're a wallaby and an eagle, and your religion is the land and sacred sites?"

"Wallaby and eagle are my totems."

"Really? I love it!"

"After my year at Boggabilla I came home to Cootamundra," Asha said. "Before I left, there weren't enough jobs in Cootamundra, so I expected to move to Wagga when I got back, only after Covid there aren't enough jobs there. I browsed the internet for options and that's when I came across indigenous models. Friends sometimes said I could be a model, so I checked pictures of models and realised I could. I rang agencies, caught a bus to Canberra, they arranged for a photographer to take my portfolio, and here I am."

"I did much the same," Sophie said. "As you know I decided to model for spending money while I study, but I'll think more about that."

"On the internet I saw a picture of an indigenous model in jeans and she was topless, but her breasts were ceremonially painted. She had her arms draped over a spear resting across her shoulders. I want to be a model like her but I wondered if I could pose like that. Now I know I can."

Matt had seen that. "That picture is amazing: beauty and tradition combined."

"That's art."

"Yes it is." Matt thought. "I'd like to do something with the shots of you and Sophie, beyond putting them into a calendar sometime in the future."

"Yes, fine," Asha said. "If my nipples are showing in any of the pictures you took, don't worry."

"Same with me," Sophie said. "I'm proud of my nipples!" and she laughed. She stood. "We ought to dress and go home."

"I could stay here forever," Asha said.

"Is this your land?" Emma asked.

"This is Wiradjuri land."

"Awesome!" Emma stood. "I've learned so much, thank you Asha. I hope your shoot in Canberra goes well and good luck with your career."

What a delightful thought? Then Matt had an idea pop into his head and the light was still good too.

"Asha and Sophie, do you mind if we take one last round of shots?"

"Yeah, sure," they agreed.

"Put on the bikini bottoms you wore when you were kissing, and straddle the fallen tree facing each other with your knees almost touching. Hold hands and gaze into each other's eyes."

Matt quickly pulled his underwear and trousers on while they posed like that.

"Good, great," Matt said as he knelt while running off seven or eight shots. Emma to his left murmured 'amazing'. Matt lowered his camera. "Thanks girls."

"That was amazing," Emma repeated as Matt stood in the shade of the tree to check those last shots. They were amazing.

"Thank you for today and that's it," Matt said. "Now we can dress."

They all dressed before Matt packed his camera bag, and tossed the elastic ring to Emma who redid her ponytail. They walked to cars nearby, with Sophie and Emma heading to Emma's old Toyota.

"Thank you Sophie and Emma," Matt offered.

"See you Matt," they echoed. "See you Asha."

"Goodbye."

Asha climbed into Matt's car where he joined her. He started up to follow the Toyota at a distance given the dust it raised.

"I can come to Canberra by bus anytime," Asha said.

"I'll let you know when we're ready," Matt offered. "You now know modelling is more than beauty."

"Sit on that fallen tree and look pensive, seduce the camera, make love to the camera. Take off your bikini top and kiss Sophie. Gaze into Sophie's eyes like you love her, which is really what you meant."

Matt laughed.

"The bus gets into Jolimont Centre late afternoons," Asha said. "Like last time I was in Canberra I can stay at the hostel nearby."

That wasn't a nice place to stay and it was inconvenient for their shoot. Matt wondered, but if Asha wasn't comfortable she could simply refuse. "I have an apartment where you can stay in my spare room," he said. "From there we can use my car to get around."

"Is that too much trouble?"

"Not at all."

"Alright; good."

They reached the Young to Cowra road where Matt turned and picked up speed.

"I just loved today, it was great," Asha said.

"Not all shoots are relaxed in the Australian bush with good company like Sophie and Emma," Matt said. "Sometimes they're rushed, frantic even, but even then there are worse ways to make money."

"What will you do with the last pictures of Sophie and me?"

"I'll enter them into a competition. If I win I'll be the winner, but you and Sophie will gain publicity and the concept, reconciliation, will be front and centre."

"Being topless is us. Our women were topless before whites arrived, so those last pictures are more us."

Matt knew that which is why he posed the girls like that. "You're right," he said.

"To think I was worried about that but it's easy!"

"Sometimes fashion is see-through."

"I noticed that."

They slowed for Young, left and right, roundabouts and the rough climb out of the shopping district, before picking up speed for the curves on the highway beyond that town. On and on, it was a great drive. A little further; Cootamundra. There Matt turned left onto Temora Street and right onto Sutton Street to stop at the modest, aluminium-clad home with lush, green grass, two trees and a veranda. After Matt tilted the sunroof and parked, Asha led the way inside.

"Mum, Dad?" she called as they walked along the corridor. Unusually the three bedrooms and a small bathroom were arranged along the right of the corridor, with a large bathroom on the left next to a partly-open kitchen. There a middle-aged man and two middle-aged women waited as Matt followed Asha into the combined kitchen, lounge and dining room. Like the rest of the house that room was unmarked, looking brand-new but with a lived-in look; the inevitable clutter of a family.

"How did it go," one woman asked while hovering.

"It was great Mum. This is Matt Taylor."

Mr Reid went to shake hands but Matt went to bump elbows instead.

"I'll get used to that one day," Mr Reid said with a smile. "I'm Jack and my wife's Ella, and this is Asha's Aunt Beth. So it was good?"

"All the girls were great and Asha's a natural," Matt said.

"Matt wants to use me again, when?" Asha asked.

"Next week in Canberra."

"You've already got your money back on your portfolio," Ella said. "This is promising. How far can this go?"

"In normal times without Covid-19, this can go a long way," Matt said. "Samantha Harris is the best known and I think the first indigenous model, and she's worth about a million."

"You're joking?"

"I'm not promising a million for Asha, but when this pandemic is over she could go all the way. She's got the look, but more importantly she's got talent and ambition."

The adults beamed at that comment.

"Do you want to stay for dinner?" Ella asked.

To refuse would be rude and Matt wasn't in a hurry to leave anyway. "Yes please, if it's no trouble."

"Its stew and I've got plenty. Come this way."

The round dining table was set for five, including a jug of water wet with condensation and five glasses.

"Where's Lochie?" Asha asked.

"With his friends," Ella said.

"Auntie; where are Jason and Sue?"

"With Lochie," Aunt Beth said.

Lochie must be Asha's brother, while Jason and Sue were cousins or part of Asha's kin.

"Is this is your full-time job?" Jack asked Matt.

"My photography is a mix of fashion shoots, this bikini shoot, weddings, promotions; anything that needs a camera. And you?"

"I work at Elouera Industries making pallets. They've been good to me."

Matt recognised the paternal undertones in that comment. Never mind, happiness or satisfaction was important. More important was a three bedroom, aluminium-clad house, either owned or rented, and a steady income. After four sat and Ella brought out the bowl of stew to join them, it was eerily middle-class, suburban Australia. Those who were racist, who called Asha abo or boong at school without really knowing her, would have been shocked. Even more shocked that Asha had the possibility of fame and fortune because of her smouldering dark looks. And the mystery of The Dreaming; maybe that seeped through. For sure The Dreaming seeped through Asha's personality which made her especially interesting. Matt ate his meal, middle-class, suburban Australia for sure. Great meal too.

"This stew is lovely," he said.

"Thank you," Ella acknowledged.

"What do you know about us?" Aunt Beth asked.

"Asha explained a bit about The Dreaming, and kin and her clan. Asha also told us about her time away. I'm no expert but I'm glad I'm from a generation where there's more understanding." Matt focussed. "Auntie is like a second mother, and cousins are more like brothers and sisters?"

"In your terminology, yes."

"That's better than us."

"We think so."

"Do you have more kin in Cootamundra?" Matt asked.

"Lots!" Asha exclaimed with a bright smile. "There's always drama or a problem somewhere but I've got support for my problems too. And support for my successes."

"That's better than us."

"I know."

Silence for a moment. "Asha is a lovely name, where did you get it from?" Matt asked.

"In a dream," Ella said.

"It might be that Asha is meant to be."

"It might be."

They finished their meal in silence, with the delicious stew regenerating Matt but now he had a long drive home. Plates were empty.

"That was lovely, thank you," Matt offered.

"Thank you for sharing our meal," Jack said.

"I should go; it's a long drive to Canberra."

"I'll show you out," Asha said.

Matt stood. "Goodbye and thank you for your hospitality."

"Thank you for looking after Asha for us."

They walked to the veranda where Matt paused to gaze into Asha's big, brown eyes. She was young and yet mature, capable, ambitious; the real deal. Matt felt like the guy in Re-Make / Re-Model by Roxy Music, not so much shy as not wanting to take advantage of his position. For sure his opportunity could come in time, and he had time.

"Next week Canberra, Asha. I'll be in touch."

"Goodbye Matt."

"Goodbye Asha."

Matt headed to his car.

Chapter Five

Yaseera strode into the Cabinet Room where she noted all her colleagues were in place, waiting. One of the few rooms in Parliament House which wasn't naturally lit, perhaps that was a subtle reminder by the architects of that magnificent building to keep cabinet meetings short, sharp and to the point. Yaseera took her chair and put her compendium on the oblong table.

"Good morning and welcome to the 47th Parliament of Australia."

A round of applause followed.

"Given events of the past two months our election policies were understandably lacking development. Our most critical issue is our economic situation." Yaseera looked to James.

"Treasury modelling suggests this economic downturn following the Covid-19 shutdown of our economy will last some years."

"This will require a living Newstart unemployment benefit until this situation passes, and for after that too."

"The cost of our proposed permanent increase is one point four billion over the forward estimates, while generating economic growth of course."

"Now to pay for this," Yaseera said. "Do we have the numbers in the house for our two percent increase to the top tax bracket?"

"We do," Lionel, Leader of the House of Representatives, said.

"Do we have the numbers in the Senate?" Yaseera asked while looking to Paula.

"The Greens say we're not going far enough, but they will support our increase in the Senate."

"We must be right with two percent if the right says we're going too far, and the left says not far enough."

Laughter.

"Now, stimulus?" Yaseera asked.

"State and territory governments have put their wish-lists in," James said. "Mostly public transport projects, like here in Canberra with their light rail extension."

"They want light rail running past the Prime Minister's Lodge," Yaseera commented. "We're playing catch-up after a period of high population growth so that makes sense. I mentioned the Anzac Hall project at the War Memorial here, remembering a controversy from architects over that proposal."

"There are two issues to that. One is the demolition and replacement of a relatively new and quite fine exhibition space, with the opposing view being it doesn't have space to show our involvements in Iraq and Afghanistan, which are Australia's longest-running military engagements."

"Understood, but surely crowded trains, trams and buses, and choked roads, are more critical? I'm still inclined to abandon the Anzac Hall project, or at least defer it indefinitely."

"If you can sell it, fine."

"Anyone else object to abandoning the replacement of Anzac Hall?" Yaseera asked while looking for body language. No response. "I've been to the War Memorial where I felt that what it shows, it shows well. I'm sure I can sell this abandonment or deferment if we do that selling on-site, showing Anzac Hall as the fine exhibition space it is," Yaseera looked to her notes. "Now on another issue, indigenous rights. Firstly, establishing an Indigenous Voice to Parliament, enshrined in our constitution so it can't be obliterated by a conservative government at some time in the future."

Lydia started. "History shows that unless a change to the constitution has the support of both major parties, it will fail. Referendums that have passed, like the 1967 Aboriginal referendum, all have that characteristic."

"In some cases it has taken two attempts to pass a referendum," Yaseera said. "On that basis I believe we should table our legislation for the referendum on the Indigenous Voice to Parliament, and for the treaty too."

"We'll be subject to scare campaigns by the Murdoch press and the opposition," Lydia said.

"Will we burn political capital?" Yaseera asked.

"These scare campaigns will paint pictures of families and businesses losing access to land they've purchased, the Voice being an extra chamber of parliament and all that we've heard before."

"Those who are educated and progressive will understand what happened in 1788, with white settlement on what was considered unoccupied land, was wrong. The Indigenous Voice to Parliament and a treaty will help to address that. Lydia, can you tell us how that white settlement came about?"

"I won't say life was all peace and harmony, but different nations occupied their parts of Australia, with each nation having unique languages and some differing cultural practices. When the First Fleet landed at Port Jackson in 1788, the Eora Nation were surprised by their pale skins, their clothing, their ships and almost everything else. In early months there was mostly peaceful interaction between indigenous peoples and the new arrivals, although there were a few skirmishes where spears were of little use against muskets. The Eora people quickly recognised this and even passed word to other nations not to fight these white people, which meant there were few incidents of indigenous retaliation. From the whites there were some massacres but disease played a larger role."

"Can we paint a picture of whites occupying formerly indigenous land by force and disease, and capitulation based on pragmatism?"

"We'll work on that concept. To think they were pragmatic enough to realise they couldn't beat a musket shows how capable they were."

"The real history is the declaration of Terra Nullius, an unoccupied land, which meant British settlers didn't negotiate a treaty like they did in other places they conquered," Yaseera said, before glancing at the clock. "We also have to change the Australia Day holiday, being the anniversary of the landing at Port Jackson which really is Invasion Day, and then be subjected to vitriol for that."

"We should change some words in our national anthem, because Australia is not young but one of the oldest cultures in the world."

"That'll mean more vitriol," Yaseera said. "Thank you all for your time; we have our chambers to attend."

Yaseera stood to be followed to the House of Representatives for the first day of the last two-week session of parliament before Christmas.

* * *

Yaseera hated the Prime Minister's Lodge, being close to a century old and looking it. Big and ochre-coloured, haunted by the ghosts of Prime Minister's past, their wives and families. Outside, lush gardens more like parklands were blighted by never-ending traffic noise from Adelaide Avenue, which once might have been peaceful but now was forever busy, while inside had heavy drapes, furnishings like living in a museum, and a bed that gave her the creeps. It was important for the Prime Minister to live there, saving taxpayer money on flying home to Melbourne which didn't have a suitable residence, anyway. So The Lodge it was, with one-hundred year old decor and furnishings to match.

"How was your day?" Kasir asked.

"My day was fine," Yaseera replied, which she was. "How was your first official day of being first husband?"

"My day was fine," he said. "The weather was nice but the garden isn't pleasant with traffic noise from beyond the wall."

"Wait until winter."

"Winter will be too cold to go outside, I'm sure."

Yaseera wondered. "I might go for a swim."

"We have a pool and it's nice weather this evening."

"I'll get changed and you can come outside to keep me company."

Yaseera went to their room where that bed really gave her the creeps, to change into a black one-piece swimsuit and a black swimming cap. The barbeque area was lovely, the pool especially, as she dived in to swim a few lengths. Swimming was good exercise and better that it relaxed her busy mind.

There were many challenges including recovery from the worst economic downturn in close to a century, meeting climate change commitments that had fallen well behind target, while being barraged by scare campaigns that told little truth, dealing with indigenous issues that should have been dealt with years ago, and making sure the nation got value for money from ever-increasing debt, which Yaseera felt wasn't the case with the demolition of a near-new display area at the War Memorial. As she swum laps, Yaseera was ever more convinced that taking the press into Anzac Hall to show it as a great facility it was, was the best way to sell her proposal. She swum to the ladder at the shallow end to climb out where Kasir had a big, white towel waiting. After drying herself, Yaseera removed her cap to let her long, black hair fall free.

"You're beautiful," Kasir said with sincerity.

Yaseera laughed. "I'm 48 and overweight!"

"Having two children does that to any woman."

"So you say and I believe you too."

"It does."

"I understand," Yaseera said, while thinking love was blind. "I wonder what's on the menu?"

"Barbequed kebabs, rice, chickpeas and a salad."

Yaseera was surprised. "Is that your influence?"

"It might be."

Yaseera took Kasir's hand to go inside, as she pretended not to notice her security detachment discreetly watching for her safety, and the many CCTV cameras tracking her. It was an honour to play her part in helping her nation in a difficult time, but also intrusive for as long as she held her position. Yaseera would change into a comfortable outfit suitable for a middle-aged woman a few kilos overweight, have a nice meal, and later they would share privacy and intimacy and a good sleep too. The best part of her evening so far was her swimming; for the future Yaseera decided to do more swimming, to relax her mind and shed a few kilos too.

Chapter Six

The Ben Chifley Building or Lubyanka by the Lake. The building overlooked the lake for those lucky enough to have a window and time enough to enjoy the view. Adam had both that morning as he watched shimmering blue in the near distance, while closer, cars streaming past, mostly heading east towards the city centre or to take the cloverleaf to southern suburbs. His office, not small but not luxurious either, had a polished maple desk sized for a director, his big, leather reclining chair, a couple of visitor's chairs, and a polished maple bookcase with a few training manuals from many years past but retained out of habit. Not a paper out of place, while his pens and clutch pencils were kept in individual compartments, one compartment per colour of pen and one compartment for the pencils, in the top drawer of his desk. The clock on the wall ticked down where, on time, his team leaders entered and closed the door behind them.

"Leon and Erin; please take a seat," Adam asked.

They sat in the two leather-covered visitor's chairs, both with clipboards to take notes.

"Anything to report for the new week?" Adam asked wearily.

Silence for a moment. "The alt-right chatter we heard about something happening here in Canberra has died away," Erin said.

"How so?"

"There were five message board postings early last week, then nothing."

"Your opinion?"

"They know we monitor such forums so they're keeping it under the radar."

"Exchanging web-based emails?"

"That's one possibility."

Adam frowned. "They could be here now but we would have trouble finding them."

"Two parties, gender unknown but more than likely male, using VPNs on the Deep Web to mask their specific location even though indications point to Sydney, possibly now in Canberra, meeting a third party, gender unknown but probably male too. In a city of 426,000 that's more than just trouble finding them."

"I understand. Monitor that forum in case there are similar postings. They might need more resources for whatever they're planning."

"We've got that forum under surveillance."

"Leon?" Adam asked.

"It's relatively quiet for my team unless something happens. This week I plan a couple of desktop exercises to keep them sharp. I'll use the training room."

"Alright, good," Adam said. "Let me know if you come across anything, Erin."

With that cue they left, for Adam to ponder the implications of that forum going quiet. Covid-19 was raging in most of the world but not in Australia. Canberra, nestled inside New South Wales, was close enough to Sydney to make the assumption that parties drove along the motorway for a few hours, and in doing so became untraceable. The bleak, inhospitable western suburbs of Sydney were already home to many disenfranchised alt-right radicals struggling to get by as casual, part-time, whatever job they could find while blaming immigration and multiculturalism for their situations in life, only to have their anger stoked by political events over the past two months. Adam glanced at the clock on the wall which showed it was his turn. He grabbed his leather-bound compendium to walk the 50 metres or so to Nicole's somewhat bigger and grander office, as deemed appropriate for a Deputy Director General. The venue for their regular Monday morning meeting was Nicole's polished maple meeting table with six, padded, leather-covered chairs, a coffee pot, cups and saucers, a water jug, glasses, a plate of biscuits, and Rebecca the personal assistant waiting to record minutes. Adam sat beside Nate, both opposite Nicole: in her forties, always immaculately dressed usually in suits, but with a short and severe hairstyle that hadn't changed for as long as Adam reported to her.

"Adam?" Nicole asked.

"The message board has gone quiet leading me to consider the possibility that face-to-face contact has been made, possibly here."

"Your reasons for this consideration?"

"There's no doubt recent political events are seen as controversial by some on the right of the political spectrum, made worse by our recessed economy and worsening inequality for much of the past decade. It's possible that some may try to exploit these confluences of events for their ends."

"Agreed. Do you want to fix our economy to prevent an attack?"

"That's beyond my capabilities, but I'm sure greater prosperity and greater equality will result in a safer Australia."

Nicole nodded her head. "Nate?" she asked.

"We're looking into the potential compromising of the issuance of security clearances," he said. "Budget and headcount cutbacks under the previous government have led to perfunctory assessments at times, while reliance on contractors and consultants has increased the numbers of clearances issued over the past while."

"How long for?"

"Seven years."

Nicole took a shortbread biscuit. "So hundreds? Thousands?"

"Many thousands."

Nicole ate some of her biscuit. "That's a problem. Any ideas?"

"All security clearances expire in time and need to be reassessed, which is no help if headcounts aren't relaxed and budget pressures eased."

"We need an economic recovery, greater equality, and a public service with sufficient resources to do necessary tasks effectively. Am I missing something?" Nicole asked.

"That's about the size of it," Nate said.

"I'll write something along these lines for the Director General, who can discuss this with the minister if he deems that appropriate. Economic prosperity might be elusive, although our new government has indicated they will increase taxes at the higher end of the scale, permanently increase unemployment benefits, and re-work our industrial relations regime, while more resources to adequately vet security clearances, if that's going to happen, will take time. Thank you Nate and Adam."

They left Nicole's office to return to respective offices overlooking respective teams who worked from shoulder-high cubicles: a desk, a chair, a laptop, a screen, and a shelf clipped to one of the partitions. They didn't have access to natural light or views across the lake. Adam pondered his next move before taking his personal smartphone from his leather satchel. He pressed a contact, it rang; he answered: "hello Adam."

"Hello Andrew. Are you interested in filling out a few hours this afternoon?"

"For sure!"

"Usual place at the usual time."

"See you there."

"Bye."

Adam ended the call and put his smartphone away, to then ponder their situation. The previous Liberal-National government unashamedly favoured the wealthy while dismantling industrial relations systems originally implemented to help those less well off. Oddly, those who were far from recipients of government favour, and indeed suffered because of reduced labour bargaining power, re-elected them multiple times. Perhaps they thought one day they would be wealthy and beneficiaries of that favour but that would never happen. No, they believed that lie, before they had enough of blatant corruption. Even if the Director

General advised action to benefit the nation's security, that would take time which they didn't have. Adam rotated his chair to admire the view once more. At least the shimmering blue lake and lush green lawns never changed.

* * *

The Royal Canberra Golf Club was an institution dating back many decades; almost as old as the city itself. To be Royal it had to be, but its age and stature was also reflected in the attractive, brick and stucco clubroom, unlike much of modern Canberra being concrete and glass. The club's age and stature was also reflected in club fees and in a restricted membership. It was for those who knew someone important, which for Adam wasn't a problem given he was third-generation public service from the upper echelons of the biggest employer in town. At a window overlooking the greens, Adam gazed across a normally delightful view with his mind oddly blank.

"What's wrong, mate?" Andrew asked.

"Pardon? Sorry? Ah, I'm not good company today."

"Tough weekend?"

Adam remembered back and involuntarily grimaced. Saturday nights were dining out nights while Sunday morning was time with Susan. The former was tolerable because of Adam's favourite Indian restaurant, while the latter was perfunctory and routine, as always. Adam wondered how to frame what bothered him. He suspected Andrew guessed or may even have the same issue.

"We have a routine we've fallen into," Adam said as he contemplated his gin and tonic. "It's agreed, no words need to be spoken. Perhaps such routines lose their sparkle over time."

"Everything loses sparkle over time," Andrew said. "There are ways to spice such things up."

"That takes agreement by two where such agreements might not be reached."

"Understood and not unique. There are a few other options, one of which I'm sure you can guess. The other option is something similar but different." Andrew leaned close. "Sugar babies," he whispered.

Adam hadn't thought about that, beyond hearing about them of course. "Do you know anyone who has?"

"Maybe. Although there's a financial reward involved, it might be more like a date. A bonus is 18, 19, 20, or older if you prefer. Don't expect a meeting of minds but don't dismiss it either. Things are tough for university students these days."

Adam sat more upright while he sipped his drink. There might be attractions in that. He wondered how to put it. "That might sparkle," Adam said.

"It might."

Adam thought a discreet search engine, not Google of course, would not only point him to the relevant sites where such arrangements could be initiated, but also give hints and tips. He sipped his drink to realise it was empty.

"Another one?" Andrew asked.

"No thanks. Another one of life's little routines is dinner at seven, so I ought to hit the road." Adam thought. "Our little discussion has given me food for thought, though."

"Don't expect an intellectual challenge but that's not the point of it."

Adam smiled to himself at that thought. "I suppose not."

Andrew glanced at his watch before emptying his scotch and water. "I didn't realise the time," before he looked to Adam. "I have a date waiting."

Adam couldn't help but smirk at that revelation, before walking with Andrew to the carpark. At Adam's black Lexus NX300 SUV: luxurious and practical, he stopped.

"Enjoy your date, Andrew."

"Always."

Adam climbed into a charcoal-grey leather seat while thinking 18, 19 or 20 at university had the potential to sparkle. He buckled up to drive home while feeling pleased about that conversation.

Chapter Seven

Alice took away their breakfast plates to stack the dishwasher while Luke thought they'd been waiting a while. Surely time was running down.

"There's one thing guys," Luke said. "John might come for us anytime soon."

"I ought to see more of Canberra before then," Mike said. "I've been to the city centre and I went for a drive to the space complex south of the city. Do you have any other ideas?"

"The lookout tower on Black Mountain is good," Alice said.

"I'll check that out."

"Go to Parliament House," Luke said. "You'll need to buy a ticket though."

"I'll buy a ticket today for tomorrow."

"I heard the War Memorial is good," Jake said. "You'll need to buy a ticket for there."

"You ought to come with me, Jake."

"Thanks Mike. We'll buy tickets today to sightsee tomorrow."

Just then, Luke's smartphone rang. John Connell.

"Hi mate," Luke greeted.

"Can I come around to discuss something?" John asked.

"Sure."

"Be there in 20 minutes."

Luke ended the call.

John will be here soon," he said. "We'll wait in the living room."

They sat: Mike and Jake on the couch with Luke and Alice opposite in the armchairs. Then knocking at the door.

"I'll get it," Alice said. Moments later, "Hello John, come in. There's space on the couch there."

John sat in the middle to place a laptop on the coffee table.

"The previous Liberal-National government had a plan to demolish Anzac Hall at the War Memorial to replace it with a new, bigger hall, in total costing half a billion dollars. Prime Minister Devi is going to announce the cancellation of this project, on Tuesday at 11 at a press conference in Anzac Hall. This is a good chance to get at her."

"Do you know Anzac Hall?" Luke asked.

"Anzac Hall is on two levels connected to the older part of the War Memorial by an upper level walkway. At the end of the walkway is a cafe on the right, while this level juts partway above displays on the lower level. The upper level area outside the cafe is where the Prime Minister will hold her press conference. A staircase connects the upper level to the lower level, where visitors can get closer to exhibits."

"Will there be visitors during this press conference?"

"Anzac Hall will be closed from 10.30 to 12."

"What's your advice?" Luke asked John.

"Plant an IED on the upper level near the cafe."

"I don't want to damage war exhibits," Luke said.

"Exhibits are quite a distance from there."

"There must be press at a press conference," Alice said.

"Press numbers will be restricted due to Covid-19 distancing requirements."

"It's a loss of life for a greater good," Luke said.

"Yes, of course," Alice said.

John opened his laptop, to stand beside Mike and Alice. He showed a diagram of the older part of the War Memorial, the walkway, and the two levels of Anzac Hall. Luke thought.

"Alice and I will go there tomorrow to check this out. If we can hide an IED, we can trigger it by using a mobile phone when we know Devi's in Anzac Hall."

"I think Alice should do that," John said. "She stands out less than you, mate."

Luke thought for a moment – yes. "I agree," he said.

John closed his laptop and sat between Mike and Jake again.

"Do you need us tomorrow?" Mike asked.

"No mate," Luke said. "Alice and I will check out Anzac Hall while you and Jake do your sightseeing. We've got until Tuesday anyway."

"You've got a good job, John, where you can come here during the day," Alice said.

"Whenever possible we work from home, which is what I'm doing today."

"Ha, so this is work!"

John laughed while Luke contemplated John, a key member of their team. He wondered before leaning close to Alice.

"This time, what do you think of Mike, Jake and John?" Luke whispered.

"No Luke," Alice whispered back.

"Are you being naughty again?"

Alice nodded her head with her finger in her mouth.

"Go to our room."

With her head down and her finger still in her mouth, Alice crept to their room. Luke strode in and closed the door.

"Take off your clothes," Luke ordered.

Alice did while Luke watched with his arms crossed. He went to the bottom drawer of the cabinet beside his side of the bed, where the long, stainless steel chain and clamp set sparkled. He took them to Alice to pinch first one nipple, already mostly erect, and clamp it, then clamped her other nipple which didn't need pinching at all. Kneeling now, Luke rubbed her pussy with his fingers, already wet and aroused, before clamping first one labia lip and her other. He stood back, arms crossed again. Nice.

"Does that hurt, Alice?"

She nodded her head.

"Put on your mesh baby doll."

Alice went to the top drawer of the cabinet beside her side of the bed, to pull out a bundle of black. She put in on, which covered but didn't hide her.

"Go into the living room and stand in the corner for 20 minutes."

Head down Alice did that, while the looks on Mike's and Jake's faces were even more priceless than last time, and especially John of course. Alice stood in the corner, nose to the wall and her cute bum exposed to all to see. Pain, yes, humiliation, very much yes.

"Has Alice been naughty?" Mike asked.

"She said no," Luke said.

"No to what?"

"Just no."

Mike laughed. "You've got the life."

In the corner of the room, Alice stood silently. Luke doubted that Alice would ever learn her place.

* * *

Asha gazed out of the window of the light rail as it sped past house after house, all modern and new, on her way to

Gungahlin. Matt texted he could pick her up from Jolimont Centre or she could catch the light rail, but Asha had travelled all the way to Boggabilla and home again, so the least she could do was catch a light rail across Canberra. So there she was late in the day as they left the last of those two-storey houses behind, brick and concrete with new trees and very little grass, and passed shops instead. So many shops, and cafes and restaurants; all new like the houses. People, so many people; many more people than you would ever see in Cootamundra or even Wagga, and this was just a part of Canberra and not the main part.

An announcement for the end of their journey at Gungahlin, so Asha stood as the light rail eased to a halt. There she pushed the button for double doors to spring open. The platform for the light rail was just two steps down, and after that Asha could wheel her case along concrete paths surrounded by all those people. Remembering the directions from Matt's text she walked in the same direction as the light rail, crossed at the traffic lights, turned left and then saw, amongst even more shops, the entrance to the apartment building which was the tallest building in the vicinity. With a bank of letterboxes to her left, Asha keyed '304' and pressed 'hash'.

"Hi Asha," Matt's distorted voice greeted. "I'll release the door and you can come up to level three."

The glass door clicked but didn't open, until Asha took one step back. There she entered a carpeted lobby, and picked up her case by its handle to climb flights of stairs. Up to floor three which was the top floor, where a brass sign guided her to the left. She saw 304 in brass on a black door which had a buzzer. She pressed the buzzer. Moments later, the door opened.

"Hi Asha, come in."

She entered, where like the lobby and staircase it was all sparkling new, and quite lovely, especially walls painted in light grey and floors in dark grey tiles. Just to the right was a long, narrow kitchen with stone bench tops, which looked almost unused. Next was a combined dining and lounge room a bit like Asha's home, with a rectangular dining table which had metal legs and grey tiles on top, and six chairs which matched, while beyond that was a couch and two armchairs in light grey leather with a low table between, in metal with grey tiles like a small version of the dining table. Big windows overlooked a balcony outside. There was a bedroom on the left with a queen-sized bed and windows to a balcony on that side, and another bedroom with a king-sized bed clearly used, and again windows to the balcony. The two bedrooms had dark grey carpet. Hiding somewhere must be a bathroom.

"How was your trip?" Matt asked.

"My trip was fine and ride here on the light rail was good." Asha thought. "This is nice here in Gungahlin with so many shops."

Matt laughed. "I'm sure you could have fun shopping here," he said.

That was true. "Yes, very much. This is a lovely place to live; you must have a good view."

"Have a look."

Asha crossed his living room past the lounge suite to the big window to look across the balcony and down to the streets she'd just walked along, and saw the light rail just over there.

"I like it here," Asha said. It was clean and modern, busy but not too busy, and had housing right in the shopping centre.

Matt came alongside. "What we shot last week at Koorawatha, and what we're going to shoot tomorrow, will help with your resume. But if you want to be a full-time model, you'll need better than the Gemini Modelling Agency in Canberra."

That was true.

"Don't worry Asha," Matt said. "Tomorrow's shoot will be good experience and will help when you move to bigger things."

"What's this shoot about?" Asha asked.

"The Canberra Chamber of Commerce will be running a campaign promoting Canberra as open and ready for tourism. Part of tourism to Canberra is shopping for fashion, having your hair styled and visiting makeup salons, and that's where you fit in. You'll be highlighting various tourist spots, and fashion and styling and so on."

"People in Cootamundra could come to Canberra to see the sights and go on a fashion shopping binge."

"I can't see people coming from Sydney to shop in Canberra, but from Cootamundra and places like that, for sure."

"This is real modelling."

"Bikini modelling is real modelling but this is more elaborate."

"You'll have fashions for me to wear and a makeup artist and a hair stylist?" Asha asked.

"Yes."

Asha pondered that. "This is more responsible," she said.

"Don't worry about that," Matt said. "You're beautiful and the camera loves you."

Asha couldn't help but grin.

"Do you want to go out for dinner? Matt asked. "My shout on expenses?"

That sounded nice. "If that's no trouble," she replied.

"It's easier to eat out than to cook, and there are many restaurants as you probably saw."

"I saw lots of restaurants!"

"What food do you like?"

"It doesn't matter; I can try something new."

"Alright, let's go."

Matt held the door before they went down the staircase together.

Chapter Eight

Right on time Matt heard the intercom. He released the outside door and moments later, opened his door. Jenny came in, dwarfed by a big, black, felt hat, to air-kiss him.

"Hi Jenny," Matt greeted. "This is Asha."

Asha got an air-kiss too. "Oh she's so beautiful!" Jenny exclaimed. "Asha, your pictures don't do you justice! I'm Jenny and I'm your hair stylist and makeup artist, and in the back of Matt's car we have your clothes for today, except this outfit," as Jenny displayed the suit-pack draped over her arm. Yesterday, Matt and I visited our shooting locations so we know where to get changed and all those important things."

Asha looked a bit stunned. "That's good," she eventually said.

"Don't worry if this seems confusing, we know what we're doing. I've seen your bikini shots and the camera just loves you! Canberra is like a big country town, so a country girl like you is perfect! Let's go to your room to get you ready. Such lovely complexion, just a little eye shadow, and pale pink lipstick with pale pink nail polish. Gorgeous hair too."

Carrying the suit-pack and her makeup case, Jenny followed Asha into the spare room while Matt leaned against the back of couch with his arms crossed. Jenny was efficient and he knew this would be quick. Not so long after, Asha emerged in a black blouse with white sequins along the seams, a white almost ankle-length skirt, and calf-high black boots with quite a few centimetres of heel, and now carrying the black, broad-brimmed felt hat that Jenny wore. Eye shadow, pale pink lipstick, pale pink nail polish, a tortoiseshell hairclip, and gold studs in her pieced ears.

"Asha can carry that hat when we shoot," Matt told Jenny. "She'll have to."

"You look great, Asha," Matt said. "Come on, let's go."

"You need a bigger car," Jenny said.

"You can fit in the back."

They headed downstairs, past the foyer and down more stairs to the carpark which was always cold, even on a warm to hot, sunny summer's day. Matt pressed the button on the driver's door to release the locks, Jenny stowed her luggage with everything else there, and slammed the tailgate.

"You need a bigger car, Matt," Jenny repeated before opening the left side passenger door. The Veloster was unusual with one big door on the right and two smaller doors on the left, and although the back was cramped it was big enough for Jenny. Asha climbed in front just as Matt pressed the start button. Soon they were off, up the ramp and out.

"Our first stop is Telstra Tower on Black Mountain," Matt said.

"Is that far?" Asha asked.

Matt realised her confusion. "For the federation of the Australian colonies to succeed, they needed a capital city that wasn't either of the two biggest cities: Sydney and Melbourne. So Canberra was planned and built, inland away from the risk of sea invasion, because this was in the days before aircraft, and in the mountains where it's cooler than further inland. Canberra straddles seven mountain peaks."

"I've seen temperatures here," Asha commented.

"It is colder here than in Cootamundra, although where you come from is cold enough on winter mornings."

"It can be very cold."

Being planned meant that main roads were laid out before houses, so driving around Canberra was a breeze. In no time they were climbing Black Mountain.

"This is gorgeous!" Asha exclaimed. "So much bush!"

Up and up and up until Matt reached the near-empty carpark, where he did a loop to park near where he planned his first shot. They climbed out. Matt reached for his camera, prepared for daytime shooting, only there were two guys at the top of the stairs. Never mind, they wouldn't be there for long.

"We'll wait here," Matt said.

"Can I look around?" Asha asked.

"Just over there is a view towards the city. I'll call you when we're ready."

She headed off.

"I hope this turns out better than you know who," Jenny said.

"Rachel," Matt said, although Jenny knew her name.

"And the other one."

"Jade. This is different."

"Asha looks young. How old?"

"Asha's 18 but different."

"That's young Matt."

Matt looked into Jenny's eyes. "Asha's been racially taunted since the day she went to school, and she's just returned from a year in a medical clinic in a shithole in outback New South Wales, where she had to deal with drunkenness, domestic violence and rapes. Asha has more life experience than girls her age, or girls much older."

"She is gorgeous."

The two men were still there.

"Jenny, can you get Asha and I'll ask those guys to move out of the way?"

Matt climbed the staircase to stop a couple of metres short, to be Covid-safe, of a pair of guys, one older and tall and one younger and short, the older one in a Harley-Davidson t-shirt, Levi jeans, boots and sunglasses, and the younger one in a white t-shirt and cheap jeans.

"Excuse me," Matt said. "We're doing a photographic shoot and I wondered if you can move out of the way a bit."

"No worries mate," the tall one said with a big smile, before looking over the balcony wall. "Is she your girl?"

"She's our model."

"Nice. See you later."

They headed down the ramp on the other side as Matt returned to Asha and Jenny.

"Asha, this is different to the bikini shoot. Today you've come to Canberra to buy gorgeous clothes, and the people who see your picture can come to Canberra and shop, or not. It's their choice not your choice; you really don't care. Do you understand?"

"I've looked at pictures of fashion shoots and I think I know the look you want."

She'd done her research, excellent. "Climb to the top of the staircase and I'll shoot from the bottom, looking up so the tower is in the frame. Hold your hat in your left hand."

She climbed, and surprisingly she strode well in those boots. It was a gorgeous outfit that suited her, although models were tall and slender because clothes, no matter the style, always hung well on them. Matt stood at the bottom.

"Please look down to me," Matt said. "Remember, you don't care if they come here or not."

She looked down as Matt ran off a couple of shots.

"That's great, Asha. Just like that."

A few more.

Matt looked up towards the sun.

"Put your hat on but tilt it backwards so it doesn't shade your face." She did. "Great." A couple more. "This is good." A few more. "Alright, that's it for here. Now we go to the cafe and lookout."

Asha bent her head back to look up the tower. "Up there?" she asked.

"Yes."

"Cool!"

Matt led Asha through the foyer to a bored-looking security guard at a small window. Matt was sure the tower was built in the 1970s, where the foyer, the small window and the entry gates hadn't changed in the meantime. In any case Matt bought entry for two adults, got two round, copper tokens which they dropped into those old-fashioned gates, to be able to get to the lift where doors sprang open when Matt pressed the 'up' button. After selecting the cafe level, the lift hurtled upwards with the metres above sea level showed on an indicator: starting at 810 metres, the summit of Black Mountain, higher and higher until they reached 870 metres and doors sprang open. The communications tower reached quite a bit higher than the observation decks.

The cafe was quiet with only one couple with coffees each. Canberra was a popular tourist destination, but with external borders closed and some state borders closed until recently, international tourism had been obliterated while domestic tourism had taken a hit. Asha's observation was spot-on: Cootamundra, Wagga Wagga, Young where Sophie and Emma lived, and other cities and towns in New South Wales were targets for this campaign.

"We're not having coffee here," Matt said. "Please put your hat on, tilt it backwards so it doesn't hide your face, and sit at a table away from those people." Matt looked around. "That one there."

"Just sit and look indifferent?" Asha asked.

"Now you're looking forward to a nice coffee, if that makes sense."

"I'll try."

She sat while Matt knelt a few metres from her table to take a few shots.

"Asha, smile at the camera but too brightly."

"Got it."

She did that while her hat was astounding. Matt took six or seven shots before standing and checking them. Beyond Asha, all that were in the frame were empty tables and chairs which was perfect. It was a hole in the wall cafe, possibly not changed since the 1970s, where Matt didn't want to show the counter or the Asian guy there watching on.

"I've got what I want. Now we go up the stairs."

Asha stood to look through the floor to ceiling windows of the cafe. "This is an amazing view."

That was a serious understatement as Matt led the way up the stairs and outside to the outside observation gallery, where it was breezy and Asha had to hold her hat. Actually, that was good.

"Stand there please, and look to the view while holding your hat."

Asha turned to look, still holding her hat, with her dress swirling and showing more of her boots. Matt's shots would show nothing clear beyond Asha, so she was the view even though her face was side-on because of the narrowness of the gallery. Matt ran off about five shots.

"I think this will work," he said.

"Can I see?" Asha asked.

Matt scrolled them, just right.

"Are we lucky with the breeze up here?" Asha asked.

"We are," Matt said.

"Where do you live?"

"This way," Matt said as he walked around the gallery to now face north-west. "Down there is the road we came along, while over there," as Matt pointed, "is Gungahlin."

"So far and so many trees. There are more trees than buildings in Canberra."

"We call Canberra the bush capital."

"I can see why."

"This way," as Matt headed east. "That's the city centre just there."

"There's a mountain and bush close to the city."

"It was planned like this."

"It's lovely."

"We should go now. In the foyer, Jenny will take you to the ladies toilet to get changed for our next destination."

Down the steps, to the lift, and down to the foyer where Jenny with another suit-pack intercepted Asha, as Matt went to his car to stow his camera. About 20 minutes later Asha now wore an almost ankle-length dress with a plunging neckline, gathered at her waist with a thin belt, in white with a panel of dark brown, light grey stiletto boots, her hair braided into one plat, and small, round gold earrings. They came to the car.

"I hardly wear dresses, mostly jeans," Asha said. "I'm going to buy more dresses, they're great!"

"They look good on you," Jenny said.

"They're practical and comfortable on a hot day."

"We'll get into the car," Matt said.

Off they went to the War Memorial, which was going to be challenging given it was the biggest tourist attraction in the city. Australians took their contributions to war very seriously. To the underground carpark where, after locking his car, Matt led the way up the ramp with Asha not quite steady on her stiletto heels. She needed to practice that. Up and up the ramp to the forecourt. There, a crowd milled around not entirely keeping a social distance. Not surprising as directly opposite was broad, Anzac Avenue leading to Lake Burley Griffin, while on the other side of the lake and some distance back was Old Parliament House which was a particularly attractive building in white, and some distance behind that set into Capital Hill, Parliament House itself, dominated by a tall, four-legged flagpole with the Australian flag flying. On a bright, sunny day, the blue lake and green lawns were magnificent.

"We see you again, mate," Matt heard.

"What?" Matt exclaimed before he recognised them. Those two guys from Telstra tower. Must be tourists. "Yes we do," he said.

"She's gorgeous, you know."

Matt nodded his head in acknowledgement while they stood back and watched. Indeed all tourists moved back and watched, probably sensing Asha was professional and this was a proper shoot.

"Asha," Matt said. "Stand close to the edge of the forecourt facing me, while the way you look is the same as outside the tower. You don't care if tourists come to the War Memorial or not; that's their loss if they don't come here."

Asha got her look right, she had that mastered, but something was wrong. Too formal.

"Jenny, can you loosen her hair?" Matt asked.

"Sure."

Jenny untied the braid and fluffed Asha's hair out.

"Again," Matt said. "Run your hands through your hair. That's right, perfect. Again. Once more.'

Matt lowered his camera while he walked to the shade of the building. There he checked his shots while Jenny and Asha looked on.

"That's good," Jenny said. "You were right about her hair."

They were good.

"We'll braid her hair for the cafe," Matt said. "Guess what Asha?"

She smiled. "There's a toilet inside for me to get changed."

"Come with me," Jenny said.

When they walked away the crowd spread across the forecourt again. Models were like celebrities who parted crowds just by being there. About 20 minutes later Asha was in a little black dress, tight as tight, bare arms, black stilettos, dangling golden earrings, heavier eye shadow, darker lipstick, and her hair braided. In no time they were driving further east around the perimeter of the lake to the southern shore. There, Matt parked in the shade of an apartment building before they walked along streets lined by many, modern apartment buildings. Until recently that part of Kingston was a neglected light industrial area, now transformed. Between two, blue-tinged four-storey buildings and onto the boardwalk which fronted the lake. The ground floors of those apartment buildings were shops, cafes, restaurants, gyms and more. Twenty2 Espresso was expecting them as Matt went inside to what seemed like darkness after the intense light outside.

"Hi Matt," Kevin, the manager greeted. "I've reserved a table close to the lake although it's quiet today.

Indeed it was quiet; there was nobody there. "Let's hope this campaign works," Matt offered.

"For sure."

"Can you bring out a flat white for the model to pose with?"

"No problem."

Back outside.

"That table with the reserved sign is ours," Matt said.

"We have to fight our way through the crowds," Jenny said as she took the reserved sign away.

"Asha take a seat, the waiter will bring you a coffee, and you can guess what you have to do."

She smiled. "I can guess."

"It's a serious coffee, though." Matt thought. "It's the most delicious coffee you've ever tasted and you don't want to miss any of its delightful flavour.

"Not quite the indifferent look and not quite smiling while looking forward to a nice coffee."

"Something like that."

"Got it."

Matt moved chairs from the next table for more room before Kevin brought the coffee. Asha picked it up to sip with a subdued almost-smile, just the right expression, while Matt knelt to take a shot, and moved and knelt, and moved and knelt, and moved and knelt. All the way around until he had the facade of the cafe in the frame. But for sure, across the table towards the still waters of the blue lake would be the best.

Matt stood. "That's it. Did you drink that coffee, Asha?"

"It was nice."

Kevin and his two staff watched on; transfixed. Like everyone they were fascinated by their shoot. Matt gestured and Kevin came close.

"Two more flat whites please Kevin," Matt ordered.

"On the house."

"Thanks."

Matt sat as did Jenny.

"How do you feel?" Jenny asked Asha.

"Today, and our bikini shoot, have been the two second-best days of my life," she said.

"What's your best day?"

"My best ever day was dancing in the big corroboree in Wagga just after I passed Year 12."

"Really?"

"It was the first corroboree in Wagga for more than a hundred years."

"Amazing! How do you feel about today?"

"Apart from the need to buy more dresses? It's been great and I've learned a lot."

"You've been great, Asha. You're right on it and the camera loves you."

"Thank you Jenny."

Their flat whites arrived which were just right. Canberra was the home of great coffee, everywhere.

"You'll regret that," Asha said and laughed.

"So will you," Matt responded.

"I know. What's next?"

"Next is The National Zoo and Aquarium. There are toilets there to change and deal with the after-effects of caffeine. After we shoot there you'll change again, and then we'll drive north to Gold Creek where there are three attractions, so you'll have a lot of changing to do there. We'll have lunch either at the zoo or Gold Creek."

"This has been easy so far. Are publicity shoots like this?"

"Publicity shoots are generally like this," Jenny said. "You need to have a certain look and build to be a model, which you have, and you respond well to Matt's instructions. In fact you have an expressive face. All models do this sort of work; say Samantha Harris worked for David Jones for a while, doing fashion shoots fairly much the same as today. Magazine shoots like Vogue or Harpers Bazaar are much the same, too."

"So this is good experience?"

"Oh yes! For the duration of this campaign you're the face of Canberra. There are hundreds of thousands riding on this."

"Really?"

"Don't worry, you've been great."

"I'm glad I didn't know that before!" Asha exclaimed and laughed.

"Just keep on going, Asha, and you'll be perfect!"

"I've noticed people watching. Obviously these clothes are lovely but there are other things. People have called me names and worse, but not today."

Matt knew Canberra was generally tolerant although many of those looking on were tourists from other places. That was a good point: Asha had gone from being called names to a star. He finished his coffee. "Come on ladies, let's go. We've got more photography to do."

Matt stood and sensed company on that boardwalk. He turned to spot those two guys from Telstra Tower and then the War Memorial. Now that was peculiar. Matt glanced at them a second time as they watched on with the tall one smiling when their gazes met. Perhaps that was a coincidence. Then he realised and jogged after Jenny and Asha, now steadier in stilettos as they walked to his car.

* * *

Matt eased his car into his parking space and pressed the button to switch off. Home at last, and although it was not long past four it had been a long day. He climbed out, as did Asha and Jenny. In the visitor's bay was Jenny's SUV, where it didn't take long to transfer a makeup case and thousands of dollars of dresses, skirts, blouses, stiletto sandals, boots, jewellery and a big hat. They would be returned to sponsoring boutiques and department stores to be sold. The final step was in Matt's apartment where Asha replaced her last outfit, a black silk blouse partly unbuttoned over a black lace bra, white bell-bottom slacks, a gold pendant, and gold and diamond earrings, with jeans and a t-shirt. With the last suit-pack in her hand, Jenny air-kissed them both.

"See you Jenny," Matt offered.

"Thank you very much, Jenny," Asha said.

"Goodnight you two and enjoy your evening."

Matt flopped onto his couch. Asha sat on a chair opposite.

"Are you tired?" Matt asked.

Asha laughed. "Yeah, I'm tired. It was nice though. I'm going to tell my family and friends to come to Canberra."

"Your kin?"

"All of them. Now I might try to use your half of a bath."

"Feel free."

"Your shower is very big, though."

His bathroom was back to front although two could shower at the same time.

Asha headed to the bathroom where soon water was running. After Asha finished and returned to the living room, Matt showered to wash away his tiredness. Indeed that worked. Soon he was with Asha again. From the time he met her and her thoughtful conversations in his car, through the bikini shoot where she concentrated hard and followed his instructions, and made friends with Sophie and Emma too, to today where she looked and acted like a professional, she'd been – surprising for her age. Asha was young, but in this case 18 was just a number. Mature, outgoing, friendly, capable, beautiful. A girl to fall in love with. For sure Matt felt love; a gorgeous, delicious, warm glow just by being in her company. Matt wondered if Asha felt the same.

"I still can't get over those people admiring me," Asha said to interrupt Matt's thoughts. "It was strange, odd; I don't know the right word."

"Ironic," Matt suggested.

"Yes, ironic. We were invaded and our land was taken from us, some were massacred and many more died from diseases that whites brought to our land. We were herded into missions, some worked on cattle or sheep stations for nothing or next to nothing, only to be booted off decades ago and end up in towns like Boggabilla. In the middle of that, some mixed-race children, maybe the offspring of rape even, were stolen from their families and raised in institutions or given to white families. But for those who weren't stolen, all the other things that happened have scarred us, some more than others. I'm lucky, my parents have a home and Dad has a good job, but even then I've been called names just for who I am. Mum and Dad say hate eats you away inside and they're right, so I ignored them. Now there's a demand for indigenous models. I wish more of my people had opportunities like this but I discovered our problems in some parts of Australia are too big. I tried to close the gap in one town, but I had a room with three locks on the door and bars on the window for protection. Now all I can do is look after one indigenous girl, respect and care for my kin, and make the most out of my opportunity. My kin, my family, love me and I know they'll be proud of me."

Matt realised something. "You can be like an ambassador for your people, the Wiradjuri Nation."

"I hope I can be. I don't hate anyone in particular but those in school who called me abo and worse, I can't wait for them to see me from today's pictures. We already have an ambassador who you probably know. Stan Grant, he's Wiradjuri like me. I've read his articles on growing up which would have been what my parents went through, and I've read his articles on other things like China and America where he's clear and easy to understand. He's brilliant and a role model to us all, and he shows whites who are still racist that there's no real difference beyond the colour of our skins."

"I'm a Stan Grant fan myself; he's clear, sharp, intelligent and articulate. Even his reasoning to stay out of politics where he would be bound to follow party lines is – astute."

"He represents us better from where he is."

Matt's glow of love was ever more persistent, and he thought, unlike Re-Make / Re-Model, it was now. "Asha, I think I could fall in love with you," he said quietly.

Silence for a moment. "I see," she said.

"You have a great personality, you're bright, capable, everything. And really, the difference is the colour of our skins."

Asha tilted her head while she looked at Matt. "There are other things," she eventually said. "My kin are my family, which if we go further becomes your family."

"I expected that."

"My spirituality...."

"Spirituality is missing in my life."

"Like most whites, I think."

"Your spirituality makes you, you."

"Do you think so?"

"Yes it does, and your kin makes you, you too."

"Don't forget elders are auntie and uncle, out of respect."

"Of course."

"There are many things you need to learn, not to love me but out of respect. Let me put it clearer. You need to know our culture so you don't accidentally offend my people, and especially not offend my kin."

That made sense. "I understand," Matt said.

"If you're prepared to learn in order to love me, then I'm prepared to love you too."

"Do you love me?" Matt asked; now quite shocked.

"You're the best guy I've ever met, and I feel – I don't know the word, no, when we're together I feel lighter and calmer and warmer than I've ever felt before. I think this is love."

Lightness, calmness and warmth. "That's how I feel," Matt said before looking into Asha's dark eyes. "There's more to love, you know."

"I know."

"Do you want to?"

"Yes I do," she said quietly.

"Do you want to make love with me?" Matt asked to be sure.

"I do."

Matt stood, Asha stood; Matt took her slim hand to lead her to his room.

* * *

Asha lay with her head on Matt's chest while he lightly stroked her hair. He stopped.

"Don't stop."

He stroked her hair again.

"That's nice," Asha murmured.

"I love you," Matt said.

"I love you too."

"You're beautiful and smart, mature and capable, young and wise."

"Go on," Asha said.

"I love you."

"You're handsome and talented, fun and nice. Really nice, and respectful too."

"Go on," Matt said."

"I love you."

Somehow they fitted.

"I don't want to overwhelm you," Asha said, "but there's one important thing you must know now for me and for my people. You must never mention the name of someone who's not with us anymore, and you must never show their image in any form. The only word you can use in relation to this is sorry business."

"I've seen warnings about images of...."

"That's sorry business," Asha interrupted.

"How much do you know about your heritage?" Matt asked out of curiosity.

"Mum's big on our heritage and I've looked things up on the internet. Early explorers and settlers wrote journals and diaries although they didn't understand what they were writing about. But if you look beyond their judgements you can get an idea. Marriages were arranged when a girl was born, so a respected elder might end up with a few wives, where some were quite young, just of marrying age. Young men had to wait but sometimes they abducted women, obviously from other clans, although there might have been love involved there. It appears some wives wanted to leave their arranged husbands. When there was an abduction, a war or really just a skirmish would follow. One clan would attack the other, and when an injury had been inflicted that was the end of it. Just because marriages were arranged doesn't mean there wasn't affection or even love, though. I'm sure you've heard of corroborees which aren't dances put on for tourists! Corroborees are where we interact with The Dreaming. Let me make it clearer; our body markings are spiritual while the music and our dance steps tell stories of The Dreaming. The word corroboree is from the language of another nation but I don't know what our word for it is. First Nations people were barred from using our languages for a long time and some of our language has been lost."

"I know you danced in a corroboree," Matt said.

"I danced in Wagga Wagga, which means 'a place of dances and celebrations' in our language."

"Not 'many crows'?"

Asha laughed. "Not 'many crows'. Now, corroboree. Clans would travel to the host clan for a corroboree, which made whites of the time think that all we did was roam from place to place."

"It could be that Wagga Wagga was the place your ancestors from the Cootamundra Clan interacted with The Dreaming."

"More than likely it was."

"What was it like to dance like that?"

"It was too good! Really, we're making progress. Stan Grant the elder, Stan Grant's father, got the meaning of Wagga Wagga corrected, which was a big thing because everything there is based on crows, so all the signs had to be changed and everything. Not so long ago he was called names, he struggled to make a living, he was poor even, and now he's important."

"If you met him, you would call him uncle."

"Yes I would. It's respectful but informal, like 'hello uncle'."

Matt understood. "Sophie was right, probably because she learned this in school. We can't unravel the past but we can move forward in a new spirit of reconciliation."

"We are moving forward, step by step." Asha sat up. "Now, what do you want to do for dinner?"

Matt knew. "I'll get some Indian delivered."

Asha laughed. "This is a city after all."

Indeed Canberra was the capital city of Australia, even if in many ways it was like a country town.

"I'll freshen up for our Indian meal, whatever that is."

Asha slid out of bed while Matt admired her cute bottom. She was beautiful all over.

Chapter Nine

At the top of the forecourt of the Australian War Memorial, a guide waited. The view behind, across the lake to Parliament House, was incredible, as most of Canberra was incredibly beautiful. Luke and Alice queued at a marked distance from a number of others who held the same ticket, Anzac Hall, for that time of the day, 11.45. To be grouped like that was a problem, as the guide inspected their tickets on Luke's smartphone before heading into the Memorial. They were taken past older exhibits, past cases of medals and up stairs to a glass-walled walkway, into Anzac Hall, which was as John described and showed on his laptop. The guide invited the group to look around while keeping a distance, where Luke guided Alice towards the promenade that jutted towards the big bomber. The Prime Minister would give her press conference somewhere in the vicinity of that promenade. Alice wandered off before coming back.

"Here, Luke."

'Here' was a seat not with legs but a sheeted-in base. Alice sat; Luke sat beside her.

"Could an IED do the job from inside the base of this seat?" Alice asked.

"It could. No, PETN will do the job, as long as I can get the top off this seat."

"There are bolts."

Indeed there were.

"Do you see CCTV?" Luke asked.

They both looked around.

"Over there, a distance away," as Alice turned her head.

Luke followed her gaze, yes. "I think, no I'm certain, if we keep beneath the barrier of this promenade, we won't be seen by that camera. Undo the four bolts, remove the top, put in the IED, bolt it up, done."

"How long will that take?" Alice asked.

"About ten minutes."

Their ticketed group numbered 30 with a guide; that wasn't going to work.

"We're not going to get ten minutes in a group like this," Luke said.

"I know. Let's check this place out."

They headed towards the cafe where there was a notice that Anzac Hall was available for hire for private functions.

"Here Alice," Luke said

She read. "Yes," she said. "What sort of function can we book? Even if we book a function, I'm sure there'll be a guide."

That was true. "We'll ask John, he's a local. He might have an idea. While we're here, let's sightsee."

They headed down stairs to view exhibits, mostly World War One and World War Two, including a bomber, submarines and many other fascinating items on display. It was truly amazing but time ran out too quickly. Soon they were on their way to the carpark for the drive to Hawker. As Luke pulled out and headed towards Limestone Avenue, he felt like a Canberran. Luke didn't need to use his GPS to get back to their flat. Car in the carport, and into their flat with airconditioning on.

"Do you want something to drink?" Alice asked. "A cup of tea?'

"Yes please."

In no time Luke sat in his armchair sat beside Alice in her armchair, sipping his tea. Nice.

"I'm getting used to being married to a Tradwife," he said.

"I've always spoiled you, mate."

"I know; you're the best."

"You're the best too. This is love, after all."

"Really?"

She punched his arm.

Just then the door opened: Mike and Jake.

"Hi guys," Luke offered.

"Do you want tea?" Alice asked.

"Thanks Alice, you're the best."

"I've already heard that today. You two, take a seat."

Alice went to the kitchen where soon the kettle was warming.

"How did your sightseeing go?" Alice asked.

"Great!" Mike exclaimed. "How did the War Memorial go?"

"We found a seat which can be unbolted, but we need ten minutes of uninterrupted time to do that and plant the IED. They book private functions in Anzac Hall which might give us the time, except there'll probably be a guide there."

Alice gave them mugs each.

"Thanks Alice," Jake said.

"Yeah, thanks," Mike said while frowning. "I have an idea; it might be crazy but hear me out. We went to the lookout tower on Black Mountain where there was a model, a photographer and a woman looking after the model's hair I think. The model was totally beautiful, I'm sure an abo. Later we saw them taking pictures in front of the War Memorial where the crowd parted like the waves of a sea, just to watch what was going on. Apart from this model being beautiful, it was quite involved with posing and then changing her hair and posing again. By coincidence we caught up with them a third time at Kingston, where they were taking pictures outside a cafe. All of the guys from the cafe were outside watching pictures being taken of the model drinking coffee, with the cafe empty. You could have emptied their till and they wouldn't have known."

Luke wondered where this was heading.

"I know what you're getting at," Alice said. "We'll book Anzac Hall to take pictures with this model, and that'll distract the guide."

"It should. I mean she's totally beautiful while the picture-taking is quite interesting."

"What do you think of Aboriginals?" Alice asked.

"I don't have a problem with Aboriginals," Mike said. "Unlike migrants who come here to clog our cities and take our jobs, Aboriginals have always been here and will always be here. Unlike Muslims who fly jets into skyscrapers, Aboriginals don't do that."

"They have The Dreaming," Jake said.

"That's right, they have The Dreaming." Mike leaned close to Alice. "You should have seen her. It's not that she's almost as tall as me and really good looking, her personality just overflowed. Apart from when the photographer took pictures and she had to look serious, she never stopped smiling. How old do you think she was, Jake?"

"Not old, 17 or 18."

"Really?" Alice exclaimed.

Knocking on the door.

"I'll get it," Alice said.

"Mate," Mike said to Luke. "Do you realise how lucky you are," as he pointed his thumb towards the door.

Luke understood; simple things like opening the door. "Yeah, I know."

"Hi all," John greeted with Alice by his side.

"Take a seat," Luke offered, where John placed his laptop on the coffee table before sitting between Mike and Jake.

"John, we have a plan," Luke said. "We'll book Anzac Hall on Monday evening for a photography session, using a model that Mike and Jake saw. This model will be a distraction to give them time to plant an IED inside a seat that Alice and I found. The IED will be a backpack with PETN, the detonating explosive, and a sim-operated detonator that Alice can dial. The top of this seat is held in place by four, 12mm bolts, and as long as they keep below the rail of the upper level, they'll be out of sight of any CCTV cameras."

"What's the name of this model?" John asked.

"I don't know," Mike said.

"That's no problem," John said as he picked up the laptop, opened the screen, waited a moment and typed. He handed it to Mike.

"Check those model websites," John said.

Luke watched Mike frowning, using the touchpad, frowning, touchpad, frowning. "Got her. Asha Reid at Gemini Modelling Agency."

"Can I see?" Luke asked.

Mike handed the laptop across which Luke balanced on his knees. He scrolled pictures.

"She's hot!" Alice exclaimed.

"She's totally hot," Mike said.

She was too. Luke thought. "I'll ring that agency now, book the model, find the photographer and the woman who does her hair and book them too, and book Anzac Hall for Monday evening, for a couple of hours to make it look genuine."

"John," Luke said, "do you have anything planned for this afternoon?"

He frowned. "Not really."

"Alice...?" Luke asked.

She put her head down with her finger in her mouth. "I can be good or I can be naughty. Which do you want me to be?"

"I want you to be good."

"Alice will be naughty again."

"Go to our room, take off your clothes, and bring me the paddle."

Alice left, head down with her finger in her mouth, while Luke glanced to Mike, John and Jake on the couch.

"A wife needs to be put in her place," Luke said.

Alice returned naked, not even partially obscured by black mesh, to hand the studded paddle to Luke. She put the flats of her hands on the coffee table with her upper body bent quite low and her bottom high. Luke took the paddle and hit Alice firmly with the slap quite distinct in the quiet room, again and again and again and again and again and again and again and again. And once more. Luke rubbed bright red flesh and not once did she whimper, although tears ran down her cheeks.

"Good girl," Luke said while he rubbed her.

"Can I dress now?"

"No you can't, Alice."

"Alright."

Alice gingerly sat in her armchair, her bottom must have been quite sore, while Luke wondered what he was up to – ah yes, phone calls to make those bookings. He took out his smartphone. He looked to the laptop where the phone numbers for Gemini Modelling Agency still displayed, before looking to Jake, John and Mike; all with eyes super-wide. Smiling to himself, Luke dialled.

Chapter Ten

Yaseera knew the history of Western parliamentary democracy and its adversarial nature, always at its worst during Question Time, which allows members of parliament to ask questions of the Prime Minister and other ministers, with the convention being the first question is asked of the Prime Minister. It would be more civil if interjections were banned, but if that was the case the Prime Minister and other ministers wouldn't directly answer their questions which would render Question Time useless. So it was what it was as they filed into the chamber just before two in the afternoon.

The Leader of the Opposition, Leo Harvey, stood from his chair opposite Yaseera.

"Madam Speaker, my question is to the Prime Minister. Will the Prime Minister confirm that she intends to put a referendum to the people of Australia to establish a third chamber of the Australian Parliament?"

"The Prime Minister," the speaker, Alana Roberts, said.

Yaseera stood.

"Thank you Madam Speaker. At the last election we took to the Australian people the commitment to establish an Indigenous Voice to Parliament, an advisory body only...," and she paused as the interjections from the opposition started. "An advisory body only, so that members of parliament are aware of indigenous issues when we make

decisions affecting the First Nations people of Australia."
More interjections. "This Voice to Parliament will not be
binding on any votes taken in this chamber, in the Senate, or
have any subsequent effect on decisions made by the
Parliament of Australia. The Uluru Statement of the Heart
believes the Indigenous Voice to Parliament is best enshrined
in the Constitution of Australia, to ensure it will remain in
perpetuity."

The chamber was more than just rowdy as Yaseera sat
while contemplating that third chamber view, which went
around and around and around. In the meantime the Shadow
Minister of Indigenous Affairs, John Foster, stood.

"Madam Speaker, my question is to the Prime Minister. Is
the Prime Minister preparing to negotiate a treaty with
indigenous people of Australia?"

"The Prime Minister."

Yaseera stood.

"Yes."

She sat to uproar while John Foster stood once more.

"Will this treaty extinguish rights to land currently held by
non-indigenous people of Australia?"

Yaseera stood.

"Is this a question or a cross-examination?" she asked.

"Please answer the question," the Speaker, Alana, asked.

"The proposed treaty with indigenous Australians will bring Australia in line with all other Commonwealth nations, which have treaties with their indigenous people, and which don't specifically impinge on non-indigenous people."

"How can you give something to someone without taking something from someone else?"

"A major part of this proposed treaty will be Truth Telling; an opportunity for our First Nations people to have their voices heard on past wrongs, which in many cases has ongoing impacts. We can't undo the past but we can change how history is viewed. Other aspects of this treaty may include land rights already vested to indigenous people on the basis of High Court precedent and subsequent legislation. Of course any treaty should include the Indigenous Voice to Parliament."

Yaseera sat to chaos which the speaker eventually quelled enough for Question Time to continue. The rest of Question Time was to other ministers including their plans for the tax rate increase, where James recited the original observation of 'trickle-down' economics, from 1930s USA, to obvious momentary shock. Knowledge of history can be valuable. Eventually Question Time was over leaving Yaseera to walk with her ministers to the far north wing of Parliament House, containing offices for ministers and the Prime Minister. The long corridors and many closed doors of Parliament House, invisible to the general public, didn't quite work. Beyond that the general public perceived parliament as chaos, shouting and interjections, which didn't reflect reality. Most legislation was passed by prior agreement between the two major parties, with relatively few bills requiring debate. This practical civility was then undone by daily highlights of rowdy Question Times whenever parliament sat.

"How did it go?" Debbie, her receptionist asked.

"The usual," Yaseera said as she entered her office. There Yaseera had much reading on the economic choices they had, and especially stimulus projects. Australia was in recession now, there was a million unemployed now, government spending was required now, and not on projects that might take years to be planned and approved before they got underway. But that converse of that was not to spend valuable money on projects with lesser utility. Yaseera set herself to reading options and recommendations while making notes.

* * *

Yaseera was glad to get to The Lodge to kick her shoes off. She collapsed into a massive, green floral armchair chair.

"How did it go?" Kasir asked.

"The usual. I suppose you watched Question Time."

"I did. I liked your one-word answer, yes. It's like watching another you."

"That's really me," Yaseera admitted. "If I gave a sarcastic answer it's because inside I'm sarcastic, or if I'm terse I'm that too, but I don't need to be sarcastic or terse to you."

"Is that right?"

"I think so. You can help me with something. These are tough times as you know, and the Prime Minister of Australia is very well paid by international standards. I believe it would be helpful and symbolic for me to take a pay cut."

"I agree."

"All ministers will then have to take pay cuts so I'll see how I go with getting agreement on this."

"Maybe business executives will follow your lead."

Yaseera laughed. "That'll be the day! They earn as much in a year as they could spend in a lifetime, so why do you think they want so much money?"

"I've got no idea."

"It's because my pay is bigger than your pay."

"Do you think so?"

"I'm sure of it. To take a pay cut would be like having a smaller dick," and she laughed.

"What do you want to do now?" Kasir asked.

"You know my routine. I swim, you watch, later we eat."

"What are you going to do in winter?"

"They have an indoor pool in parliament house. It won't be as nice as coming home, talking with you, swimming with you being there, but it'll keep me fit in a job where I have to sit for too long."

"It'll be interesting for members and staff to swim with the Prime Minister."

Yaseera had thought of that. "When I'm in the pool, I'm Yaseera Devi not the Prime Minister."

"I think that's a good thing."

"I think it's good too."

Yaseera went to their room to change. She'd already lost a few kilos although there was room to lose more. That didn't matter, she was a mother of two and mothers always put on weight, and Kasir loved her regardless. Life wasn't bad. She didn't like The Lodge but it had a pool which rekindled her love of swimming, while there were challenges ahead but she was in a position to help resolve some of those challenges. Yaseera felt life was really good as she went downstairs to swim laps, for fitness and more importantly for relaxation.

Chapter Eleven

Adam finally made it this far. Mostly they contacted him, messages were exchanged; he then gave them his prepaid mobile number for texts which went on for longer. But when the time came to arrange dinner or meeting over coffee – nothing. Silence. After two did that, Adam suspected that meeting face-to-face opened the door to the next step, which became too much. Sarah was 20, studying commerce, slightly chubby which in her pictures looked quite attractive, especially her picture in a lace leotard, and youthful with a fresh complexion, no need for makeup or even hair styling with her brown hair hanging loose to her shoulder blades. After several texts she agreed to meet in the cafe at the Chifley shopping centre, some distance from where Andrew lived in Red Hill but close to hotels in Woden should things turn out well. At the cafe Adam realised why his previous contacts failed; such things were not insignificant when you're 18, 19 or 20. Then Adam saw Sarah, a bit shorter than average and nicely curvy; quite attractive in a floral-patterned summer dress which suited her figure. Adam stood; Sarah's eyebrows raised before she crossed the room. You could tell her age from her complexion; the near-perfection of youth.

"Paul?" she asked.

"I'm Paul. It's good to meet at last."

"This is my first date!" she exclaimed. "Well, not my first ever date but my first date like this."

Adam kept quiet about his lack of experience. "Would you like a coffee, Sarah?"

"I'll have a cappuccino."

Adam ordered and paid, before returning to Sarah which might not be her real name either, but unlike a married ASIO Director of Intelligence she didn't have to be as discreet.

"You know so much about me!" Sarah gushed, which Adam did and which was a hint.

"I'm a senior public servant, you know my age, 48, and I didn't tell you but we need to be discreet."

"Oh discretion!" she all but shouted. "Of course."

The coffee arrived which Sarah sipped, leaving a milky mark.

"Ha!" and she giggled before wiping with a paper serviette. Already Adam was having second thoughts until he thought of Sunday mornings – no. He would give this a chance.

"You said you would mentor me," Sarah said.

"I can help you with my experiences of life and career. I can help with my experiences in many things."

She blushed and giggled again, which was starting to get annoying.

"Can you mentor me in love?" Sarah asked quite seriously.

"Love's one of those things you have together or you don't. It's intangible and perhaps destined never to last forever, or not for long enough."

She didn't understand any of that. Then Adam knew he couldn't. He knew he still loved Susan, even if love wasn't as intense now, and he knew he would never get satisfaction from someone he really didn't care for.

"I don't think this is going to work," Adam said. "I'm sorry for wasting your time. I can pay you for this date.'

"Oh no, is it me?" Sarah gasped with her eyes wide.

"No it's me. I thought I was somebody I wasn't."

"You've not done this before."

"That's right."

"I won't take your money, Paul. If this isn't good for you, it isn't good for you."

"Thanks for understanding."

Sarah finished her coffee, wiped another milky mark, smiled brightly before standing.

"Thank you for the coffee, Paul."

Adam stood. "Thank you for your time, Sarah."

"Goodbye."

Adam watched Sarah leave, quite cute in her dress swaying across well-proportioned hips. Momentarily he wondered if he should call her back but knew he shouldn't. Instead he would do what he should have done all along, try harder with

Susan. Adam ordered and paid for another flat white before returning to his table to contemplate how to rekindle something that once burned bright but now just smouldered. The waitress brought Adam his coffee but he was deep in thought and didn't notice.

* * *

Adam drove east along Hindmarsh Drive amongst Saturday afternoon traffic. He was certain Sarah naked would be a delight, while her youthful innocence and perhaps even enthusiasm would be more than just delightful, for the moments that took. Later, showering to wash away the scent of sex with another woman, and later still, pretending nothing happened would take away the glow of those momentary pleasures. Adam suddenly had an idea, so he turned left at the next traffic lights to enter Woden Plaza. He parked in a short-stay spot near the main entry, what he wanted to buy wouldn't take long, and soon he was on his way again.

Adam turned off Hindmarsh Drive to enter the shady streets of Red Hill, a more recent suburban development than the original Canberra suburbs closer to the lake, being mostly developed post-war. But like all older suburbs, blocks were large while trees and gardens were mature and well-established. Although units were becoming more of feature of Red Hill, the area where Adam lived hadn't yet suffered that fate. His house dated from the 1980s when the original, basic government-built house was demolished. This spacious house had four bedrooms, a study and a rumpus room; with more than enough room for a family of four, as did the landscaped garden, but that wasn't the point. Red Hill *was* Red Hill. Adam turned into the curved driveway, reached for the remote before waiting for the roller door to open, to park alongside Susan's smaller Lexus SUV. There he slid out of his Lexus to grab the present and climb the stairs with Susan in the kitchen waiting for the kettle to boil. Adam eased close, his approach masked by noise of the kettle, to kiss her on her cheek.

"What!" Susan exclaimed before turning around.

Adam handed her the bunch of flowers.

"Oh, that's lovely!" Susan exclaimed as she took it. "What's this for?"

"No reason. Just to thank you for being you."

The kettle switched off but Susan ignored it.

"I'll put these in water straight away."

Adam watched Susan go to the pantry cupboard to reach for a glass vase. Never model-thin, after two children and as years passed she'd put on a bit of weight. Adam observed Susan at the bench and really not too much weight. In fact not much more than young Sarah, but those jeans, or slacks at most other times, didn't suit Susan as much as a summer dress suited Sarah. Adam imagined Sarah in winter perhaps at university, in a dress with knitted tights for the cold, still showing her nice curves and attractive, chunky legs. Adam wondered why Susan always wore jeans for casual wear and slacks for going out but then realised that Susan, unlike Sarah, didn't care how she looked. Adam felt almost overpowering darkness as Susan arranged the bunch.

"I'll put these on the dining table," she said, before returning to flick the kettle on. Once boiled she made a cup of camomile tea.

"Do you want one?" she asked.

Adam pulled himself together. "No thanks, I had a coffee while I was out.'

"You never told me why you went out."

"It wasn't anything important," Adam said while glad he didn't have to lie more than that. "Do you want to go to Japanese tonight?"

"You don't like Japanese."

"It's not my favourite but I don't mind it. I know you like Japanese so we should go."

"Alright, thank you. I'll make a booking after I've had this tea." She glanced at the kitchen clock. "Then we need to dress. Sorry, I need to dress. You always look – smart."

"You should wear a dress," Adam said.

"I like the freedom of jeans or slacks."

"It's good weather for a summer dress."

"If you want, I can wear a dress."

Adam was pleased; little things like that made a difference. Not so long after, Susan emerged from their bedroom in an almost ankle-length, grey-patterned dress gathered at her waist, over black shoes with a few centimetres of heel. Simple and nice. Nice which suited her like that dress suited Sarah. By coincidence Susan had brown hair to her shoulder blades but usually worn in a ponytail.

"Do you like this dress?" Susan asked.

"Very much," Adam admitted.

"You're dressed-up Mum!" Michael, their younger son exclaimed.

"Dad and I are going out for dinner," Susan said. "When we're out, please behave."

"Always," James, their older son said.

"I booked at Onred," Susan said.

That was close to home, in the nature reserve on the hill where parking wasn't a problem. The view from there on a balmy, summer's evening was going to be pleasant.

"Let's go," Adam said, before heading down to the garage and his SUV. In no time they were being shown to their seats.

"Do you want the set menu?" Adam asked.

"That's fine."

Adam ordered that and two glasses of white wine before taking in the view. It was magnificent in fact. He turned to Susan.

"How's work?" he asked.

"Same old strife and conflict," she said. "Mary's bitchy, as always, and bullies Michelle and Ann, but what can I do? Sometimes she even bullies me."

"Bullies her manager?" Susan was grade EL1; about one level less than Adam and close to Leon and Erin in seniority.

Susan sipped her wine. "If I talk with her about her behaviour then I'm a bully. The only thing I can do is make a formal complaint, get HR involved, get made-up accusations thrown back at me which could be a problem, and end up with a reputation I don't want to have." She put her glass down. "Do you have these problems?"

"You know I can't talk about my work.'

"Just hypothetically."

"Hypothetically no." Adam thought. Entry requirements were stringent which might be the difference, but he kept quiet on that because that denigrated Susan's department. Adam wondered how to frame things diplomatically. "There are responsibilities involved and those responsibilities might make the difference."

"There's responsibility where I work."

"I'm not saying there isn't, but...," Adam thought about his two teams on which the nation's security hinged. "I really shouldn't say what the difference might be."

"Secrecy is one thing I don't like about your work."

"I was working there when we met."

"I still don't like it."

Adam sighed. Susan, perhaps like many women, married a man, and then spent the rest of her life trying to change the man she married. In the beginning Susan thought dating a then intelligence team leader was like dating James Bond. By now she should have realised the reality of his career was secrecy. The waiter brought their first dishes to rescue a strained atmosphere. The next courses were consumed in silence with Adam thinking his spontaneous gift of flowers was long forgotten, for no good reason.

"I'm surprised Michael liked this old dress," Susan eventually said.

"I like your dress." Adam chose his words carefully. "These days it's possible to be feminine and equal."

"That should be the case, but to wear a dress to work seems like my mother when women were lesser."

"You could wear a suit with a skirt."

She frowned. "Maybe."

Adam had the right observation. "You have a good figure for skirts and dresses."

She smiled. "Thanks for the compliment."

"It's the truth."

"Thanks."

The rest of the evening was lighter- hearted and the drive home too, before they ended up in their bedroom. There Susan contemplated their walk-in wardrobe.

"You say I have a figure for dresses?" she asked.

Adam snuggled up behind, holding her lightly. "You do."

Susan reached for night ware while easing away from Adam's hug. She held up a black satin nightie.

"This will do for a warm evening," she said while undressing.

"You could sleep naked."

"I'm don't like sleeping naked, unlike you," as bra and panties were removed

"Pyjamas aren't comfortable for me. Things get in the way."

Susan smiled. "So you say and I believe you." She pulled the nightie on before kissing his lips. "Goodnight and thanks for the nice meal and company."

Adam momentarily cupped her bottom through satin. "My pleasure."

They slipped into bed where Adam turned his light off. This was going well.

Chapter Twelve

The leafy, shady streets of Yarralumla were more than just lovely; they were part of original Canberra. After many delays, in 1913 work began on building Canberra, although a war delayed that. Work resumed with old Parliament House, the Prime Minister's Lodge and Government House ready by the mid-1920s, as well houses for a small number of public servants and other necessary buildings, only for work to come to a halt with the Great Depression of the 1930s. Economists of the time cut government spending and balanced budgets in order to cure the depression, which of course made it worse. Then another war further delayed development which meant Canberra didn't really get going until the mid-1950s. For a long time Canberra was regarded as sterile which probably it was in those days, but the setting: the mountains, valleys and the man-made lake, and the many bush reserves of native grass and gum trees, made Canberra unique and quite beautiful. Now in 2020, Canberra still had those reserves and trees as well as an established look far from sterility.

Yarralumla was landscaped in the 1920s for temporary cottages and barracks housing construction workers of the time. Now, century-old trees shaded quiet streets while extensive, native treed parklands originally fronting the Molonglo River were a feature of the suburb. Those cottages and barracks were removed in the 1950s to be replaced by simple government-built public servant houses on massive large blocks, while later Yarralumla found itself on the shores of the newly-flooded lake with parklands now lining Lake Burley Griffin. In some cases those government houses were demolished to be replaced by new, larger dwellings, in other cases modern unit developments hid behind the many trees, while some of the original 1950s houses remained but were rebuilt to the extent of being unrecognisable. There on a massively large block was one of those originally small, pokey, public servant houses greatly extended in more recent times, surrounded by grass, native shrubs and mature trees. Probably worth close to two million. Matt turned onto a paved driveway to park in the shade of a gum tree. He strode to the house as the door opened for Jenny to air-kiss him.

"Hi Jenny,"

"Come in."

Inside was bland white, with beige carpet in living rooms and polished boards in much of the rest of the house, with one of the many bedrooms converted into their workroom. On a big screen was a shot from the cafe at Kingston while Andrew was at the computer.

"Hi Andrew," Matt greeted.

"Hello Matt. I've selected the shots we need from yesterday and sent them to the Chamber of Commerce. I'll show you."

Andrew scrolled each location, one by one. He'd edited and corrected exposure; easy given they were in RAW format. The shots Andrew chose were all quite good.

"Thanks Andrew."

"Thank you Matt, they're great as usual. The model is perfect. The other model from the bikini shoot was great; why did you pick this one?"

"Asha's ambition is to be full-time professional while Sophie isn't sure. I knew Asha would come up well and I hoped this would help her. Asha's role model is Samantha Harris."

"Interesting," Jenny said. "Sam Harris has spent a lot of time doing workshops for indigenous girls, judging competitions, mentoring and training too. In fact there has been a lot of effort put in by many to find a girl, but as far as I know only two have become professional. Now you've stumbled across what they've been looking for."

Matt had looked into that on the internet. "They've been working with indigenous girls in central Australia and remote Western Australia. Asha is from Cootamundra while Samantha Harris has a somewhat similar background from Tweed Heads."

"They've absorbed both cultures," Andrew said.

"I think having lived amongst whites they straddle our culture more comfortably."

"She is gorgeous," Jenny said. "Have you fucked her yet?"

"It's not fucking her," Matt said firmly.

"But have you?"

Matt smiled and shook his head. "Yeah."

"What was she like?"

"Jenny!"

"Come on."

"She's beautiful."

"I know that."

Matt thought it won't hurt and would get Jenny off his back. "Like on the shoot she's pleasant, eager to learn and she's done her research."

"Really? That's straddling cultures."

"Probably."

"Now the APP competition," Andrew said.

"Forget about the girls kissing, I'll use the shots of Asha and Sophie holding hands."

Andrew selected the folder on his Mac and scrolled.

"Those shots are eerie," Jenny said. "I've never seen someone with fairer complexion than Sophie, let alone her blonde hair and light blue to grey eyes, while Asha is genuinely brown with jet black hair and dark eyes, yet they're clearly about the same age and built almost like twins. Incredible. And there's the love in their eyes. More than incredible."

Andrew frowned as he looked to the big screen while scrolling. "The third is the best," he eventually said. He turned his chair to face Matt. "You should use that. I'll enhance exposure and put it on the cloud for you. I'll email you the link."

"Thanks Andrew. Now the other reason I came here is I would like to use your studio to do some freestyle shots of Asha for her portfolio. Casual wear and lingerie."

"Sure, no worries."

"Clothes?" Jenny asked.

"What do you think?"

"White. Tight, white slacks, a sheer white bra, sheer white panties, white canvas shoes and a light grey chiffon wrap. I have a wrap you can use and you can buy the rest at Gungahlin."

"I'll get Asha now and we'll go shopping."

"What's she doing this morning?"

"Window shopping."

"What else? You know if she goes further with her career you might lose her."

Matt had thought of that. "Asha might have to base herself out of Sydney but that doesn't mean I'll lose her."

"You're a Canberra man."

"Sydney isn't my place, and I don't know if Asha has been there, but after Cootamundra and Wagga, Sydney might not be her place. But the Southern Highlands, Moss Vale, Mittagong, Bowral, might be."

"Then it's just commuting time."

"That's right. I'll fetch her now."

Matt headed out to his car. There he texted Asha that he would be home in 20 minutes, before pulling out for the long in distance yet quick in time drive across the western side of the city.

* * *

The studio was a north-facing bedroom with a big window catching natural light. Like the rest of the house it was painted white, and it had equipment in the corner: a couple of folding screens, flash umbrellas although they wouldn't be needed, seats, a stool, some potted plants. After being air-kissed by Jenny and bumping elbows with Andrew, Matt took Asha to the studio.

"This shoot is part-nude," Jenny said with the wrap draped over her arm. "Do you want me to oil her skin?"

"Yes please Jenny," Matt said. "Asha, can you strip to your bra and panties?"

Asha removed her slacks and blouse. Although her bra and panties were sheer they obscured where she needed to be obscured. Jenny returned with a bottle of baby oil to pour some in her palm and wipe it over Asha's arms, torso and legs.

"Because this is natural light, this oil will glisten and subtly highlight your skin," Jenny said.

"What's this shoot for?" Asha asked.

"The portfolio Gemini arranged got you this far but it's a bit pedestrian," Matt said. "I want to capture the inner you, and I want you to experience freestyle posing for when less experienced photographers use you."

Jenny snapped the top of the bottle closed. "You're too beautiful, Asha. Relax and enjoy."

Matt put the stool in the corner of the room before setting his camera.

"Pull on your slacks and shoes and sit on the stool to show me how beautiful you are," Matt said. "Your pretty face, your arms, your lovely long legs, your gorgeous hair. Especially your hair. Don't hold back, just relax and go."

"Pose after pose?" Asha asked.

"Yes."

Matt stood to use his camera as Asha pulled off some stilted poses.

"You're beautiful," he murmured.

She relaxed a bit as Matt circled past her, shot after shot, to eventually be laying on the floor highlighting Asha's long, shapely legs as she stretched them out while rolling her head, ruffling her hair, turning her face, turning side-on.

"Great Asha," Matt reassured her.

Still she did the poses, more and more relaxed. So many and so good. Matt stood.

"Now, lean with your back against the window," Matt said as he brought a white screen to stand opposite. That would reflect the light making Asha brighter than the light behind her. He adjusted his camera.

Matt did a couple of shots of Asha standing still. "Just hang on for a moment," as he checked the exposure of what he took. "These are upper body shots: your face, hands and hair."

She started, and like on the stool she got more and more relaxed.

"Asha, please take off your slacks and shoes."

She did before Matt tossed the wrap to Asha.

"Please stand in the corner away from the window so I can do full body shots. Play with this wrap. Hide, reveal, discreet, bold, sexy; whatever takes your fancy."

She did that and did it well.

"No wrap now, just on the stool."

"In my underwear?"

"You're beautiful in lingerie."

Matt sat cross-legged on the floor with Asha's long legs highlighted from down low as she easily pulled off the poses, before lying on his side.

"That's great, Asha."

More and more before Matt stood.

"Can I see?" she asked.

"It's better for you to get dressed, sorry about the oil, and I can show you properly."

Soon they were in the workroom with Matt's camera plugged into Andrew's Mac, and Asha almost as large as life on the big screen. Without saying a word, Matt scrolled them one by one.

"Some of these are good," Asha said. "This is different."

"I'll pick seven or eight for your portfolio. From now, if you're with someone inexperienced who wants to do fashion or part-nude, it'll be you, not them, who makes the shoot work."

"They're great," Jenny said from the doorway.

Asha looked to Jenny. "Just two weeks ago I never imagined part-nude or those topless shots with Sophie," she said. "Now it's easy."

"Your comfort shows in your shots."

"Our women used to go topless."

"Until our people made that shameful. You have to put that behind you because you're beautiful, including your breasts."

Asha nodded her head. "I am beautiful," she said.

Matt looked to Asha with his head tilted. It was rare for women, even beautiful women, to have that degree of self-awareness. Interesting.

"Now I have good news for you, Asha," Jenny said. "Excuse me Matt."

Matt got up for Jenny to lean over and open Apple Mail. She double-clicked an email.

"Asha; please read that aloud."

"Asha Reid, a model of the Wiradjuri people from Cootamundra, has come to Canberra to see the sights, buy a new wardrobe, buy jewellery too, and try different hair and makeup styles. Let's go with Asha on her adventure." She looked up. "Cool!"

"We always put model's names on shoots but this is different,"

"This is good for my people. Everyone who sees this will know that I'm First Nations and I can do this job. The real problem for my people is lack of jobs."

"That's right; this blurb is good for all First Nations people. Now, the other good news is we've been hired to do a private photo shoot on Monday evening at seven at the War

Memorial. Matt will be photographer, Asha will be the model, and I'll do hair and makeup and everything else. Matt, you and I are meeting Luke and Alice Monk at the War Memorial at eleven on Monday morning."

"This is great!" Asha exclaimed. "I'll have to tell my parents I'm staying on in Canberra."

"Is that a problem?" Matt asked,

"This shows progress in my career after just two weeks. They will be pleased, very pleased."

Matt glanced at the time on the computer.

"We better go, Jenny. Thanks for the use of your studio and I'll see you on Monday at eleven,"

"See you then Matt," Jenny said. "Now you two, enjoy your evening."

"Goodbye Jenny and thank you," Asha said.

"Enjoy."

They headed out to Matt's car where soon he was on his way.

"Jenny always says to enjoy our evenings," Asha said.

"Do you?" Matt asked.

"Oh yes, very much. Does she know?"

"She can guess."

"A lot of white women are blonde, like Sophie and Jenny."

"Some are natural blonde like Sophie, but many dye their hair."

"How do you know Sophie is natural blonde? Oh, I know!"

Matt had trouble keeping a straight face over that revelation. Matt still grinned as he drove along the freeway as it climbed past Black Mountain, to be soon home in his apartment. But he'd been indoors too much that day.

"I'll get something to drink and we'll sit on the balcony," he said.

"Cool!"

Matt poured two big glasses of lemon cordial with soda water and took them to the table outside. Later they would make love and later still entertain, but there was something he was interested to learn.

"I could sit out here all day and watch life go by," Asha said before sipping her drink.

"It is lovely here. You told me about arranged marriages and sometimes abductions. Do you know more?"

"It's a big confusing so I'll tell you what I know and maybe we can make sense together. The settlers wrote about arranged marriages, and sometimes young men abducted young women and they eloped into the bush. Then they were married. Sometimes a wife would have sex with another man of her husband's clan, and for this she would get beaten and sometimes get speared. But explorers and settlers also wrote, and this is early on, that when they visited a clan which they called a tribe, and stayed the night, they would be offered to have sex with someone's wife. These settlers wrote, and I'm using their words, that native men prostituted their wives. At the same time we have men's business and women's business, and clan decisions came from all in the clan, not a leader because we don't have leaders, and not just the men of our clans. So if there was an important decision to be made, all men and all women would discuss the issue to reach a decision. This is why I say women play a bigger part in our culture. This is quite different to men lending their wives to visitors, don't you think?"

Matt sipped his drink while he thought and there was a theme there. "Clearly sex was transformational. When an eloped couple went into the bush, they would have had sex and therefore they were married. They were literally transformed. Similarly, a wife has been transformed by sex with her husband, and sex with another man then became a crime. Being unfaithful must have been a crime for the woman to be beaten or speared."

"But what about sex with visitors? It was also written by some settlers that wives of a clan hosting a corroboree would have sex with men visiting the corroboree."

Matt thought more. "Maybe to have sex with another member of her husband's clan was a crime, but sex with a visitor was just sex or simply good hospitality. What we don't know is if men told their wives to have sex with these other men, or if women told their husbands they were going to have sex these other men, or if it was just an accepted practice where no words needed to be spoken."

Asha sipped her drink. "That's true. The writings of explorers are our world through their eyes, where their wives were like property."

"Exactly." Now Matt had a question. "What about birth control?"

"Ah, this is bigger than that. Sophie said we have an affinity to the land which is true. Each clan had their area of land within their nation, where they would ceremonially burn part of that land to flush out wildlife to be hunted and eaten, and then they could gather food from there. This also burned dry grass, fallen leaves and twigs from that part of their land; so that when there was a lightning strike they wouldn't get a catastrophic fire."

"Like we've now fucked-up your land and had those terrible fires early this year?"

"You said it," Asha said with a bright smile. "But we were custodians of the land and all the creatures of the land, so once that part of their land sustained the clan for a while, they would move to another part to allow it to recover."

Matt understood; unlike whites they didn't exploit that land and its wildlife until there was nothing left.

"This means clans were on the move from time to time, and also walking to corroborees and initiation ceremonies, which we call a burbang. To do this they couldn't have lots of babies and toddlers. How they achieved this we don't know. I do know and please don't take this the wrong way, but it was recorded in some cases that when twins were born, one would be killed or left to die. I don't know if our nation did this but it has been seen in remote places."

"That's called infanticide," Matt said. "Western morals and values come from Greece and Rome going back maybe 4,000 years, and we can't apply those values to a culture going back 60,000 years. It was what it was and that's what they needed to do to survive. First Nations aren't the only people in the world to have done this, anyway."

"I didn't know that."

"I've heard of infanticide in other places."

"There's one other thing I know about marriage. I told you that when women reached marrying age they would be given to their arranged husband, or abduced by a young man they loved, and obviously marrying age was their first menstruation. Because of their diet it seems they didn't menstruate until about 16 or 17. In fact, close to my age now."

"I understand. By then they would have known what to do."

"I'm sure of it. We didn't have shame, like Jenny said, so boys and girls knew what was different. Of course sex wasn't in public but it would have been difficult to be totally private."

"Do you know how they did it?"

"Woman squatting above."

Matt pictured that. "That sounds hard on the legs," he said before thinking more. "A man could hold a woman's legs to make it easier for her." He sipped his drink. "Do you want to try it?"

"Now?" Asha asked.

"Why not?"

"A bed isn't the same as in a lean-to or behind a tree, but I'd like to be how my ancestors were."

Matt had a wicked idea. "One day, do you want to go for a drive to somewhere private, outdoors?"

"Yeah! We don't need to go as far as Koorawatha Falls, but there are lots of places like that."

"But now on our bed and we'll see if can make this work."

Matt grabbed the two glasses and followed Asha inside. This was going to be good.

Chapter Thirteen

After making love, Asha liked to lie with her head on Matt's chest, and she liked Matt to play with her hair. She had lovely hair, thick and lush.

"That was good," she murmured. "You were right about holding my legs."

"Did you come?"

"You took so long I came."

"Good.'

"You're good to me."

"That's because I love you."

"I love you too."

Matt knew Laura was going to say something and he ought to sort that out now. "You're not my first, of course."

"First girl or first model?"

"First model. She was nice but there was something missing. Sometimes life is like this; you learn from your mistakes."

"What was missing?"

"There were looks and a sense of humour but not the deeper thinking you have."

"Ah."

Now for tonight. "Do you want to be my girlfriend?" Matt asked.

"I want to be your girlfriend but we need to do this properly. We should go home and tell my parents before we tell anyone else."

Fantastic idea! "Yes, you're right. That's your deeper thinking. After that, the next people we tell are my parents. I know. Do you cook more than breakfast?"

"My mother has taught me how to cook."

"How about after we tell your parents, we invite my parents here, and you can cook for us as my girlfriend?"

"That sounds right."

"I have a friend and his partner visiting us tonight. I'll get a meal delivered."

"I like Indian food."

"You can have your Indian food."

"What do we call me?"

"Asha."

"That will work, to be fair on my kin."

"I'm listening and learning."

She ruffled his hair. "I know. I talked about us with Sophie and Emma and they both told me older men were better. Now I know they were right. A young guy wouldn't be so accepting."

Matt was surprised and not surprised. In fact that's what he liked about women. He liked the way they thought deeply about things, except beautiful but frivolous early twenties white girls.

"We need to get ready," he said.

"We do."

"My shower's big enough for two."

"Alright but don't wet my hair."

"I won't."

Asha slipped out of bed. "I know why you want to shower with me."

"Why?"

"You like seeing me naked."

Matt laughed. "I do," and then he realised. "That's also what was missing."

"What?"

"You understand me."

Silence for a moment. "Let's shower."

Matt followed Asha to the bathroom.

* * *

The intercom rang where they were fashionably late. Matt buzzed them up where moments later his door buzzer rang. Matt opened the door.

"Hi Paul and Laura; come in."

Paul dressed like an Australian guy, tonight in a black t-shirt, knee-length khaki shorts and fortunately not thongs but not much better with white socks and sandals. Laura dressed like an Australian woman, tonight in a tight, white t-shirt stretched across her bra straps, black yoga pants stretched across her bikini briefs clearly showing, and black sandals with a wedged sole. Some women could pull of yoga pants, Asha like most models could, but the average woman had too much hip and arse. As far as her bikini briefs went, options were a g-string, boy shorts, or simply go commando. Asha wore her white slacks and the white sandals they bought at Suzanne Grey earlier that day, with her white cotton blouse.

"Good to see you again, mate," Paul said as he handed across a bottle of chilled white wine. "How have you been?'

"I've been busy which is good. Paul and Laura, this is Asha."

"Oh my!" Laura gushed. "You're gorgeous! Are you Ngunnawal?"

The look on Asha's face was priceless. "I'm Wiradjuri from Cootamundra."

"You must be one of Matt's models?"

"I've just shot a campaign promoting Canberra tourism. I'm sure you'll see it soon."

Matt thought he'd help Asha's sarcasm along. "It'll be on national and regional television, print, online of course, and posters."

"I'll look out for it."

"I have another shoot coming up," Asha said. "This is why I'm here."

"It's good to meet you, Asha," Paul said. "I'm a photographer but I don't have the eye for people so much."

"What do you shoot?"

"Static stuff: businesses, their products; all that advertising stuff. Matt's into models and weddings and things like that. You should see some of his wedding shots."

"Come in and take a seat," Matt offered.

Paul and Laura sat on the couch facing Matt sitting in one of the armchairs and, surprisingly, Asha planted herself on the thick armrest. Nice touch.

"Laura is a medical practice receptionist," Matt said.

"We met when I went to the doctor," Paul said.

"Every couple meets somewhere," Asha said. "My parents met at the supermarket where my mother works."

"That's almost the same as us."

"Yes it is."

Matt had an idea. "Do you want me to show the reconciliation picture?" he asked.

"Yes, show it."

Matt grabbed the tablet from the low table to power it up. There he opened the picture Andrew put on the cloud.

"You might be interested in this, Paul. I'm entering this in the APP award for portraiture. I call it 'reconciliation'."

Matt handed the tablet across where Paul frowned while Laura also looked on. Silence, silence, silence.

"This is great, mate," Paul eventually said. "If you don't win with this I'll be surprised." Paul looked up to Matt while Laura was now red and flushed. "This is art," Paul said.

"The white model Sophie came up with the idea of reconciliation," Matt said. 'Younger people have a better understand of past hurts and the need for healing. I came up with the idea of holding hands like that."

"I'm proud of that picture," Asha said.

"Is it hard to pose like that?" Laura asked.

"No." Asha smiled slyly.

Paul handed the tablet back. "You're going to win with this."

Matt switched it off and put it down.

"Are you into social media, Asha," Laura asked.

"I have Facebook but I don't use it much. I ought to post about these past few days but I haven't had the time. Mostly I spend time with my – family. We practice music and dance, that's my cousins and me, and I paint traditional art."

"What does traditional art mean?"

"Like our dances, our art tells stories from The Dreaming."

"Until I met Asha I didn't realise how empty and pointless our Western lives have become," Matt said.

"Does this give you ideas?" Paul asked.

"I've always been inclined towards Buddhism. I think we need more in our lives than a new car or our next meaningless purchase."

"Emma had a Buddhist tattoo," Asha said. "She was the other girl on the bikini shoot. She was very – calm. There was something good about her."

"I'll look more into Buddhism," Matt said.

"That sounds good," Paul said which Matt thought he didn't mean.

"Are you boyfriend and girlfriend?" Laura asked.

"No," Matt said.

"When it's right for it," Asha said.

Laura frowned.

"What do you do in your free time, Laura?" Asha asked.

"Too much Facebook, that's for sure! I should get off my smartphone and take up a hobby."

"Do you connect with your family?"

"I should do more of that. We waste so much time in a virtual world we lose touch of the real world."

"That's me," Paul said. "It's time to get off my smartphone."

Just then the intercom rang. Matt let the delivery guy in and waited by his open door to be handed three paper sacks.

"Come on guys while its hot," Matt said.

The table was already set including three wine glasses, four tumblers and a jug of freshly-made lemon cordial. They sat where Matt spread around the dishes and placed the Indian bread on a plate.

"Help yourselves."

"I like this food," Asha said as she dished up rice and lamb.

"After Cootamundra, it must be a culture shock here in Canberra," Paul said.

"Home and family will always be home and family, but life might take me on a journey away from there for a while."

Matt poured a glass of wine while Asha poured from the jug.

"You're about the same age as Matt's last girlfriend, Rachel, but very different," Laura said. "Do you think that's your spirituality?"

"I don't know Rachel," Asha said. "The only thing I know is you can't separate me from my family and my beliefs."

"I think Matt's right; we need something," Laura said. "Is Buddhism good?"

"It's about balance and harmony and not religious dogma," Matt said. "My religion is better than your religion has done so much harm that collectively we've turned away from all beliefs, rather than searching for a belief that isn't dogmatic or destructive."

"This means two of us on our computers tomorrow, not doing social media but searching for the meaning of life."

Matt tore off a piece of bread to soak up the spicy gravy of that lamb dish. Fortunately during the nine months he dated Jade, Paul and Laura never met her. He didn't want to explain two models in his past, and he knew from experience that Jenny would be discreet about both. Nothing to be ashamed of, except making the same mistake while expecting a different outcome, but this time wasn't a mistake. The meal was lovely the company less so, but friends were friends even if you didn't have as much in common as you once thought you did. It was a reasonable way to pass a Saturday night, especially as he had a wedding to shoot tomorrow afternoon and evening, as was often the case on weekends. Mandatory social distancing had made weddings smaller, but smaller receptions were now friendlier than hundreds of guests. Briefly Matt wondered what a First Nations wedding would be like but suspected it would be older women cooking and all kin there on the day. Really, that's all you needed.

Chapter Fourteen

Adam woke with morning's light seeping around drawn curtains. He snuggled up to Susan smooth and curvy in her satin nightie. In his arms she stirred.

"Good morning," Adam murmured.

"Good morning," Susan replied.

They lay like that for a while before she eased away to slide out of bed, to the ensuite. Adam felt that way so when Susan returned, and removed that lovely satin nightie, he slipped out to the ensuite too. By the time he got back after splashing his face with water to take away remnant tiredness, the doona was pushed down and Susan was on her back, naked. Adam felt his hardness as he ran his gaze from head to toe, still beautiful and she always would be. Adam lay between spread legs to put his head on her shoulder where she rubbed his hair for a moment.

"Remember, Michael has cricket."

"Yeah," Adam sighed as he slid down the bed to feast where he'd just admired her the most. He stopped and put his head up. "Do women really understand how men feel?" he asked.

"This is why we're doing this."

"No, how much we love every part of you, like here," as he brushed his finger past dark hair, "and here" as he stroked a soft thigh; surely the softest, smoothest part of her body.

"Here," as he ran his fingers around the curve of her buttocks. "Everywhere."

"I understand," but Adam knew Susan didn't as he went back to between her legs, wet now. He knew her well, sensed her journey, briefly imagined how it felt, until she came. He slid up her body while she guided him, and then Adam began his journey. Adam went to kiss Susan but as always she turned her head away; for some reason she didn't like to kiss during sex so he nibbled the side of her neck instead. Head turned, nibbling and making love, until he came. Love, sex, was freely given and should have been nice but felt – empty, always. Deep down Adam wondered if she enjoyed it or just did it for him.

"Hug me," Adam murmured.

Susan did and that felt better. He loved her, her body aroused him: in a simple but classy dress, in a brief satin nightie, and especially naked. They conversed at times, they connected intellectually and had things in common, but maybe they didn't gel with sex. Really, they never had. But love, sex, was shared which was something.

* * *

Body to body, kissing, Yaseera hugging Kasir skin to skin, as close as two people can get. Together on that peaceful, Sunday morning. He had his style, slow and gentle with love, which Yaseera adored. No rush, no hurry, just love. And then a change as Kasir knelt upright and braced his hands on Yaseera's thighs. Harder now, harder and harder as he bent forward to kiss her again. Still hard now and still kissing until he took his head away just as he came. Yaseera shivered as she sensed his peak. Kasir overcome with his peak lay with his head beside her head, too exhausted to kiss. She hugged him tight until he kissed her again.

"I love you," Kasir murmured. "You're beautiful."

Yaseera rubbed his curly hair. "I love you too but I'm not beautiful."

"But you are."

She smiled. "Alright, I won't argue."

"What do you want to do today?"

"Shower and breakfast then Skype with our children."

"They'll be staying here soon."

Yaseera was looking forward to the end of the school year and their children staying.

"We have two daughters like your parents had two daughters," Kasir said.

"Being a female in Australia is getting closer and closer to being equal."

"You were already involved with politics when I met you. Was that because you were oldest of two daughters with no sons?"

"I really don't know," Yaseera said. "I could go to university to study law so I did, and I got involved with politics there. Later I joined the local branch of the Labor Party. I had no plans beyond helping, but family issues intruded on Mike and he retired. Two women and one man stood for pre-selection and somehow I got it. You better get up now."

Kasir rolled away. Yaseera headed to the bathroom to shower, wash her hair and get ready for a day of relaxation before the grind returned on Monday. Later that day they would catch up with Sajia and Najam at boarding school, and soon their children would be in Canberra for seven weeks holiday. Yaseera looked forward to that very much.

Chapter Fifteen

By the time Matt showered and shaved, Asha was in the kitchen at the hotplate with the rangehood running. Her research went beyond model poses to what models ate for breakfast, where smoothies or yoghurt were possible but eggs were favourites for the majority, while tea was common but coffee was acceptable. Matt went to the sink to rinse his filter machine before part-filling it with fresh water and two scoops of coffee for two mugs.

"What is it this morning?" he asked.

"Omelettes. Take a seat and it'll be ready in a moment."

"We're like an old, married couple."

"Ha!" with a bright smile.

He got his omelette and a mug of coffee with a splash of skim milk. Model diet too.

More cooking until Asha was with him. She picked up her knife and fork.

"Did you ever expect this?" Matt asked.

"Never! Your friends aren't what I expected."

Matt knew but wondered how to explain it. "Paul and I were mates in university and I don't want to lose us."

"Well, Laura might become Buddhist thanks to you. I don't know what that means other than it seems good for Emma." Asha ate some of her omelette and sipped her coffee with a splash of skim milk. "How do you know Jenny and Andrew?"

"Canberra is a big city like a small town. My father's an accountant and they're his clients. They gave me a chance after I graduated and it worked out. The calendar was theirs as well. They manage promotions like business conventions although that's dried up now. Jenny's qualified in hair styling and makeup and she's learned about photography while being on shoots."

"That's why she knows about body oil and things like that. Do they have children?"

"No they don't."

"That's a pity; Jenny's lovely. How old do you think she is?"

Jenny wasn't model tall but she was model-slender, preferring to wear slacks that hung a bit loosely, often white with blouses that had white patterns. Fair complexion, blonde hair, and despite her slender build her face glowed except for lines around her eyes which gave away her age. "Jenny looks mid-forties to me," Matt said.

"That's why I expected to see children in that big house. It seems you're more into women than men. You're closer to Jenny than Andrew, you've got me now, a past model, and I wouldn't be surprised if there are others. Perhaps if you lose Paul you've got less men in your life. But it doesn't matter you're more into women. I'm no expert but somebody told me love without lust seems empty. Paul and Laura seemed empty."

Matt was curious about that comment. "What's love and what's lust?" he asked.

"Love is here," as Asha touched her head, "and here," as she touched her heart. I don't know for men, but for women lust is kind-of overpowering!" she said with a bright smile.

"Do you have love or lust?"

"It feels like I've got both. What about you?"

Matt thought. "I think for one girl who was part of my life for a while I had love, and I think for another girl I had lust." There was another one, Jade, who was also lust and not love, but she would remain a secret. "You can guess how I feel about you."

"I can guess."

"What are you doing today?" Matt asked.

"Laura gave me an idea. I'll post on Facebook what I've been doing here in Canberra."

"Do you have many Facebook friends?"

"I don't have many: Mum and Dad and my cousins, my school friends and few others. The hard thing is to post what I've done without it sounding like I'm boasting. With the first shoot I wrote about Sophie and Emma, you, that I learned and lot and had fun, and later we swum together."

"Did you write that we swum naked?"

"No I didn't! That was fantastic but others would never understand."

"I was joking."

"I know you were. I like your sense of humour. Seeing as you have a dishwasher I'll stack our plates later, but now I'll post."

Asha went to the couch to curl up with her long legs all but filling it. Frowning, she studied her Galaxy. Matt sat in one of the chairs to pick up the tablet left there last night.

"You're going to look into Buddhism," Asha said without lifting her head from her smartphone.

"Yes, I will," Matt said.

"Can you put on some music? I like that music you played in your car."

"Sure." Matt powered up the amplifier before grabbing the CD and sliding it in.

"Roxy Music," Asha said.

"These are compilation CDs covering Roxy from 1972 to 1982. This one starts with the sounds of a party where you can hear this song playing in the background, like at a party."

"That's clever. What else do you do in your spare time, apart from listening to Roxy Music?"

"I like reading. I download ebooks onto my tablet. In winter I follow football."

"Oh no!"

"Not the run and crash into each other type of football. I like AFL based in Melbourne, following Collingwood which is a Taylor family tradition. If we get serious you have to follow Collingwood too."

"Do I have to?"

"Don't worry, I'll explain the game. During winter we'll go to a top-level game at Manuka. When you see the entire field rather than what television can show, it makes more sense."

"A winter's day watching football sounds good."

"AFL is based on a First Nations game," Matt said.

"I didn't know that. Sometimes wars between clans were skirmishes with spears. Other times they played ball games. Which clan won the game, won the war."

"Over forbidden love."

Big smile. "Mostly. Love is part of the eternal cycle of life."

"A lot of places in Australia have First Nations names," Matt said. "Cootamundra."

"We say it as two words: Coota Mundra. White settlers misheard Marrambidgery and called it the Murrumbidgee River. Other places especially rivers and creeks were named wrongly. I don't know which creek this is, but whites asked our people what the name of it was; only there were two dingoes or dogs fighting nearby. Our people said 'mad dingoes' and that's what the creek's named! The creek which runs through Young near where we did the bikini shoot is named Burrangong, which means 'meeting place of kangaroos by the water'; so that was another misunderstanding. This song is amazing!"

"It has great lyrics."

"Planting potatoes by the score."

"Yeah."

"I'll let you get on with your research."

Matt turned to his tablet to start at Wikipedia which he hoped would give a balanced overview of what was not so much a religion as a way of life. Then it became confusing when the aim seemed to be to reach Nirvana but most followers had the aim of a better rebirth. From there it became complex with different schools of thought, a variety of paths, early texts, later texts. Matt ploughed on: the five precepts he understood and seemed a logical way to live a good life. The full set of precepts was significantly more restrictive, including celibacy and vegetarianism, but those were intended for monastic life which ultimately led to Nirvana. That explained why most followers of Buddhism merely aimed for a better rebirth. Meditation made sense and was something Matt was sure would help him. Vegetarianism wasn't a big thing but it was inconvenient, such as that evening when he shared a meal with Asha's family. He thought reducing his meat intake, which he didn't eat that much, might be a compromise. Matt then read about texts and traditions which confused things again.

Matt took a link to Western Buddhism which showed him two options, East Asian and Tibetan. He took a link to Tibetan Buddhism where things gradually became clearer. He felt it was about harmony, balance, moderation, treating people decently, and again meditation. Sex had no strict rules, but Matt felt that sex within a loving and monogamous relationship, like with Asha, was harmonious, balanced and did no harm. Yet at the end of that page, Matt wasn't at all confident that he had the answer to life.

"Are you making progress?" Asha asked.

"Yeah, I am," Matt lied.

"Do you want lunch? I'm making a salad."

"Do we have ingredients for a salad?"

"I've been shopping at Coles."

"I'll have a salad, thanks."

"Come to the table."

Matt sat at the table which had knives, forks, a jug of lemon water and two glasses, to be presented with a plate with a healthy serve of a model's salad: lettuce, feta cheese cut into cubes, avocado, tomato, cucumber, chicken and olive oil. Asha joined him.

"You don't mind, do you?" she asked.

"This salad looks great. Where did you get the chicken?"

"They sell cooked chicken at the supermarket. You know I could get to like Gungahlin."

Matt knew that as he ate his salad. He checked his watch where it was already past one. Time was getting away.

"I need to dress up and leave for the wedding ceremony after this. I'll follow them to the reception which is at four."

"Are you really making progress with your research?" Asha asked. Clearly she didn't believe him.

Matt wondered. "I need to digest what I've read," he said.

"Do you want to learn some of my beliefs?"

That sounded promising. "Yes, thank you."

"When do you finish this wedding shoot?"

Matt thought. "I'll be finished by six."

"Come home after your shoot, we'll have something to eat, and for after then do you know a private place in the bush away from city lights where I can show you the stars of the night sky?"

There were patches of bush on the banks of the Yass River, not far and easily accessible. "Yes, I do."

"We'll go there after we eat."

Matt was intrigued by that. He finished his salad while hoping an explanation of The Dreaming would help him. He really hoped it would.

* * *

189

Matt headed north on Sutton Road towards Gundaroo.

"Your car is rough on bumps," Asha commented.

That it was. "It's a sporty car."

"But not a sports car?"

"It's bigger and heavier than a proper sports car, but it's nice to drive and it's big enough for my work."

"I really don't understand the difference."

Matt slowed for Gundaroo, a village of a few hundred with a general store, a cafe and a winery, where at the crossroad he turned left. Fifty or sixty metres later he passed the last buildings; there were only a few houses and the winery on that street. A bit further on he stopped close to the river, switched off and climbed out. It was quiet now except for tinkle, tinkle, tinkle, tinkle.

"Your car makes a lot of noise when you turn it off," Asha said with a frown.

"That's the hot turbocharger cooling."

"I hope that's alright."

"It is."

Asha looked around. "This is good here," she said.

"I'll take you to the river."

Matt held Asha's hand as they eased past native shrubs to be close to the meandering Yass River, where grass was soft and lush beneath a few gum trees. Asha knelt.

"Now we'll make love," she said, before unbuttoning her blouse. Matt unbuttoned his shirt while Asha unzipped her skirt, removed her bra and panties, and everything to be naked. Matt was naked too, kneeling face to face as Asha wrapped her hand around where he was hard.

"This is your penis," she said. She took his hand and placed it between her legs, and used her fingers to spread his fingers to rest either side. "This is my clitoris."

Matt rubbed her clitoris while Asha whimpered, then rested her mouth on his shoulder. She held his back and nibbled his shoulder as Matt rubbed while cupping her buttocks. Rubbed and rubbed as she bit his shoulder, bit him and bit him, body stiff, whimpering more. Body stiffer; bit him hard and gasped so Matt stopped.

Matt lay on soft, cool grass to let Asha straddle him, feet flat as she put him inside her. Like last time he held her bottom to take part of her weight as she rode him. Rode him, beautiful in near-darkness, rode him and rode him. Matt felt it, a little then more, then more and more. Then closer, and closer more. He heard himself when he came. Asha stretched her legs back to lie lightly on him.

"Imagine not one-hundred years ago but one-thousand years ago on this river bank, and over there are lean-tos with elder men and elder women, men and women our ages, children, dingoes, and fires for the cool night to come. Here, away from the camp, we're private when we make love. Now, not one-thousand years ago but ten thousand years ago. Still the same camp: lean-tos, elder men and elder women, men and women our ages, children, dingoes, and fires for the cool to come. And us here making love because this is the eternity of life. Now, not ten thousand years ago but sixty-thousand years ago. Still the camp over there, the friendly chatter, the fires, and us here by the river making love. Can you imagine this?"

It was hard to imagine 60,000 years of the eternal cycle of life but that really happened. Matt had seen pictures of remote camps, taken a hundred years ago or even more recently as remote parts of Australia were explored, where life hadn't changed for 60,000 years. "Yes, I can imagine it," Matt said, with memories of those black and white pictures in his mind.

Asha climbed off to lie on her back beside Matt still on his back. "Baiame tossed an emu egg into the sky, where it struck dry wood and burst into flames, illuminating a dark world for the first time. Baiame saw how much the world was improved by light so he decided to rekindle the woodpile each day. Baiame is the creation god of my people, but like all men Baiame is only half, so Baiame has a wife, Gurigada. Gurigada has a body like rock crystal. Baiame and Gurigada and the other creation spirits of The Dreaming climbed a rope in the sky, and then passed through a fissure between rocks to reach Wandanggangura, the sky world, beside the Murrumbidgee River which we call the Marrambidgery River, where they live for eternity. We on earth have two spirits, warangun the good and harmless spirit, and djir: the darkness we all possess. When we leave this world our warangun spirit has to climb the same rope to reach the same fissure. But the journey from there isn't easy because the entry through the fissure is only revealed from time to time. This entry is guarded by the Moon Man who has a penis so long that he keeps it tied around his body, and the Sun Woman who has a clitoris so big that it covers the fire that Baiame first created. Your spirit must not be afraid to pass the Moon Man and the Sun Woman. Then your spirit will encounter two ancestral men from The Dreaming, both with erect penises. These men will ask questions but your spirit must not answer. They will sing funny songs but your spirit must remain unmoved to pass this test. Then your spirit will encounter two ancestral women who will dance sensually, and again your spirit must remain unmoved. If your warangun spirit passes these tests it will be let into Wandanggangura to be with Baiame, Gurigada and the other creation spirits of The Dreaming.

"Baiame was now living in Wandanggangura, the sky world, hiding in the Yarran Tree surrounded by bushes beside a waterhole, waiting for an emu to come there to drink.

When an emu came, Baiame speared the emu which ran some distance before it fell from its injury. Baiame ran after this emu but tripped over the roots of the Yarran Tree to fall hands-first to the ground. Now, follow my fingers," Asha said as she pointed to the millions of stars so clear that night. "See those brighter stars there, there, there, there, there, there; that's Baiame lying upside-down on the ground, holding the first boomerang which we call a barrgan."

Matt frowned as he followed Asha's fingers to the constellation Orion. That could be the outline of a man holding a boomerang or really a barrgan.

"Now, the emu in the sky, which we call Dinawan, is the darkness in the stars there, also fallen to the ground."

That darkness was in the Milky Way. Matt thought he saw something.

"Is the emu is on its back?" he asked.

"Yes it is. As each year passes, season by season the stars move across the sky, showing Baiame and the emu, then Baiame chasing the wounded emu, then Baiame falling over the roots of those stars there which are the Yarran Tree," as she pointed out the Southern Cross, "and now at this time of year, we see Baiame and the emu fallen. The next one is easier. If you look there you'll see a vast galaxy of stars with a gash down the centre. Look," as she pointed.

Matt saw it quite clearly.

"That's the Marrambidgery River beside which our spirits will live for eternity."

"I see that."

"Also you can see in the stars the Rainbow Serpent, which we call Wawi, and the other creation spirits of The Dreaming, but that's not important for you. What's important is you now know where my spirit will go when my time here is complete.

"We First Nations people feel sad about what white people took from us, some feel angry about what's been done and what continues to be done, even by neglect, but we also feel sorry for white people because you have no Dreaming. Poor white people, you have no Dreaming."

"I understand," Matt said; which he did. "Thank you."

"I could sleep naked under these stars tonight, even though it will be cooler later."

"Me too but I don't think we can. But this is an evening I'll never forget."

"Let's lie like this for a while longer."

Matt was in no hurry to leave the stars of The Dreaming.

* * *

Matt lay in the darkness of his bedroom while beside him, curled up in her pyjamas, Asha slept soundly. Poor white people, you have no Dreaming; truer words had never been spoken.

Chapter Sixteen

Covid social distancing restrictions meant the War Memorial, once perpetually busy, now had entry tickets to restrict visitor numbers. Online Jenny bought four, one-hour tickets for 11; while a guide, not a volunteer but an employee of the Memorial, was due to meet them. Private photo shoots weren't that common, they were expensive after all, but sometimes businesses used Andenny Promotions to shoot to their specifications. Usually these shoots were advertising but until they met their customers, Luke and Alice Monk, they wouldn't know.

"How are you today, Matt?" Jenny asked.

She probably noticed. "I'm trying to make sense of the meaning of life. Do you have any ideas?"

"Sometimes I've thought about that, but usually I distract myself by doing something else and the urge to know goes away."

"At the moment I really want to understand."

"When you discover it, let me know."

Just then through the inevitable crowd on the forecourt, a couple emerged from the carpark ramp hand-in-hand: he was as tall as Matt but broad and muscular, tanned and creased, Matt guessed mid to late-forties and not a gram of fat. She was dwarfed by comparison to her husband, with fair skin, some lines around her eyes showing probably mid-forties, and shoulder-length, dark-red hair not uncommon amongst women of Irish ancestry. Unlike many Australian women where the average these days was size 14, she was trim in tight jeans and a blue blouse. Matt watched as they paused to look around.

"I think they're your clients," Matt said.

"You're right," Jenny said.

Matt and Jenny walked side by side to stop two metres short. The guy approached so Matt backed away, until the guy stopped and shrugged his shoulders.

"Hi, my name's Luke Monk and this is my wife Alice," he said with a distinctive British accent, but not posh by any means.

"I'm Jenny Mason, you spoke with my husband and business partner Andrew Smith, and this is Matt Taylor who's our regular photographer."

Luke went to bump elbows with Jenny first and Matt, who then bumped elbows with Alice, as did Jenny.

"Before we collect our guide," Jenny said, "can you tell me the purpose of this shoot?"

"Yeah, no problems. I served in the army for two tours of Afghanistan so the military is a part of me, but until I came to Canberra I never expected to see this museum which shows the entirety of Australian military history. You might have picked my accent which is originally from Birmingham, which like all of Britain is doing it tough with Covid-19. After coming here the other week I came up with the idea sharing this wonderful museum with my past homeland in a different way to normal websites, and brighten a few lives there."

"I understand," Jenny said. "We'll go inside and collect a guide to sort out what you want for tonight."

Jenny went to within a couple of metres of a volunteer to ask for their guide while Matt stood by Jenny and the Monks kept their 1.5 metre distance. Covid-19 social distancing was getting annoying after such a long time. Shortly after, a middle-aged man in a green uniform approached.

"Jenny Mason?" he asked.

"I'm Jenny Mason."

"I'm Mike Gillies, and I'm to show you Anzac Hall so you can plan for your function tonight. Please follow me."

They went into the memorial, a place that Matt, like all in Canberra, had visited quite a few times. There was familiarity in many exhibits like the landing boat from Anzac Cove, the intricate World War One dioramas, which were like beautiful toys and not representations of mud and death, and countless other treasures seen countless times but never seen too often. They passed the thousands of medals donated to the museum to climb steps to the glass-walled walkway which led to vast Anzac Hall, which had small groups distanced from each other, and volunteer guides distanced from their groups.

"Mike," Luke said to their guide. "Will it be alright to photograph a model against these exhibits?"

"Beyond distancing requirements, many of our exhibits like the Lancaster bomber here, will make excellent backdrops for any photograph."

"What do you think, Jenny?"

Jenny looked around. "This shoot will take time as we need lights and reflectors."

"I understand. Is your model available?"

"Asha Reid has been booked for this evening."

"Can your model do a bikini shoot for us?"

Jenny looked around the vast hall. "Asha can do a bikini shoot but I don't believe that matches the theme here. Most of these exhibits are from World War Two and earlier, where bikinis didn't exist then. For here, I would pick a one-piece swimsuit for our model."

Luke frowned.

"I find one-piece swimsuits attractive, feminine and surprisingly revealing," Jenny said, "especially on a model like Asha. They're cut higher here," Jenny said as she drew a half circle against the hip of her white slacks. "This will make her legs look longer and more feminine than a bikini. Also one piece swimsuits stretch tighter to reveal a model's mons pubis, which is discreetly erotic."

"Come again?"

"Her pubic mound."

"Ah."

"What about shoes for your model?" Alice asked in a similar British accent to her husband; quite pleasant to the ears.

"With a bikini shoot we would use stiletto sandals, but I believe that style is too modern for here. In the 1940s, sandals or pumps with heel heights up to several centimetres," Jenny said with her fingers spread about that distance, "were the fashion footwear of choice."

"So 1940s swimwear and shoes?"

"Not exactly. At the time of these exhibits, women's bathing suits were quite modest. So we'll dress our model in a high-cut one-piece swimsuit imitating the 1960s, with 1940s-style shoes. It's more that a bikini doesn't belong here, but a high-cut one-piece doesn't look too much out of place even if it's not historically correct."

"That sounds good," Luke said. "Is tonight at seven enough time for you to get ready?"

Matt looked around. "Give me half an hour and I can plan my shots. Jenny?"

"I'll go to the Canberra Centre to check out Myer and David Jones. No, I'll go to Ozmosis, they stock quite a few brands of swimwear. I'll also call into Florsheim who are conservative with their women's shoes, so I should find the heel size and type I want from there." Jenny looked to the Monks. "We'll be on the forecourt just before seven."

"Okay, we'll see you then."

They walked away still hand-in-hand while Matt took the small notebook and pen from his trouser pocket.

"I'll head off to shop now, and I'll meet at your place at half-five," Jenny said. "Asha can dress, as little as that is, and I'll do her hair and makeup."

"What do you think about makeup?" Matt asked.

"Asha's complexion needs little to make her sparkle, although the heavier eye shadow and lipstick at Kingston suited her."

"I'm no expert but my recollection of the 1940s and 1950s is bright red lipstick."

"With bright red nail polish to match. I'll use pink and pink like most of the publicity shoot. Add to that a little eye shadow, a tortoiseshell hairclip, gold studs in her ears, and she'll knock them out."

Matt knew she would.

"Sorry about talking about your girlfriend's pubic mound," Jenny whispered.

"Asha isn't my girlfriend yet."

Jenny looked a bit startled.

"We're going to tell her family before anyone else," Matt said.

"That's – the right thing to do."

"She's like that."

"Sorry about talking about your almost-girlfriend's pubic mound."

Matt couldn't help but smile while shaking his head. "Don't worry, she's a model." Guys could drool over her pubic mound if that turned them on, or her breasts when Reconciliation was released, but for a model it just was another shoot. Matt wandered off, frowning as he took notes. There were many gorgeous items of military hardware which if highlighted by a model in a once-piece swimsuit, Jenny had that right, would look amazing. Matt went down the stairs to be amongst the many exhibits there. His possibilities were almost endless.

Chapter Seventeen

Matt climbed the ramp from the underground carpark, his camera bag on one shoulder and a flash umbrella on his other shoulder, with Asha by his side and Jenny trailing, holding a small case and also with a flash umbrella on her shoulder. They reached the forecourt, where Luke and Alice Monk waited with two casually-dressed guys who seemed familiar.

"They're the men we saw at Telstra Tower and here," Asha said quietly.

Matt frowned. They were those guys which was odd – no.

"One of them complimented you and would have wanted you for this shoot," Matt said quietly. "They must have checked online until they found you."

"Ah, yes. They would have found me easily."

That was right as Matt closed to be within two metres of the foursome. One odd thing: one of the younger men wore a backpack. No, not so odd; everyone used backpacks to carry things.

"G'day," Luke greeted. "These are friends, Jake and Mike, who decided to tag along."

"Good to meet you all," Jenny said; now holding the flash umbrella. "My name's Jenny Mason, this is our photographer Matt Taylor and our model, Asha Reid."

"I'm looking forward to this," Alice said. "Australia and Britain are like this," she said with fingers intertwined. "This will show a different side of Australia in a fun way."

"From Britain, do you know our war history?" Matt asked Alice.

"I know about Afghanistan and Iraq," Alice said. "This museum is older than that."

Matt glanced at his watch showing 10 to 7. There was time. "As you know Australia started as a number of British colonies, so in 1914 when Britain declared war on Germany for invading Belgium and France, Australia felt obliged to go to this war. A volunteer army was raised, which when combined with New Zealand volunteers became the Australian and New Zealand Army Corps, or ANZAC. Anzac's first engagement was at Gallipoli in Turkey, but that failed. Then Australian troops went to the Western Front in France and Belgium, where victory eventually came. In 1939 when war broke out between Germany and the rest of the world, basically, again Australia felt obliged to go to this war. Then in 1941 Japan declared war on the rest of the world too, but this time threatened to invade Australia which I think is the ultimate example of Australia's heroism. Japan defeated nation after nation until the Kokoda Track in Borneo, where Australian reserve troops stopped Japan's previously unstoppable advance. Shortly after this at Milne Bay in New

Guinea, a combined Australian and American force, but mostly Australians, inflicted the first defeat on Japan."

"That's fascinating."

"The real history in this Memorial is a small nation playing a major part in the victory on the Western Front, and later fighting for survival against a Japanese military that seemed undefeatable." Matt glanced at his watch again. "We should go inside."

A guide waited where Jenny spoke and then followed to Anzac Hall.

"Now I know why this is called Anzac Hall," Alice said from a couple of metres to Matt's side.

"I don't think there's much glory in defeat, but perhaps Gallipoli in 1915 was unwinnable because of the terrain there. The true glory is a couple of years later when Australia led the way to victory against Germany, literally with France and Britain trailing."

"Did this happen?"

"To this day the French have never forgotten that Australia liberated their nation from an invader."

They climbed the steps to the walkway to Anzac Hall, to stop outside the cafe.

"Asha," Jenny said. "There are toilets next to this cafe where you can prepare your first outfit."

In this case preparing meant removing her white slacks and white blouse, given her hair and makeup was done and she wore a black, high-cut, one-piece swimsuit under her clothes. Already showing were black sandals with chunky, five centimetre heels, and her own studs. As this was an after-hours private function, the cafe was closed.

Jenny led the way downstairs to be amongst the exhibits there, while their guide stood to one side. Matt set up a flash umbrella next to a massive wheel of the Lancaster bomber 'G for George', the memorial's iconic exhibit. Nearby Alice read the plaque outlining this bomber's history, 90 missions, and what it represented in regards to Australia's involvement in the war against Germany. Asha approached looking gorgeous in her swimsuit. Jenny had that right: it was feminine, attractive, revealing bordering on erotic, while sympathetic to exhibits such as a 1940s night bomber.

"Asha?" Matt called.

She came to him.

"Stand to the side of this wheel and look up to the cockpit there."

"Did people fly in that?"

The cockpit was a large, plexiglass structure sitting above the fuselage proper, with room for maybe four flight crew. "Yes they did. The night sky was full of anti-aircraft fire and pieces of deadly shrapnel, while enemy night fighters were guided by radar to fire bullets at them, yet they sat in that."

"They were brave," Asha gasped.

"Keep that thought in your mind as you look up."

Matt ran off a couple of shots with the flash blanking out the many shadows of what was a mostly dark exhibit, no doubt representing night bombing.

"Now, stand in front of the wheel and I'll take you from front-on. This is going to be a 1940s pin-up shot, so cross one leg slightly at your knee while you smile happily with your hands on your hips. You're being photographed to boost the morale of brave airmen who might not live for more than a few weeks, but at the same time discreet between your legs as models were at that time."

"I understand."

Matt took several shots while Jenny set the second flash umbrella based on her copy of Matt's notes.

"Asha," Matt said. "Stand in front of the bomb bay, those two long doors hanging down, and peer inside."

"They carried bombs in there to drop on the enemy?"

"Yes they did."

Asha bent forward and looked inside while Matt took his shots from side on and back on, capturing her bottom. Once-piece suits were revealing of the feminine form that way, too.

"That was good, Asha."

"To think this aircraft flew in a war and dropped bombs, and men flew in it and were scared."

"They were men your age."

"They must have been scared."

That went without saying. Matt checked his notebook. Luke originally wanted a bikini shoot where the next shot would reveal Asha in a different way to wearing a bikini. He walked with Asha to where Jenny had set a flash umbrella a distance from a number other aircraft.

"Now Asha, that big bomber is from the 1940s and World War Two. These aircraft are from 1918 and World War One. Although they're painted, they're made from canvas stretched over wooden frames."

"That's more dangerous than the other one."

That was for sure. "This time you're a visitor, so stand there as you contemplate the two aircraft ahead of you. One arm folded around your waist while resting your chin on the point of the finger of your other hand," Matt said as he demonstrated that pose.

"Do you want a serious look?"

"Serious but not too serious. Contemplative"

"Like this?"

"Great Asha."

Matt took a few shots, where if Luke wanted to see her pubic mound as promised by Jenny, now he had it. Matt checked his shots on his camera and so far they were good. He looked around to see Luke and Alice a few metres distant as was the rule, but no sign of the other guys. They must have been exploring although that was odd. Always men, like their grey-haired guide standing two metres close, watched the model doing her poses. It might be the era of #metoo, but put a beautiful young woman in a swimsuit into the frame and men subconsciously did what men have always done, stopped and looked. Woman was God's most beautiful creation even if you didn't believe in God.

"Now Asha changes?" Jenny asked.

Matt checked his notebook which he'd marked after Jenny came to their apartment to prepare Asha, and to show the idea she had while shopping at Canberra Centre.

"Yes she does," Matt said.

"Asha?" Jenny called.

"What is it?" Alice asked.

"Jenny has designed a different look for our model while staying within the themes of this exhibition." Matt thought. "What do you think so far?"

"It's good."

"Good."

Jenny had already placed a flash umbrella at the Milne Bay exhibition. Shortly after Asha was by his side in a black satin bra, black satin panties, a black garter belt, black stockings and the same black sandals.

"I love this outfit," Asha said quietly.

"You look beautiful wearing anything and you look beautiful wearing nothing," Matt whispered. "You look especially beautiful in that."

"I feel – you know."

Somehow lingerie did that.

"Go to that little tank to peer inside the turret on top," Matt said. "Stand with one leg bent backwards at your knee."

Asha posed with her hands on the rim of the turret; just right. Her leg bent like that looked period.

"Great Asha," as he took a few shots before checking.

Jenny moved the other flash umbrella as Matt gave Asha her instructions for his next shot. They went on, shot after shot, until almost every item of military hardware had been framed by the most beautiful model in Canberra. The last exhibit, Asha pinup-posing while leaning against the tracks wrapped around the World War One tank, was just another picture, playful and a bit sexy while staying within theme. But after taking it, Matt contemplated the tank. That tank, forever still and silent now, once killed enemy soldiers, while the young men inside were no doubt scared or even terrified, because a well-aimed artillery shell would have obliterated them. Indeed, every exhibit in that hall was death, destruction, fear and bravery. Matt removed the flash to fold one flash umbrella while Jenny packed the other flash and folded the other flash umbrella. Asha was upstairs to dress in white probably over black lingerie.

"What do you think of our shoot?" Jenny asked Luke.

"It's great," he said. "It's just what I wanted."

"Thank you.

A few moments later Asha returned.

"Now we can go," Jenny said.

They climbed steps to the upper level with Matt still contemplative of death and destruction, fear and bravery. Contemplative of something else. The word beautiful didn't do Asha justice, while she'd absorbed a lot these past weeks and was able to play that back, which not all models her age did as capably. Yet despite her looks and talent her prospects were limited. That was – unfair. In spite of a good shoot and their client pleased, Matt felt a bit down. No, he felt a lot down.

They walked along the glass-walled walkway with Jenny leading, the Monks and their friends next, where Asha came to Matt's side.

"Are you alright?" she asked.

Matt wasn't going to lie. "I feel a bit down."

"I'll give you a kiss to make you feel better."

Asha kissed his cheek and took his hand. She was right, that made Matt feel better.

"You know a lot about history," Asha said.

"My father likes Australian history and I've read some of his books. I also know that Australian history post-invasion is like this," as he held his thumb and forefinger about two centimetres apart, "compared to the entirety of Australian history which is like this," as he spread his arms as wide as they would go.

"Did you know some of what I've told you?"

"I knew some but not the detail of it, or the perspective you give. Keep sharing if there's more."

Asha swung his hand playfully which made Matt feel even better, even if they were living through a once in a hundred year pandemic and the many impacts that was having.

Chapter Eighteen

Alice eased the Mazda close to the kerb in Ferdinand Street two blocks north of the War Memorial, amongst large, modern and no doubt expensive houses. She got out to check herself in dark-tinted windows: black silk blouse, white slacks, black ankle high boots with a few centimetres of heel, simple gold earrings, and a gold pendant with opals. All good. She grabbed her smartphone from the pocket of the door, to lock the car and stride south towards the small carpark next to Anzac Hall, noting a CCTV camera in one corner and a second camera on the grey building further south. Alice continued to head south now using a downhill path beside that big, grey building, then down a flight of steps to be directly above the underground carpark. As Alice crossed a courtyard she checked her watch to see Prime Minister Devi was due in about 20 minutes time. Up the steps to the forecourt, across that to the Memorial proper, where Alice joined the queue for a tour of the Galleries and the Commemorative Areas, due to leave in five minute's time. The queue eased forward; Alice showed the guide her ticket downloaded to her smartphone, who nodded to allow Alice inside.

Being a tour of the older part of the Memorial, they were free to wander. Having been there twice, Alice knew the way as she passed displays of war memorabilia, those Great War dioramas were particularly fascinating, then past medals before discreetly climbing the steps to the walkway to Anzac Hall. At the end of the walkway, two bulky security guards in blue uniforms stood next to a sign showing the hall was closed from 10.30 to 12.

Alice returned to the older part of the War Memorial where she pretended to study the many medals on display. It seemed almost every medal ever awarded to an Australian soldier was there. Then four men in dark suits dwarfing Yaseera Devi, like Alice in a black blouse with white slacks, swept past. Alice turned her head to watch them go up the steps to the walkway where security guards would stand aside to let the Prime Minister and her security detachment past. On the upper level of Anzac Hall outside the cafe, press waited to hear and film Devi's announcement. Alice was unmoved – collateral damage for a greater cause. She went into a side gallery of desert-camouflaged tanks and jeeps, but like much of the War Memorial they were from past conflicts and not Afghanistan or Iraq. In the corner of that gallery Alice took the prepaid, Nokia mobile from the right pocket of her slacks where one contact showed on the LCD screen. Heart beating fast Alice dialled that contact; dialling, dialling, connected – moments later 'boom'. Head down Alice marched out of the desert warfare gallery, south past Great War galleries, and outside to the forecourt. Now she was safe

before they had a chance to react. Alice retraced her steps
down to the courtyard, up to the path beside the grey
building, across the small carpark and further to her car.
There Alice pressed the remote, opened her door, placed her
smartphone in the pocket of the door, before climbing in and
buckling up. Alice started up and drove away – easy.

* * *

The intercom rang where Matt checked the screen. Jenny.

"Come on up," Matt said as he held the button.

Moments later he heard the buzzer on his door, to open it
and receive an air-kiss.

"Come in," Matt invited. "Asha's gone shopping. Her
research includes model diets. Today for lunch we're having
salad, and she makes nice salads."

"Ah, of course. I came around because last night I sensed
something about you."

That was observant. "There's a lot of death and misery in
that place, but that wasn't what I felt so much. I ran those
poses with Asha and she starred, as always. She's got the
potential to be a great model but her opportunities are now –
limited. Overseas travel simply isn't possible for I don't know
long. You need a valid reason to be allowed to leave
Australia where I'm sure a fashion show doesn't count, while
quarantine restrictions make that practically impossible."

"Until we get a vaccine."

"That depends on how effective these vaccines are. Even if they are effective it will take time to vaccinate however many billion in the world."

"Why did Asha choose modelling?" Jenny asked.

Matt remembered. "This is ironic. She wanted to get a job in Wagga, but because of the Covid-19 economic downturn there weren't any jobs."

"That's ironic. Andrew like most men likes to watch documentaries. I watched one with him on the 747, which I thought would be boring but it was fascinating. The 747 as you know, carried many more passengers than before, and I didn't know this but it had more economical engines. So for the first time international travel was cheap enough to be available for the masses, which includes models flying to New York or Paris or wherever. The first 747 flew commercially in 1970 but it would have taken time for it to have made a difference in ticket prices."

Matt was shocked. "I didn't know that." He thought. "Before then, flying was for the rich."

"Not a supermodel flying to New York to do a show, especially when you've got thousands of local models who can walk a runway."

"Until cheap air travel when they could fly supermodels all around the world, which they did."

"Yes. Asha has opportunities though. Sydney always has modelling work, except there are more would-be models than gigs."

"Come in and sit," Matt offered.

They sat on the couch.

"Possibly the old ways will return to us at some time in the future," Jenny said. "In the meantime we've got a talent which we should nurture. This is your decision but if I was Asha I would stay here with you, and if opportunities come up like a shoot or a show in Sydney or even Melbourne, she can travel there. It's only a few hours by car or bus to Sydney and an hour flying to Melbourne. If Sydney becomes a bigger thing, then you might move there or thereabouts."

"Being on the books of a top agency in Sydney would help her," Matt said.

"You told me Asha's role model is Samantha Harris who we know has been helping First Nations models. I'll see if any people I know can give Asha's portfolio to Sam Harris, or better get them in a room together. Harris should put the pieces together; they have similar backgrounds, which is obvious when you think about it. This might help Asha get signed by a top agency there."

"If you can do this, that's great."

"No promises!" Jenny exclaimed. "We have a star; you saw it even if you wanted to fuck her. How is that going?"

"We're in love and in lust." Jenny was earthy and really laid-back. "I've only had a few, despite what you imply, where Asha's relaxed and natural, and at times even other-worldly."

"With sex?"

"Yeah."

"Wow!"

Matt had to clarify that. "Don't stereotype please; this is Asha, her personality and perhaps some influences on her life. You can't put a label on white girls and say they're all like this or all like that, can you?"

"Or white men."

"That's right." Matt remembered a recent discussion where this was a good time. "Now that we're being personal, why didn't you have children?" he asked.

"Me? Well, my parents were social drop-outs, they were called hippies which I'm sure you've heard of, and they lived in a commune in Nimbin which you've probably heard of too. It was drugs especially and sex too; lot's of sex. When I got older I needed to get away except Sydney did my head in. After supporting myself there sort-of, I met Andrew who decided to help a poor, confused soul, and even fall in love with her. Children? I never had the urge. Maybe that's from my background."

Matt was surprised. "You ended up in Canberra."

"Andrew wanted to go home, but not the public service of course. I rode along until I got here, and then I realised this is a city with something like the calm and quiet of Nimbin."

"Do you have drugs and sex in your background?"

"Both. Magic mushrooms and weed mostly, they're harmless. By the time I left, heroin was the drug of choice. I used it once or twice but I didn't like it. Oh yes LSD; I had some good trips on acid."

"Sex?"

"A few, many, too many. Later I discovered that's empty but it's all I knew."

"How did you get connected with Andrew?"

"That happened by accident, but I'm not your average Canberra woman which he might have been attracted to. Me? I liked his adoration. For women, in case you don't know, you can't be loved too much. Maybe with love comes trust or something like that. For whatever the reason, the love a man gives, gets reciprocated."

Matt now knew that. "You have a fascinating past, Jenny," he said.

"That part of my life did me no harm. With a different background I might have had children, but with a different background I wouldn't have loved Andrew as much. Probably, certainly, being raised in a commune helps my career now. Our work is about our clients, our valued photographers, our models, and the art we create together. Children from communes are either mentally disturbed for life, or they're free-wheeling and arty. I hope I'm more the latter," and Jenny laughed.

"You're arty, Jenny. You have a great eye."

"Thanks."

"You're great with people too."

She laughed.

Just then the door opened.

"Hello Jenny," Asha greeted.

"Hello Asha," Jenny replied. "We've been talking about you but now we need to stop!"

"Don't stop just because I came home! Do you want lunch; I've got plenty."

Matt looked up to see Asha put two shopping bags on the kitchen bench.

"No thanks Asha, I need to go because I have people to ring." Jenny paused. "No, thank you for the invite; I'll stay for lunch. I heard you make delicious salads."

"You have been talking about me!" Asha exclaimed.

"Only talking about good things," Matt said.

"One thing I didn't say is you were perfect last evening, as always," Jenny said. "Those shots came out superb."

"That was down to you, Jenny, and Matt," Asha said. "My costumes suited the museum while Matt's poses and what he told me made it easy. Enough of the self-congratulations; I'll make lunch."

Asha went to the kitchen while Matt watched her put her shopping away before getting out a large bowl, a chopping board and reaching for the knife holder.

"One of your past girlfriends must have been into cooking," Asha said.

"That was Linda," Matt said. "We met at university and later we lived together."

"You must have been young."

"I was your age, no." Matt remembered. "I was a bit older than you when we got attached. Later, after we graduated, we moved in together."

"After her came the model."

"They don't count," Jenny said.

Matt couldn't help but glare at Jenny while Asha stopped chopping to look at Jenny.

"There was more than one model?" Asha asked.

"There were two models," Matt said as he got his thoughts into order. "After Linda and I broke up I was vulnerable I suppose, and I felt something for Jade but it wasn't right for either of us. Later I met Rachel who I told you about. She was fun, she had a nice sense of humour, but that wasn't right either. Now I know what was missing."

"Yeah, alright, I suppose so."

Asha didn't sound convinced while Matt realised he should have told the full story of his past when he had the chance.

"Matt's right," Jenny said. "Rachel was fun, quite different to Jade."

Frowning, Asha resumed chopping. Beside him, Jenny was flushed red.

"Lunch is ready," Asha said while she carried the big bowl to the table already set with knives, forks and plates. Jenny and Matt sat while Asha brought a jug of lemon water and three glasses. Matt waited for Jenny to serve herself before dishing some of the salad: kale, dates, almond, sliced apple and olive oil. Tasty.

"This is lovely," Jenny said. "Matt and I have just had a good conversation. I've had one boyfriend, Andrew, but I had a few other men. I don't know how many, I never counted."

Silence. "Does Andrew know this?" Asha eventually asked.

"He knows a bit but not the whole thing, so please don't tell him." Jenny ate. "I told Andrew there were one or two who didn't matter. I was embarrassed and I suppose I didn't want to put him off or even lose him." Jenny ate some more. "There's not a rule that says one or a few, or more than a few."

Asha's eyes were still wide apart.

"Don't worry," Jenny said, "that experience made me appreciate love with one when it came."

"You live together and you work together too," Asha said.

"We're quite different where Andrew does one part of our business and I do the other part. What I'm trying to say is we work in the same business but doing different things, like me here now."

"Did you study art or something like that in university?"

"I lived in a commune where my parents were into art and other things. Most of the adults in the commune did sketching, painting, sculpture and ceramics, and that's how they made their money. I went to the local school, I passed year 12, and then I left for Sydney. As soon as I could I changed my name, I just couldn't stand Blossom and all that it stood for."

"They called you Blossom?"

"Yes they did. I had a doll which I named Jennifer, I don't know why, so that's where my name comes from."

"How many brothers and sisters do you have, Jenny or should I say Blossom?"

"Ah yes. The world is under strain from population growth, this is one thing I was in agreement with my parents. If a couple have two children that's zero growth, but if a couple have one child, that's population reduction on an already overpopulated planet. But not all had that idea.

Some thought birth control was unnatural so they ended up with six or seven children, and then they wanted bigger houses but Nimbin was a commune so that created disputes, beyond disputes over population growth against what's natural."

"Do you see your parents now?"

"I rebelled, I went away, and later we went back. I'd grown up, they liked Andrew, and they were pleased that I had a creative career. Nimbin today is just a shadow of what it once was, but there's tourism there so they can make and sell their art. It was a bit sad to see aged idealists when our planet has gone from bad to worse in the meantime."

Jenny finished her salad.

"That was lovely Asha but I ought to go home now." She frowned. "I should have texted Andrew to tell him I was staying here and to make himself lunch. Oh well."

Just then, Matt heard sirens and helicopters. More and more sirens as a jet flew past very low. Very fast and very low. Asha frowned.

"Don't worry," Matt said. "Because we're the capital we sometimes have war memorial ceremonies here, and the airforce often do flypasts like that."

A phone rang in Jenny's bag. She fished it out.

"Hello Andrew," she greeted and then listened. "I haven't heard anything; I'm with Matt and Asha." There was a pause.

"You're joking? Really? Alright. Thanks Andrew, bye." Jenny looked up. "Andrew said there's been an explosion at the War Memorial when the Prime Minister was visiting there."

Matt reached for his iPhone.

"Matt, turn on the television," Asha said. "The ABC will have it."

Good idea. Matt grabbed the remote, powered the television where it was already tuned to the ABC and a flustered-looking female reporter not from Canberra, so probably a Sydney newsreader, reporting an explosion at the War Memorial in Canberra, with no information on what might have caused it, if it affected Prime Minister Devi who was visiting at the time, or if there were casualties. The airforce was mobilised which explained the jet and maybe the helicopter although that could be police, just as another jet roared past. The reporter stated ambulances were on their way while police had cordoned off roads in the area.

"This is eerie," Jenny said. "We started the year with fires, then a pandemic and now this. Do you think this is terrorism?"

"The War Memorial with the Prime Minister visiting would have to be a terrorist target," Matt said.

Jenny frowned. "I'm sure they have a plan for such things."

"They must have. They had the airforce flying in no time."

"That's right."

The reporter had more information on the War Memorial explosion where Anzac Hall was damaged."

"That's where we were!" Asha exclaimed.

"Yes we were," Jenny said. "I hope that's a coincidence."

"I'm sure it is," Matt said. "Seven of us went in, we did a photo shoot, and seven of us left a few hours later. Now it's 16 hours after we left."

"Yes, you're right."

"It's a museum," Asha said. "There must have been visitors there, and staff like that guide for us."

"If the Prime Minister was visiting they would have kept visitors away."

"But not the press or War Memorial staff," Jenny said.

"This could be bad," Asha said.

Meanwhile on the ABC, everything remained unknown and confused. Jenny stood.

"I ought to go home," she said. "Thanks for lunch and your hospitality, and our day was really nice until the roof caved in, metaphorically speaking! I know what you'll being doing for the rest of today and we'll be doing the same. Goodbye."

"Bye Jenny," Matt said.

"Goodbye Jenny," Asha echoed.

Jenny left. In the meantime their lunch plates stayed on the table while eyes were glued to the television broadcast which remained confused and hypothetical. Apparently there was going to be a panel to discuss today's event in Canberra, with the obvious assumption this wasn't a random accident.

"I'll stack the dishwasher," Asha said.

"Are you alright?" Matt asked.

She tilted her head. "Jenny didn't tell Andrew because she was embarrassed and didn't want to put him off. Andrew still doesn't know but if he found out – well, they've been together for a while now. These things happen, I suppose, but don't keep secrets from me."

"I won't."

Matt returned to the television where it still remained confused. He guessed it would remain confused for a while. No.

"I've just had a thought," Matt said. "If the Prime Minister was accounted for, we would have heard."

"Sometimes you're too clever but this time you're right. Someone would have said they're all alright."

That was for sure as the television droned on.

* * *

Alice fumbled with her key in the lock of their apartment; only then did she realise her hands were shaking. Eventually she unlocked the door to enter the living room where Jake, John and Mike were side-by-side on the couch watching the television with the sound turned low, just loud enough to hear.

"How did it go?" Alice asked.

"I think you did it," Mike said. "If the Prime Minister survived they would have said."

"YES!" Alice shouted while punching her fist in the air. "You've got no idea how good it felt to dial that number!"

Just then the door opened for Luke to enter.

"How did it go?" Alice asked.

"I couldn't see much from where I was, as I expected. How is it on the television?"

"No reports of casualties or anything much," Jake said.

"If the Prime Minister was safe they would have said," Luke said. "Alice, you did it."

"We all did it," Alice said.

"Yeah, we did," Luke agreed. "Now that this is over, it's time for all of us to get out of Canberra."

"Are you going, mate?" Mike asked.

"Alice and I are going, soon. Soon, not now. Alice, are you going to be good or naughty?"

Alice thought. "Do you want me to be good?" she asked.

"I don't want to punish you, but if I have to, I will."

"What's this good and naughty about?" Mike asked.

Alice looked to him. "Sometimes Luke wants me to do things but I can't help myself; I just have to say no. I could say yes but it comes out no."

"Do you like being punished?"

"A naughty girl deserves to be punished."

"So Alice, what will it be?" Luke asked.

Alice looked to Jake, John and Mike. There was pleasure in sex, pleasure in pain and pleasure in humiliation. She left the room to remove her clothes, grab the paddle and return to hand it to Luke. Alice bent over with her hands flat on the coffee table to await her punishment for refusing Luke's request to fuck the members of their team. She held her eyes open, looking to Jake at the far end of the couch. The first blow was a shock, delightful and burning. Luke knew how to punish a naughty girl. The next blow was even more delightful, and the next and the next, as Alice felt her eyes watering. Later that evening they would fuck with Alice on top so Luke could squeeze and pinch her sore bum, merging pleasure with more pain, but for now it was just pain, and searing, gorgeous pain it was.

Chapter Nineteen

Adam sat with Nate and Rebecca at the meeting table in Nicole's office. Waiting, waiting; until Nicole strode in, flushed red and sweating, and sat opposite. She opened her compendium.

"At the War Memorial we have seven fatalities including Prime Minister Devi, two security guards, one War Memorial guide and three members of the press. A further 11 have been taken to hospital with two in a critical condition. I don't need to tell you how serious this situation is. Adam, what's your take on this?"

"Without doubt this is related to those forum posts that went quiet last week," he said.

"I need to review those posts myself."

"I'll ask Erin to go through them with you when we're finished here."

"Its possible an IED was planted in the upper level of Anzac Hall."

Adam frowned while he thought. "Anzac Hall is quite dark where it might be possible to hide an IED there because of the darkness."

"The other issue is this event wasn't made public until this morning's media release at nine, which makes planting an IED amongst visitors and War Memorial staff quite a difficult undertaking, unless there was a security leak. Even if there was a security leak, I was told there are thorough inspections of Anzac Hall by security guards after closing time, and after any evening functions." Nicole turned the page in her compendium. "This is simple: Nate, your team will investigate Parliament House for possible security leaks, while Adam, your team will investigate the War Memorial. Australian Federal Police are currently interviewing witnesses and gathering physical evidence which we will have access to in the usual manner."

"Is War Memorial CCTV affected by this explosion?" Adam asked.

"War Memorial computer servers are in their administration building some distance from public galleries and Anzac Hall. Adam, CCTV should be your priority, starting now."

Nicole stood; they stood to leave her office. When he reached his team, Adam asked Erin to see Nicole and be prepared to show all relevant forum posts. Then he asked Leon to come into his office and close the door behind. Adam repeated Nicole's summary before pausing to think.

"Take a seat, Leon," Adam said while sitting to turn to his computer. He looked up the government directory where Australian War Memorial was one of the first entries, and Director Michael Albertson in charge from April 2020.

Adam paused to think that was a tumultuous eight months before dialling. Two rings and answered by a woman.

"Agent C11, Director of Intelligence ASIO," Adam said. "I need to speak with Mr Albertson."

"I'll let him know."

Moments later: "Michael Albertson."

"Agent C11, Director of Intelligence ASIO. Our priority is to get a copy of your CCTV files."

"I understand. I'll tell our Director of IT, Gerard Wood, to be expecting you."

"Two agents will be on their way shortly." Adam paused. "How are you?" he asked.

"This is terrible. You read about these things and see them on the news, but until it happens.... Damage can be fixed but lives lost are – tragic."

"My condolences to you and your staff, and to families who have lost their loved ones. We'll be there shortly."

Adam hung up before turning to Leon.

"Book a car and get a plug-in hard drive. There's no rush; it's only ten minutes from here."

"Yes Adam."

He left while Adam paused to think. Despite Covid-19 restrictions, hundreds came and went through the Memorial each day. While CCTV was helpful, unfortunately they didn't have access to broad-ranging facial recognition. Their only hope was Anzac Hall cameras caught what happened. Adam opened the War Memorial website to check where the administration building was. Leon came to the doorway.

"Car's ready when you are, Adam."

"Thanks Leon," Adam said as he grabbed his suit jacket from the coathanger on the back of his door. "Drive along Fairburn Avenue to enter from the north."

Adam, with compendium in hand, followed Leon to the carpark level. Nearby his Lexus waited which Adam knew would be waiting for a fair while. They climbed into a white Toyota Camry sedan, Adam in the front passenger seat, for the short drive to the War Memorial, where as expected, Fairburn Avenue was cordoned off with three police cars and six officers in their bulky vests. One strolled lazily to the Toyota as Adam pressed the power window button, annoyingly the same as his Lexus. As the officer closed, Adam reached for his ID card to simply hold it up. It took a couple of moments to register before orders were given to clear plastic barriers.

"To the right, Leon, and then a carpark on the left."

That took them to an empty carpark where Leon slotted the Toyota in place. From there it was a short walk to the hushed administration building where three receptionists were guarded by two security guards and two police officers. Adam showed his card.

"Agent C11, Director of Intelligence ASIO. Gerard Wood is expecting us."

"I'll let him know."   Quick phone call. "He's on his way."

Wood was in his forties, like much of the public service. When public servants got to age 55 they took packages and left, often to return as contractors. Widespread redundancies were becoming a security problem. Adam and Gerard Wood faced at a distance with handshakes belonging in the past.

"If you follow me," Gerard Wood said, "I'll get our people to help you."

They went deeper into the ground floor of the 1950s administration building. Grand and with character, including a broad staircase leading to upper levels. They bypassed that to end up in a cramped space of pokey offices and a server room behind a glazed wall.

"You want a copy of our CCTV files?" Wood asked.

"Going back," Adam thought, "six weeks if you can."

"Not a problem," as Leon handed the hard drive across.

That was given to a younger guy, contractor for sure, who went to a workstation to plug it in.

"Do you know how many feeds?" Adam asked Wood.

"CCTV was upgraded about two years ago. We have 28 feeds."

That meant they had a big job on their hands but that was good. One or more of those feeds must show something.

"Do you want coffee?" Wood asked.

"No thanks," Adam said, as they waited. "CCTV monitored by who and where?" Adam asked.

"Monitored by security guards on the ground floor here."

That number of feeds was only as good as the guards checking them. Waiting, waiting, until the younger guy stood with the hard drive in his hand. He gave it to Wood who gave it to Adam.

"Thank you for your cooperation," Adam said.

"I'll show you out."

Soon they were in the Toyota heading to the police cordon which was quickly cleared as they approached. Literally minutes later, they were in the basement carpark. Silence as they rode the lift to floor three with Adam thinking. Lift eased to a halt, doors glided open; they stepped out.

"Leon," Adam said. "Wait in my office."

Adam asked Erin to join them, and when Adam hung his suit jacket and sat, they sat.

"There are 28 CCTV feeds where, including your team Erin, we have 22. I'll get extra resources to make up the difference. In case they set an IED on the day and later escaped, start your surveillance from two hours after the explosion and work backwards from there. Anything odd, unusual or out of the ordinary, tell me."

"Yes Adam," Erin said as she and Leon stood to leave. Adam left his office to ask Nicole for the extra six agents he needed. As he walked through hushed Ben Chifley building, Adam felt like was like searching for that elusive needle.

* * *

The email arriving sound woke Adam from semi-dozing. From Nicole to all staff: *'Parliament House IT Contractor John Connell has gone missing. CCTV from Parliament House on Monday November 23 shows Connell in the company of an unidentified male. Connell is the younger and smaller of these two men.'* She attached a screen shot. Adam composed an email to Leon and Erin.

'If you see either or both from Nicole's email at the war memorial let me know straight away'. Send.

Adam resumed his wait; gazing out the window as dusk settled across Canberra.

"Excuse me Adam," Erin said from the doorway of his office, as Adam spun his chair around. "Niki found the older male from Nicole's email."

Good, excellent! Adam followed Erin to Niki's cubicle where the CCTV image was paused on a slightly blurry shot in one of the galleries.

"I'll play it," Niki said.

Adam watched a memorial guide in a green uniform, a mid-forties, blonde-haired women in white with a white umbrella on her left shoulder and a case in her right hand, a tall male maybe late-twenties, with a white umbrella on his left shoulder and a soft, brown bag on his other shoulder, and beside him a tall young woman dressed in white slacks and a tight, white blouse, with a mid-brown complexion and long, black hair. Next came the male from Nicole's email, quite tall and muscular beside a female, less than average height and slim, then two young males, one taller and one shorter, and both in dark t-shirts and jeans. They flashed past the camera in no time.

"Can you play it again slowly?" Adam asked.

Niki did as Adam stared at the screen. "Stop there."

They were all on the screen with the time showing 6:58 Mon 14 Dec, after closing time, while those umbrellas were odd. Indeed this group was odd.

"I've seen that darker-skinned female," Erin said. "She's part of an advertising campaign for Canberra tourism." Erin frowned. "Unusual name I can't quite remember, but I remember Wiradjuri from Cootamundra. She's a model. Aah. I think those umbrellas are for professional flash photography. This must be a photography session in the Memorial."

"Move it forward a couple of frames, Niki."

She did.

"Stop." Adam stared at the screen. "One of the two at the rear has a backpack."

"Yes, he does," Erin said.

The next step was clear. "Erin, all of your team and tell Leon too, check all feeds from 6:30 on Monday to when they leave." Adam thought. "I'll surf the net to find that advertising campaign and get the model's name. She's First Nations."

"She is. She might be on a modelling agency website."

Adam realised the significance of that. "If there's an agency, they might have details of who booked her."

Back at his computer, Adam found the campaign which included a shot from the forecourt of the War Memorial. Asha Reid, a model from Cootamundra and really gorgeous. He searched model agencies to scroll endless attractive young women and handsome young men until he found Asha Reid at Gemini Modelling Agency. He looked for a New South Wales driver's licence but found nothing with that name, and looked for a Canberra licence but found nothing there. Passports, nothing, Centrelink had her date of birth, October 10 2002, and home address: 30 Sutton Street, Cootamundra. He looked at the time on the taskbar, 7:11, too late to contact her agency. Adam went to Erin.

"Any luck?" Adam asked.

"Lots!" she exclaimed. "Look at this one from inside Anzac Hall."

The model was in a black one-piece swimsuit, classy, beside the Lancaster bomber talking with the photographer before he stepped away to take pictures, with the security camera showing flash reflected by the white umbrella. They did another pose and a third as Adam watched for about ten minutes before they went away.

"Another one here," Erin said.

A little later, posing by World War One aircraft.

"And here," Erin said.

Now the model, Asha Reid, was in black lingerie beside a small tank.

"This is the last before they go outside," Erin said.

Timestamp was 8:48 with the group leaving through the walkway. The guide led while the photographer had his head down and was frowning, until the model, dressed again in a white blouse and slacks, came alongside. They talked for a moment before she kissed his cheek and took his hand, to walk on jauntily by his side.

"Stop there!" Adam ordered. "Go back and play it slowly."

Erin did.

"Stop!"

Right on the kiss.

"Those two are in a relationship," Adam said.

"They're a photographer and a model who work together," Erin said. "Relationships often start at work, like here."

That was true, but a model as beautiful as that girl. Adam felt a twinge of jealousy, especially her bright smile when she kissed him, and the happy, bouncy way she swung his hand as they walked on. Spontaneous and playful; something Adam hadn't experienced in a long time. No, never.

"Back it up and play it again slowly," Adam asked.

The older woman with blonde hair, the male from Nicole's email holding hands with the female next, then the two younger males – wait, he didn't have his backpack.

"Stop!" Adam ordered. "The backpack is missing, Erin."

"You're right!" Erin gasped. "This is when they planted the IED. But where in Anzac Hall did they plant it, and why with a model, a photographer and that older woman?"

Good questions. "I found the model's agency but that will have to wait until they're open."

"Pity."

That was true. Adam thought.

"Email me screenshots of the group leaving: one showing the photographer and model, one showing the older woman, one showing the male from Nicole's email with what looks like his partner or wife, and one of the two younger males."

"Will do," Erin said.

Adam went to his computer to compose an email to Nicole:

'Have found the unidentified male from your email at war memorial for what looks like an after hours photographic session in Anzac Hall with what looks like his partner or wife. With this male and female are a First Nations model Asha Reid, a Caucasian photographer, an older Caucasian woman, and two younger Caucasian males, screen shots attached. We have identified the model's agency. Will contact memorial director now for details of this photographic session and will contact the model's agency tomorrow when they're open.' By then Adam received an email from Erin with the four screen shots, which he copied, pasted and sent.

Moments later from Nicole: *'Adam, concentrate on the unknown male and partner / wife for now. Nate, concentrate on John Connell.'* Moments later Adam received his email as Nicole forwarded it to all staff. Ignoring that, Adam opened the image of the model and photographer: spontaneous and playful for sure. Apart from being one of the most beautiful young women Adam had ever seen, and she was young too, there was more to this model than her dark beauty. For sure she had more personality than Sarah when they briefly met, who Adam really couldn't stand. Workplace romance, lucky young man, although he wasn't young. Not old but older. Adam sighed, duty called. He looked up the Government Directory before dialling a mobile number.

"Michael Albertson."

"Agent C11, Director of Intelligence ASIO. We spoke earlier. We've identified a private photographic session in Anzac Hall, on Monday evening between 7pm and 8:48pm."

"Yes, that sounds right. We take bookings for private functions in Anzac Hall."

"Can you tell me the parties involved with this booking?"

"Personally now I can't. I'll ring around but at worst this might take as long as tomorrow morning before I can get these details."

"It would be useful to know sooner rather than later."

"I'll see what I can do."

"After this call I'll text you a number for you to contact me or my team."

"Thank you Agent C11."

Adam ended the call, texted Michel Albertson, before asking Leon and Erin to come to his office.

"Our priority is the unidentified male and the unidentified female who look married or in a relationship. We have every driver's licence picture in Australia, and passport and other government-issued documents. If we were allowed to run facial recognition, we'd find them like that," as he clicked his fingers.

Leon shrugged his shoulders while Erin nodded her head in agreement.

"Split your teams," Adam said. "Some will visually match pictures against right-wing terrorist suspects currently under surveillance, while the rest will trawl CCTV for other appearances by this group. Almost certainly they reconnoitred the Memorial before planting this IED. At midnight, half of your teams take four hours sleep, and at four, the other half sleep until eight. Any questions or suggestions?"

"Your sleep, to be fresh?" Leon asked.

"Later I'll bring a sleeping bag in here and shut the door. If it's a major breakthrough like a positive identification, wake me, but if it's more coming and going just email me, and we'll catch up tomorrow morning at eight."

"I understand," Erin said.

They left while Adam felt hungry. He'd get someone to take a car for a pizza run to – Manuka was the closest. That would go down well with team of mostly twenty-somethings. Leon pulled out his personal smartphone to text Susan although she would expect Adam not to be home anytime soon. As Adam texted, his team worked on.

* * *

The television droned in the background but Matt had enough of that.

"Do you want me to turn it off?" he asked Asha.

"There's nothing more we can learn tonight."

243

Matt picked up the remote and pressed the red button. Silence.

"How do you feel?" Asha asked.

"I feel a bit depressed. How do you feel?"

"I feel a bit down. I expect most of the country feels down. Let's talk to get our mind off things. How old are you Matt?"

"I'm 26."

"You seem older."

"Going to university made me grow up, and now having my own business. Guys in past years, like Steve Jobs of Apple, were well into it by the time they got to my age. That other IT guy, Bill Gates, he was young when he made his mark."

"Now it's your turn to ask me a question," Asha said.

There was one. "How did you get that job in Boggabilla?"

"That goes back a few years. When I turned 16 I worked three Saturdays out of four at the Woolworths supermarket. Near the end of my Year 12 they put up a notice at school for a receptionist at Boggabilla Aboriginal Medical Clinic, which needed awareness of indigenous cultural issues. I looked up Boggabilla where my people are doing badly and I thought I could help there. I spoke with my English teacher who helped me write my resume, the supermarket manager gave me a reference, and I got the job. It was hard yet good. I kept in touch with my family and friends through Facebook; I'd shown Mum and Dad how to use it. My problem was I couldn't find a decent guy which was lonely outside of work, and the violent crime there was a bit frightening. Indigenous guys in Boggabilla are – not really employable and many girls aren't either, but I encouraged the doctor and nurse and they found my replacement at nearby Goondiwindi."

"Why aren't girls there employable?" Matt asked.

"They're born and raised in families destroyed by drink, drugs and hopelessness. At maybe seven or eight, some guys are into petrol or glue, and some girls too. Drink and drugs, weed and meth mostly, comes later. With nothing to do there, some girls end up pregnant in relationships when they're too young. Other girls don't bother much with school, I think because they come from families which didn't bother much with school, or there's no point because there aren't jobs for First Nations anyway. You'd see boys and girls on the streets during the day when they should have been in school."

Matt thought. "It must have been hard to hold a responsible job while surrounded by your people not having the same opportunities as you."

"At first it was hard but I tried not to let it get me down."

"I'm glad you went to Boggabilla because you wouldn't be here with me now. Maybe you're naturally mature, but I'm sure you grew up even more while you were there."

"I did. Now my question: why did you become a photographer?"

"I've been fascinated by photography since I don't know when. Like you I worked in a supermarket on weekends only I used my money to buy a bridge camera. From there it was university and an artistic way to make a decent living. Now my turn," and Matt thought that he knew so much about Asha already. Then it hit him. "You're quite confident in yourself; how did that come about?"

Asha frowned. "My father's the oldest of his kin and I'm the oldest of our kin. My family is my brother and my cousins, especially my girl cousins, with me being older more of the leader."

That made sense.

"You're more into women," Asha said, "why is that?"

Yeah! "I'm the youngest with two older sisters. I had school friends and we did boys things together, while I was comfortable with my sisters and their friends when they came to our house."

"We're like opposites being oldest and youngest," then she yawned. "Sorry."

"Do you want to go to bed, just to sleep?" Matt asked.

Asha sort-of smiled. "Tonight, can you hug me?"

A hug for love and a hug for security. "Let's go to bed and hug."

Together, they headed to the bathroom to get ready for bed and a hug.

Chapter Twenty

Adam slept well but felt dirty. A splash of water and a cup of coffee didn't make up for his morning shower, shave and breakfast. On that thought he rubbed his chin where that showed. Opposite, Erin and Leon waited while Adam read two emails. He looked up.

"You found CCTV of the unknown female crossing the north-eastern carpark to enter the Memorial about 20 minutes before the explosion, leaving a few minutes after. Clearly this woman detonated the IED from inside the Memorial, possibly by mobile phone," Adam said. "She either had her car parked out of camera range or was meeting an associate. You also found CCTV of the unknown couple, the older woman and the photographer at the Memorial earlier on Monday at 11. They went inside with a guide, looked around Anzac Hall and departed. Michael Albertson called where the evening session was booked by Andenny Promotions Pty Ltd. Directors are Andrew Smith and Jenny Mason, with the registered office a house at 26 Irwin Street, Yarralumla. You matched Jenny Mason's driver's licence photo to the CCTV. This is excellent, thank you both." Adam looked to his pad. "Leon, ring Gemini Modelling Agency on...," Adam looked up to see Leon ready. "Numbers are 6282 8700 or 0411 512 781. Get their address, pay a visit, and find out what they know about the War Memorial photography session. If possible get the name, address and mobile of the photographer, and the address and mobile of the model...," Adam looked to his notes. "Asha Reid."

"I wouldn't be surprised if the photographer and the model live at the same address," Erin said.

Adam felt that twinge of jealousy again. He looked to his pad for inspiration, no, for reference.

"We don't know if Jenny Mason is involved with this plot or not, so we'll put her under surveillance, starting now. We have her mobile number from the booking, we know her address, and you can find her car details. Erin, put together a surveillance roster, trace all calls and slip a tracker onto her car. Leon, as soon as you find out what you can from that modelling agency, call me."

"Will do."

Adam checked notes previously jotted. "I'll ring the Memorial to see if they have ticket details for the earlier visit at 11. We may get the other parties' names that way." Adam looked up. "Any questions?"

Heads shook before they left while Adam reached for his smartphone. He dialled from the call log.

"Michael Albertson."

"Agent C11, Director of Intelligence ASIO. Thank you for your response to my team. Since I called last evening we've identified persons of interest entering the Memorial earlier on Monday morning at 11. I wondered if you have ticket details for them."

"We ticket by name and contact number as is required for Covid-19 tracing."

"These tickets might have been booked by Jenny Mason."

"If you can wait for a moment, I'll ask my PA to check."

"No problem," Adam said.

Two or three minutes later. "Agent C11?"

"Yes," Adam replied.

"There were four one-hour tickets for 11 to be accompanied by one of our guides: Jenny Mason on 0418 998 777, Matt Taylor on 0426 398 661, Luke Monk on 0489 623 115, and Alice Monk on 0489 773 661."

Adam finished writing that down. "That's good," he said. "Thank you Mr Albertson, we can work with that."

Adam ended the call before logging into Telstra to search those numbers for Taylor and for Luke and Alice Monk, but had no luck. He checked Optus where he had success for Taylor, being apartment 304, 45 Gungahlin Place. Staying with Taylor, Adam checked car registration using name and address, to find a red 2017 Hyundai Veloster and its registration number. *Veloster?* He'd never heard of it so did a quick check to find low, wide and sleek, a real chick magnet. Turbocharged too. If working with models wasn't enough, a car like that – well. Moving to the last provider Vodaphone, and still no trace of Luke and Alice Monk. Adam sighed; they were false names.

Adam texted Leon that he had Matt Taylor's mobile and address, before emailing Matt Taylor's mobile, address and car registration to Erin for call tracing and surveillance, including a tracker on his car, and Luke and Alice Monk's mobiles for call tracing, for what that was worth. Those sims would have been discarded. Adam reclined his chair to ponder his next moves. In reality, how to find a man and a woman, both with false names, who might have fled Canberra after successfully assassinating the Prime Minister of Australia. An email arrived from Nicole: *meeting my office five minutes* Adam sighed before grabbing his compendium, slipped his notepad inside, and trudged to her office where Nate and Rebecca sat opposite Nicole, looking bright and fresh. Adam sat beside Nate.

"Adam?" Nicole asked.

"We've identified the name, address and mobile of the promoter of the photographic session, the name, address and mobile of the photographer, the name of the model, while the other man identified at Parliament House and later at the War Memorial goes by the name Luke Monk, with what appears to be his wife Alice Monk at the War Memorial. I can't be certain but Luke and Alice Monk appear to be false names."

"Nate?"

"IT contractor John Connell hasn't been to work this week, he hasn't contacted his work, he's not been seen where he lives since Monday, and his mobile is switched off."

Nicole frowned. "Adam, you verify Luke and Alice Monk or otherwise, take that to the next level and let us know. Nate, you trace John Connell as best you can."

"I put surveillance on the promoter and the photographer," Adam said.

"Why?"

Good point, until a reason came up. "With something as important as this we can't take chances."

A pause. "Yes, agreed. You'll put surveillance on the model?"

"Once we identify where she lives, although she might be in a relationship with the photographer.'

"The screen shot you emailed gives that impression. Adam, Luke and Alice Monk are your priority, as John Connell is Nate's priority. You both know what to do."

Adam walked briskly to his office where he got comfortable behind his computer to search Canberra driver's licences first for Luke Monk. One match but the picture wasn't their man. New South Wales had six matches but not their man either, nor did any other state. Next passports which had 11 Luke Monks but no matches. Canberra rates for Luke Monk matched to the address of driver's licence who wasn't their suspect. Similarly, New South Wales rates for all Luke Monks matched to driver's licences so they weren't their suspects either. Adam then did the same for Alice Monk but didn't find her licence, passport or rates notice. Adam emailed Leon to check all hotel, apartment and tourist park guest registrations in Canberra and nearby, including Airbnb, for Luke and Alice Monk.

Adam opened the screen shot of Luke Monk, cropped it so only his face was showing before doing the same with Alice Monk. He composed an alert.

'The attached persons of interest are wanted in relation to recent a terrorist attack in Canberra. They go by the name of Luke Monk and Alice Monk but have other identities. If either or both are apprehended, contact the sender agency of this alert.'

There was a group email address for all law enforcement agencies in Australia. Adam attached the two images and sent. *With luck,* he thought.

'Nicole, Luke Monk and Alice Monk are false names. An alert has been sent to all law enforcement agencies to that effect.' Send. Moments later from Nicole: *'Nate has sent an alert for John Connell.'* They were getting nowhere fast.

Adam's phone rang with a call from Leon.

"Leon," he answered.

"The agency gave me Asha Reid's address as 30 Sutton Street, Cootamundra, and I have her mobile. Reid signed with the agency on Monday, November 16, with her first booking being Andenny Promotions and Matt Taylor on Friday, November 27, at Young in New South Wales. Then came two bookings in Canberra, both with Andenny Promotions and Matt Taylor. A Canberra advertising photography session was on Wednesday December the second, preview already released, and the War Memorial which we know about."

"Thanks Leon. I've put Matt Taylor under surveillance which might locate Asha Reid."

"On my way back."

Adam ended the call before pondering their next moves. Really there wasn't anything beyond what surveillance might reveal. He went to Erin.

"I'm going home to shower and change. If anything happens, call. If not I'll be back in an hour or two."

"Right Adam."

Adam headed to the lift. He needed that shower, shave and clean clothes.

* * *

Erin saw Leon approaching her workspace.

"Hi mate," he said.

"Adam's gone home for a few hours, while we're waiting for surveillance to bear fruit.

He yawned. "I might go home for an hour to clean up."

"I'm managing things, and if something comes I'll call Adam."

"See ya."

Erin watched Leon leave with her head totally empty. Only having four hours sleep did that to a girl. Curious, Erin went through the surveillance videos until she found the photography session. There she watched the photographer, Matt Taylor, speaking with Asha Reid before backing away. The second picture was the same sequence but quite different. Daniel came to sit on her desk,

"What are you up to?" he asked.

"I'm looking at the photography session at the War Memorial." Erin slid the clip backwards. "Look at this: they talk and then she looks up to the cockpit I think, but look at her expression. Thoughtful. Now here they talk again and she poses, this time hands on hips and her legs crossed a bit. Big bright smile. They talk again and this time she peers inside, eyebrows raised looking curious." Erin looked up to Daniel. "It's not what I expected."

"Did you want to be a model?" he asked.

Erin couldn't help but smile at that memory. "Every schoolgirl wants to be a model. I don't know why: maybe we know about famous models and we want our chance for fame, or maybe it validates we're alright in the looks department. For me it validated I wasn't tall enough!"

"How tall do you need to be?"

"At least 170 but this model's 175."

"That's tall for a woman."

"Then put her in heels." Erin contemplated the paused image. "She's wearing old-fashioned shoes with a fair bit of heel, but beyond that, it's like acting. This expression, that expression, the other expression."

"Yeah." Daniel leaned close. "You don't have to validate your looks now, you know."

She looked up to him. "Thanks."

"You're as good as her; just not as tall."

"Ha!"

"It's true. Summer and bikinis are my favourite."

"I like her one-piece," Erin said. "Despite showing less skin, somehow it shows more."

Daniel looked at the screen. "You're right, you know."

"I'll get one."

"I'll look forward to that for when we get some free time."

"With the model and the photographer I mentioned workplace romances, having had that experience."

"Ours is a relationship now."

"This crisis will be over soon enough and then we'll – relate again. With Covid-19 under control we ought to go away for a few days."

"Great idea. You really wanted to be a model?"

"Every schoolgirl wants to be a model."

Daniel laughed before returning to his team. Erin contemplated the model looking into the aircraft paused on her computer screen. Already she was the face of Canberra the lucky thing.

Chapter Twenty One

Matt woke in an empty bed after sleeping well. But despite that he felt – odd. He got up and went to the bathroom, and after dressing went to the living room where Asha was on her smartphone. She looked up.

"How are you?" she asked.

Matt felt better after a hug and a good sleep, but not quite right yet. "I feel restless," he said.

"Do you want breakfast?"

"Toast will be fine."

"I've made coffee."

Matt poured a mug, added skim milk because that's all they had but that didn't matter, while Asha toasted multi-grain bread, which with margarine filled an empty stomach. Asha sat opposite.

"Are you still restless?" she asked.

"Yeah, a bit."

"I'm sure that's from what happened yesterday."

Matt needed to get his mind off it.

"Do you want to go for a drive?" he asked.

"Yes, let's go for a drive."

Matt wondered. "Crookwell is about an hour an a half north, and there's a nice cafe there where we can have lunch."

"What do we do between now and lunchtime with an hour and a half drive?"

"On the way we can stop for love in the bush," Matt said.

"Fine, good; but make sure we don't get caught!"

"That's not my plan."

"Do we go to the same place as last time?"

"In daytime we would get caught there! There's a bush reserve close to Crookwell with lots of trees. We just need to be away from the road. It's a back road so it's not busy."

Asha looked to him.

"It'll be good," Matt said.

"Love in the bush is always good."

"This time I'll take a blanket. I've got a couple of blankets I don't use."

"I'll put on shoes for the bush, and we're both in jeans so that's alright." She stood where Matt admired her delightful curves.

"I really want to get those jeans off you!" Matt couldn't help but exclaim.

She looked down to him. "Me too."

Already Matt felt better. Dwelling on what couldn't be changed didn't help, while love in the bush did no harm. Matt got up to follow Asha to their room to put on his gym shoes, which were best for walking through scrub.

* * *

Matt lay on his side while Asha still lay on her back. He brushed a strand of hair away from her face.

"It's odd but I sense someone," she said.

Matt glanced around. "There's nobody here. Besides, even if there was, what would they see? A couple in love making love."

"That really was making love. I like it like that."

"Me too."

Asha sat up and looked around. "There's a wallaby watching us," she said. "A curious wallaby." She lay down again. "My totem. Every plant and animal has a spirit, so we only hunted, fished, or ate plants necessary for our survival, and no more. We never hunted our totems. The skins of animals we hunted for food were used for clothes and blankets in cold weather. I'm sure you understand why we used those skins."

Matt did. "I understand."

"Kangaroos and wallabies always look curious when they watch us. It's like 'what are these humans doing in my bush?'"

"That wallaby would have been genuinely curious if it saw us making love."

"The way we just made love, face to face, yeah." Asha sat up. "As much as I could lie naked in the bush forever, your cafe beckons."

Reluctantly Matt got to his feet to put his hand down to help Asha get up, given how languid she looked. He looked around but nothing moved, except for a curious wallaby watching. Matt dressed, Asha dressed beside him, before Matt folded the blanket to follow Asha to their car.

Chapter Twenty Two

Adam left for home at seven in the evening; leaving instructions to call if anything happened. He had a feeling they'd lost Luke and Alice Monk, and worse they were expected to know about such people before anything happened. Nicole was in deep shit, Adam not so much. Nicole was probably going to be transferred to counting paper clips until she had enough of that and resigned. That wasn't a problem for Nicole; former ASIO operatives were in demand in the private sector.

After parking his Lexus, Adam climbed stairs to the house where Susan and the boys were in the dining room, eating. After greetings, Susan warmed leftover lasagne and vegetables while Adam poured a glass of red wine. Now life was back to normal, including everybody at the table knowing not to ask. Later, Susan stacked the dishwasher while the boys went to the rumpus room. Matt put on Mozart before Susan brought him a glass of port.

"Thanks." Adam pondered the port. "Obviously there's been no breakthrough because you would have heard. Some suspects are under surveillance and we'll see what happens."

"Are you worried?"

"We're supposed to know about these things before they happen, but that's Nicole's problem. If we had widespread facial recognition I believe we could apprehend the main parties behind this."

"Really?"

"You know not to tell anyone."

"My lips are sealed. Are you alright?" Susan asked.

Adam needed something. Then he remembered his inevitable emptiness which would make things worse. Pity. Instead he sipped his port.

* * *

Luke unlocked the door of room 18 and held it for Alice to carry her backpack which she dropped on the second of two beds. She turned around to face Luke.

"Now we're in Sydney," she said.

"From now we use our real names."

"Yes Jason."

"Yes Belinda."

"Are you pleased?" Jason asked.

"You wanted me to kill that Paki, I did. I'm going to miss our children, though."

"You know we don't have a choice."

"I know."

"You missed out with Mike, Jake and John," Jason said.

"Why did you want to share me?"

"Because you're sexy and I wanted to show you off."

"I didn't want to be shared. Was that naughty?"

"You've already been punished for that."

"I'm still upset about Max and David. Is that naughty?"

Jason thought. "You're their mother; of course you're upset. Come here," Jason said gently.

Belinda eased close for Jason to hug her.

"From now on, it's just you and me," Jason said.

"I know," Belinda said. "I hope our sons will have good lives with good wives."

"Me too, although I know there's no wife as good as you."

"I'm not good."

He hugged her tight. "You're the best wife in the world."

"Sometimes I have naughty thoughts."

"Like...?"

Belinda moved out of his hug. "Just now when you hugged me, I really didn't want you to."

Jason crossed his arms while planning what to do. "I'll have to punish you for that thought. Take off your jeans and panties and lie face down on the bed," Jason said as he pulled the thick, brown, leather belt from his jeans. "This time I want to hear your pain."

Belinda was already part-undressed and face down as Jason doubled his belt Smiling, he ran his hand over her soft, smooth flesh, before standing back to lash her there. Silence, so he did it again. Still silence, so he did it again, and again and again and again. Jason stopped for a moment to quietly observe Belinda, her hands bunching the quilt of the bed with the pain she'd endured, and still she refused to cry out. Jason lashed once, twice, three times as hard as he could. Once more hard across her bum and she moaned, deep and low.

Jason dropped his belt to sit on the bed and rub her bottom, bright red now.

Belinda lifted her head with tears running down her cheeks.

"I'll be better next time," she said.

Jason rubbed her red bottom. "I know you will."

Jason kissed Belinda there, red and swollen. She knew her place.

* * *

Jason and Belinda sat in the back of their car with Max driving and David in the front seat; not a word spoken. The entry roads to Port Botany were like a maze, but a maze including many big semi-trailers in a hurry. Max did well to get them to the carpark at the rear of the Patricks Terminal building where he eased the white Mazda 3 into a space. They all got out, David to open the boot containing two backpacks with all their worldly goods, two visibility vests and two white hardhats. Soon dressed in yellow-green fastened with velcro, passes in place around necks, hats in place too, final goodbyes, hugs from all. Then following white-marked walkways beneath big, primer-red coloured cranes; berths on one side and containers on the other. It was almost amazing to be able to drive in, park, and walk deep into the port, with the only person in sight being a security guard near the Patricks Terminal building. But it was a busy port that relied on trucks and cars being able to come and go without delay, and workers to get to those cranes and sailors to their ships, without delay too. Jason headed towards their ship, the APL Phoenix not so far along. Blue with a white superstructure part-way along the hull, APL in big, white letters on the side, and stacked with hundreds of containers mostly in blue, primer-red and dull yellow. To get passage on this ship, even though it was bound for the UK which wasn't an ideal destination, was thanks to the Dinky-Di Crew. Without that, Jason never would have agreed. As for the others: John, Mike and Jake, they were on their own to get caught sooner rather than later. That didn't matter: Luke and Alice Monk had disappeared to never be able to come home. Their real identities mightn't ever be known but their CCTV images were well-known. In their backpacks were new identities for England, while for now they were Jason and Belinda Rogers.

Beside the big ship was a steel ramp of steps with sturdy handrails, where a sailor, Mick Taylor on his pass, kept guard. Jason's and Belinda's passes were inspected before they were given access to steps climbing seemingly to the sky; higher and higher and higher, to the deck near the white superstructure. There, passes were inspected by another sailor, James Thomas, holding a clipboard. At a distance the APL Phoenix looked immaculate, but close-up seawater had taken its toll with streaks of rust here and there, and more than here and there.

Two ticks on a clipboard. "Catch the lift to the tenth floor and cabin ten," James Thomas said.

A door hung open allowing Jason to step over metal and enter the white superstructure where a lift waited, doors open. Into the lift, press '10', doors glided closed, and away. Higher and higher until the lift eased to a halt and doors slid open to a quiet, empty corridor of light-brown laminate walls, a blue rubber-tile floor, and blue doors with brass numbers. Just along was '10' where Jason turned a handle to enter a small room also of light-brown laminate walls and a blue rubber-tile floor. A window at the far end, two single beds on the left with their sides several centimetres above mattress level, a wardrobe on the right, and a couple of plastic chairs with soft blue cushions. A light brown curtain hung between the two beds but was hooked and tied to the wall. Belinda dropped her backpack on the bed closest to the door.

"This would be cosy for two sailors," she said. "I assume these are to stop us falling out of bed in rough seas," as she wrapped her fingers around the raised sides of her bed.

That was probably right.

"Now what?" Belinda asked.

"Three meals a day."

"And...?"

"Lots of whatever we can get up to."

"Lots of sex, and I'll be extra naughty to pass the time."

Jason dumped his backpack on the bed closer to the window, to look out across the port. Because of Covid-19 there were few flights and overseas travel was only allowed for special reasons anyway, but biometric identification meant they would get caught. To slip out as crew of a container ship was brilliant. One way or the other, their months at sea would pass.

Chapter Twenty Three

Leon and Erin entered and sat. Adam looked up.

"Please report," he asked.

"We've completed a search of all hotels, short-term stay apartments, Airbnbs, tourist parks and serviced apartments. No guests going by the name Luke Monk or Alice Monk are currently booked or have been booked during the past four weeks."

"Thanks Leon. Erin?"

Erin looked to her compendium. "We now know Asha Reid lives with Matt Taylor. Yesterday they went for a drive to Crookwell."

"Good," Adam said.

"They took a stop on the way and later had lunch in a cafe in Crookwell. Erin giggled. "Sorry," she said while now bright red.

"Anything else?"

"Jenny Mason walked to the shops to buy milk."

Adam sighed while Erin was still flushed.

"What is it about this drive to Crookwell?" Adam asked.

"The surveillance team was Joshua and Lachlan. When they saw the tracker moving, they followed at a distance. North out of Canberra, through Sutton, Gundaroo and Gunning. They kept heading north until the tracker stopped at a bush reserve six or seven kilometres before Crookwell.

Joshua thought a bush reserve might be the scene of a covert meeting so they tracked them on foot. It was a meeting of sorts. I'll show you."

Adam stood for Erin to take over his computer.

"As they closed, Lachlan put his camera on video so there wouldn't be any fake shutter sounds. When they heard voices they hid in a gully and filmed from there, for what that was worth."

Adam looked over Erin's shoulder to see a video of Matt Taylor and Asha Reid naked while hugging and kissing. Quite a lot of hugging and kissing before they lay down with Taylor between Reid's legs now. Quite a while of that before he slid up her body, as men do, but this was different. More than just close, it was like he wanted to climb inside her. And more than just close, she hugged him tight and crossed her legs at her ankles like she wanted him to climb inside her. That really was making love, kissing all the way. The camera moved to spot a kangaroo, no a wallaby watching the couple. By the time the camera moved back, Taylor was kissing Reid all over. His kissing went on and on like he worshipped her. His kissing *was* worshipping her. Adam realised he had his mouth open but he'd never seen anything like it. He felt flushed, like Erin.

"Did they have to film all of that?" Adam asked.

"Obviously not," Erin said.

Adam thought. "If it was a genuine meeting in the bush, fine, but if it's intimate again, please don't."

"I shouldn't have to tell them but in their shoes, that's – I don't know."

"It's...," Adam couldn't find the words either.

"It's passionate," Erin said.

Yes, passionate. "With that video in the case file, we have to hope Nicole doesn't go rummaging. Thank you both."

They left for Adam to replay in his mind what he'd just seen. Passionate, yes. Passion in the bush followed by lunch in a country cafe. *What a life?* She loved him, she must. He loved her, he must. If Adam asked Susan to go for a drive to Crookwell, and on the way make love in the bush, she wouldn't. If a miracle happened and she agreed, it wouldn't be like that. If Adam didn't have love with Susan, what was it? Friendship. Susan and he were friends; they could converse like Adam could converse with Andrew and his other friends and their wives. Susan and he were friends with once a week empty sex. Feeling odd, Adam checked a car out with no real plan, only to find himself in Gungahlin town centre. Unlike Woden Plaza near Red Hill which screamed 1970s, being enclosed, crowded and noisy; a shopping centre you got away from as soon as you could, Gungahlin was a modern replication of a traditional strip shopping centre except it was built along one main street and three cross-streets. Spacious, open, airy.

Adam sat on a bench in the broad centre median of Gungahlin Place, looking towards the Metro1 apartment building at number 45, and up to apartment 304 on the top floor. Matthew Taylor aged 26, arts graduate from University of Canberra, son of Frank Taylor, commerce graduate and CPA, and Laura Taylor receptionist for her husband's practice. Clients of Frank Taylor included Andenny Promotions, Andrew Smith former public servant, and Jenny Mason: born in Lismore Base Hospital and raised in Nimbin, New South Wales. Matthew Taylor first lived with Linda McCain, a fellow arts graduate, for three years although they might have had a relationship before then. After McCain came Jade Manson, a model who dated Matt Taylor for nine months while living in a share house, followed by Rachel Blair, another model who lived with Matt Taylor for almost two years. Now Asha Reid aged 18; a model from Cootamundra. Asha Reid passed year 12 and then took a year's contract as receptionist for Boggabilla Aboriginal Medical Clinic before signing at the Gemini Modelling Agency here in Canberra. Her parents were Jack Reid, a factory hand at Elouera Industries for 14 years, and Ella Reid who worked at the IGA Supermarket in Cootamundra. She had a younger brother Lachlan, and shared her house with a divorced aunt Betty Ryan and her two children, Asha Reid's cousins, Jason and Sue. It was bound together: Matt Taylor worked for clients of his parents as well as specialising in wedding photography, while having a string of model girlfriends. If that passion in the bush was any indication, there were no surprises that Matt Taylor attracted beautiful models into his orbit. Asha Reid came from a settled, extended family. Although young she probably knew love.

What then of Susan Colton? Father John Colton a retired former public servant grade EL2, mother Alice Colton, also retired and also a former public servant, grade APS6. Younger brother James Colton who she hardly saw, married with two children. Susan's parent's marriage was cold and empty and might always have been. Unlike Asha Reid, Susan Colton didn't know love. Adam wasn't any better, where his next promotion, a big house and an expensive SUV mattered more than things that really should matter. Sadly, James and Michael were heading along the same path. Adam looked up to apartment 304 again. Matt's love den, first his live-in girlfriend, attractive by any standards, followed by three models. A life photographing beautiful models and bedding the most beautiful of the beautiful. When Matt Taylor had a few hours free, he took them into the country to make love with them there. Life wasn't fair. Adam wished he could teach Matt Taylor how unfair life really was.

After gazing for far too long, Adam left to retrieve the ASIO Camry from the shopping centre carpark. By the time he got it back to the carpool it was close to time to go home. He went upstairs to check with Erin that she rostered all-night coverage in the office and for the two surveillance targets, which she had of course. Adam sat at his desk to check emails where at that moment an email arrived from Nicole, also to Nate: *'meeting my office five minutes'*. Adam sighed before grabbing his compendium. Adam sat beside Nate while Nicole's normally tidy hair was quite unkempt.

"Nate?" Nicole asked abruptly.

"We've got the family of John Connell under surveillance while we've identified three friends who are under surveillance."

"Any girlfriends?"

"Not that we've identified."

"Nate, please look into the two younger males attending Monday evening's photographic session. I don't know how you're going to find them, though."

"We'll have another look at CCTV and see if that sheds any light on who they might be."

"Adam, you've been chasing Luke and Alice Monk," Nicole asked.

"That trail has gone cold given they're false names."

"Have you identified a home, apartment, rental accommodation, hotel room or serviced apartment in that name?"

"There are no properties using that name now or in the recent past. I assume they've used either real names or other false names." Adam thought. "The only parties we have a lead on are the promoter of the photographic session at the War Memorial, and the photographer and the model at that session." Then Adam realised he could teach Matt Taylor a lesson about how unfair life really was. "I propose these three witnesses be detained for mandatory questioning," Adam said.

"Are you sure detention is justified?"

"I can't guarantee these witnesses aren't involved and therefore I can't guarantee they may alert Luke and Alice Monk."

Nicole drew a deep breath. "I agree," she eventually said. "Adam, prepare a briefing note for the Director General to that effect."

"I can't guarantee that access to lawyers isn't a security risk, especially given the severity of this situation."

"I agree. Include in your briefing note the recommendation that these witnesses be denied access to legal representation on the basis of the security risks that may entail."

"Assuming the Director General signs this off, do you think the Attorney-General will issue this warrant, given this is a new government?"

"I'll look into that. You can go now, Adam, to prepare your briefing note."

Adam strode to his office, feeling pleased. With luck he would have Matt Taylor, Asha Reid and by necessity, Jenny Mason, in detention within 48 hours. That would take the wind out of Matt Taylor's sails, as Adam opened the template to be used when preparing a briefing note for a Special Powers Detention and Questioning Warrant.

* * *

Leon and Erin sat opposite while Adam laid the green folder on his desk.

"Erin, do Matt Taylor, Asha Reid or Jenny Mason have set routines?"

"None have set routines. We've tracked Taylor to two weddings where he was photographer, while sometimes he and Reid go out together as you know. Once Mason came to visit Taylor and Reid."

"What's the earliest they've gone out?"

"So far, never before nine."

Adam opened the folder.

"These are three Special Powers Detention and Questioning Warrants for Matt Taylor, Asha Reid and Jenny

Mason. Leon, Superintendent Robson of the Australian Federal Police is expecting you to contact him in regards to the best time of day to detain Mason, Taylor and Reid, which will be eight tomorrow morning for all three. Leon, you will accompany one team of Robson's men to detain Taylor and Reid. Erin, you will accompany the second team to detain Mason."

"We've rarely used these powers," Leon said.

"We've never had a terrorist attack planned to this scale before, let alone executed. Because of the severity of our current situation, Taylor, Reid and Mason are being denied legal representation. It's all in the warrant. If they ask about legal representation, tell them that's not available. Leon, once you contact Superintendent Robson, he will arrange for Canberra Prison to keep these three in detention until we can interview them." Adam paused for that to sink in. "Do you have any questions?"

Silence.

"You both know what to do," Adam said.

They left while Adam couldn't help but smile.

Chapter Twenty Four

Matt heard hammering on his door.

"I'll get it," Asha said. "Seeing as you've got no clothes on."

"You sleep naked now.'

"I do but my pyjamas are here."

She slipped on white and floral cotton to go to their door where that hammering was quite persistent. Matt slid out of bed to rummage through the wardrobe until he found a pair of briefs.

Moment's later raised voices; Matt went to the doorway to see one guy in a dark blue suit holding two pieces of paper, and four police officers in blue uniforms overlaid with bulky vests of equipment like handcuffs and tasers.

"Asha Reid and Matt Taylor?" the guy in the suit asked.

"I'm Asha Reid and that's Matt Taylor."

"I'm Agent B18 from the Australian Security and Intelligence Organisation or ASIO, with a warrant for your detention and questioning."

"What are we being accused of?" Matt asked.

"You're not accused of anything. This is a warrant for witness detention and questioning."

"You can't do this!"

"Under the ASIO Legislation Amendment Act of 2003, we have the power to detain and forcibly question witnesses in special circumstances. Under this act ASIO has the power to deny legal representation, which has been exercised in this instance."

"What?" Matt asked with his head swimming.

"I suggest you get dressed, Miss Reid and Mr Taylor, so we can take you into detention now."

Asha eased past Matt into their bedroom.

"I'll close the bedroom door for a moment," Matt said.

"That's fine," Agent B18 agreed.

"What is this?" Asha asked quietly.

"This is from the photo shoot at the War Memorial, which must have something to do with the assassination there. Get dressed in something comfortably casual, answer their questions although it seems you don't have a choice, and I'm sure this will be fine."

"This doesn't seem right."

"This doesn't seem right to me, either," Matt said as he grabbed a light grey shirt and dark grey slacks. "That ASIO agent was specific so we'll just have to do what they want."

"Alright," Asha said as she mucked about finding matching bra and panties, as she always wore matched colours, then a light blue blouse and jeans that hung a bit loose. Comfortably casual.

"Hurry up," was the voice outside.

Matt pulled on blue suede shoes and tied laces while Asha put on the white sandals from her freestyle shoot. Matt opened the door, for his arm to be taken by one of the police officers, as bizarre as that seemed, down the stairs to Gungahlin Place, around through the walkway towards the shops at the rear where two police Holden Commodores, garish with dayglo stripes, waited in the short-stay carpark there. Matt was forced into the backseat of one, Asha was forced into the backseat of the other, and away they went as a convoy of two. Matt felt intimidated by the two silent police and the guy in the suit; he felt like a criminal even though he hadn't done anything wrong. Being forcibly detained as a witness was wrong, very wrong, but it all seemed legal. When they picked up the Majura Parkway, Matt knew their destination was the relatively newly-built Canberra Prison just beyond the light industrial estate of Hume. Indeed, the police officer eventually turned into the prison carpark. Another police car was already there, with Matt not surprised to see a woman in black slacks and a black suit, for sure a female ASIO agent, and two police officers escorting Jenny inside the clean and sparkling reception building in shades of green. It looked brand new even though the prison was about a decade old now.

Prison guards wore plain blue uniforms, where an older male had more stripes on his shoulders than the younger male and the younger female. Matt guessed fifties for the one with more stripes and thirties for the younger two.

"There are three trays with your names," the older male said. "Place all money, mobile phones, watches, jewellery and any other valuables into those trays."

Silently they did.

"Reid and Mason, please go with Sally McInroe to be searched and allocated a uniform. Taylor, I'm Sergeant Jack Smith and you will come with me.

Matt was taken into a windowless room somewhat bigger than a toilet cubicle. He was told to strip including underwear, which he did, to be searched including up his arse which he didn't like, more that two other guards watched that happen, and then was told to pull on his underwear, some grey overalls folded on a seat, and a pair of cheap, velcro-fastened sandshoes. While he did that he knew Asha and Jenny would be searched anally and vaginally, which was even more intrusive. No, unacceptable.

"Your number for the duration of your detention is on your overalls: 1289672. Come with me."

Matt was reduced to a number. He was led along a mostly glass-walled closed walkway overlooking the grassy fields of Canberra Prison, to a steel-framed glass door, and through that into a prison cell building which was again sparkling clean in shades of green, right down to soft, rubber-like green floor tiles. Light, bright and airy. Matt was shown to a dark green door, hanging open.

"This is a solitary confinement cell for the duration of your detention."

Matt went inside to a bed already made with a sheet and a pillow in a case, a couple of folded blankets on the end of the bed, a stainless steel washbasin with a cake of soap, a stainless steel toilet bowl, and the only view being through a small glazed window in the door looking out to the corridor. Confined and lacking privacy at the same time. Sergeant Jack Smith shut and locked the door, leaving Matt to contemplate that Australia was no better than China or any other totalitarian nation. Something was seriously wrong.

* * *

Asha couldn't believe their cell was in close proximity to male prisoners. After searching which was terrible, she and Jenny were shown to a cell with two single beds, a stainless steel washbasin and a stainless steel toilet. The only natural light was a small window in the door looking out to the corridor.

"1289777 and 1289785, this is your cell. You'll be locked inside for the duration of your detention here, while meals will be brought to you. Do you have any questions?"

"The window in the door doesn't give us privacy," Asha said.

"That's a problem, 1289777. Is there anything else?"

Asha shook her head before the door was shut and locked.

"I'm sorry," Jenny said.

"This isn't your fault," Asha said. "That shoot at the War Memorial seemed straight-up."

Jenny shrugged her shoulders.

"I'm sure this won't be for long," Asha said.

"There's only one thing," Jenny said. "First Nations people sometimes have problems being held in custody."

Asha thought through the answer to that. "After I finished school I worked for a year in a medical clinic in outback New South Wales. For First Nations people who live there, too often life borders on hopeless. It might be imprisonment is a final step in a lifetime of endless hopelessness."

"Not custody itself?"

"My life's good, once this mess is sorted out."

"At least we can keep each other company. Matt's probably on his own."

That was probably true. Asha hoped their detention wouldn't be for long.

Chapter Twenty Five

Matt was in solitary confinement as a witness although yet to be interviewed. While he waited he was served lunch of egg sandwiches on commercial white bread, an apple and coffee. Matt asked the guard for something to do and was given an ancient hardback novel with yellowed pages: Wreckers Must Breathe by Hammond Innes. At least that old novel passed the time, until a surprising dinner of coconut beef with rice and boiled vegetables. Not top quality but decent. Then lights out. Matt tried to sleep but his mind was too active. Sleep took ages.

After a breakfast of commercial toasted muesli and coffee, the door opened for what Matt assumed would be the guard to take away Matt's breakfast tray and cup. Instead the guard with a name tag 'Sutton' lurked at the door.

"Prisoner 1289672," Guard Sutton said.

"I'm a witness, not a prisoner," Matt said firmly.

"Yeah, well – okay. Whatever you are, you have an interview. Come with me."

Matt followed the guard past closed, solitary confinement cells to the steel-framed glass door, and along the walkway to end up in the reception building. To the left was an open door where the guard stood to one side. Inside the windowless room was a table, two chairs, a video camera on a tripod, and a middle-aged guy in a charcoal suit. Matt knew he was to go inside where the guard closed the door behind.

"Matt Taylor, I'm Agent C11, ASIO. Please sit."

Matt stood, glaring in anger. He was sure this guy was behind their detentions.

"Please sit so the camera can record this interview," Agent C11 said.

Still glaring, Matt sat.

"The purpose of this interview is to gain information in relation to a recent terrorist attack at the Australian War Memorial. Under the ASIO Legislation Amendment Act of 2003 you are required to answer all questions. Failure to do so carries a penalty of five years imprisonment. Do you understand?'

"I understand," Matt said.

"In addition, under the terms of the ASIO Legislation Amendment Act, you do not have access to legal representation."

"I know."

"We have viewed CCTV footage from the Australian War Memorial where, on Monday December 7, you met with Luke Monk and Alice Monk around 11 in the morning, before a photographic session at seven that evening. Did you have any suspicions regarding either Luke or Alice Monk?"

"Not initially. When we met again in the evening, Luke Monk had two guys we'd seen a couple of times during a shoot the previous week. One of those guys admired Asha, he told me that, and I assumed they wanted Asha for their shoot. One odd thing; these two men disappeared for about 10 minutes while I was posing Asha. My experience is men like seeing models being posed, especially a model like Asha who's quite striking. Later I noticed them watching us again."

"When and where did you first see these men?"

"It was during a shoot on Wednesday December the second first at Telstra Tower at 10 in the morning, then on the War Memorial forecourt, and later at a cafe on Kingston foreshore. Twenty2 Espresso."

"When you left Anzac Hall after the photographic session, you seemed upset. Why was this?"

"That shoot was the third time I've worked with Asha and the fourth time I've photographed her. She's got the perfect build for a model, she's attractive and she's talented. Photographic modelling is harder than it looks, but from our first shoot she made it seem easy, no, effortless. She has the potential to get as far as a supermodel and earn big money, but with Covid-19 restrictions her opportunities are limited for I don't know how long. That's why I was a bit upset."

"She kissed you."

Matt remembered. "Yeah, she did. That made me feel better, and to be realistic, her opportunities to star might still come in time."

"Do you know where the two men went for those 10 minutes?"

"I was busy posing and photographing Asha."

"Those men planted the IED at the War Memorial."

Matt shrugged his shoulders.

"You don't seem surprised?"

"As events have unfolded I had a feeling they might have been involved. Like I said, they'd seen Asha being photographed and I thought they checked model agency websites until they found her. Asha is probably the most attractive model in Canberra so there were no surprises they would have wanted her."

"What do you know of Luke Monk?"

"He said he's originally British and he told me a story about wanting to share the War Memorial with people in Britain. Andrew Smith handles bookings before he or Jenny Mason contact me. You'll have to speak to Andrew to find out what he thinks of Luke Monk."

"Do you have an exclusive arrangement with Andenny Promotions?"

"It's not exclusive but they use me for their model shoots. I think I've done all their model work for quite a few years now."

"You get on well with models."

"Is this part of the interview?" Alright, it seems I work well with women."

"Like Asha Reid?"

"Asha is talented as I said, and these days being indigenous is an advantage. We're playing catch-up, in modelling as well as across the nation, which makes this a good time to be the new indigenous face. I've been mentoring her because of her talent and potential."

"Alright Matt. That's all I have for now."

Matt leaned closer. "How long am I to be detained here?"

"You'll be detained until ASIO has gathered all the information it needs. You can go know."

Agent C11 opened the door for Matt to be escorted to his cell. He hoped this wasn't going to take too long but he had a feeling he'd read a few novels before their detentions were over.

* * *

Asha was led into the small room where a guy in a dark suit, perhaps her Dad's age but fastidiously neat, especially his short hair parted to one side, sat on one of two chairs. A video camera on a tripod had the red light on, recording.

"Asha Reid, I'm Agent C11, ASIO. Please sit."

Asha sat on the other chair.

"The purpose of this interview is to gain information in relation to a recent terrorist attack at the Australian War Memorial. Under the ASIO Legislation Amendment Act of 2003 you are required to answer all questions. Failure to do so carries a penalty of five years imprisonment. Do you understand?'

"I understand," Asha said.

"In addition, under the terms of the ASIO Legislation Amendment Act, you do not have access to legal representation."

"I understand."

"On the evening of Monday December the seventh, you undertook a photographic session at the Australian War Memorial. Did you have any suspicions about Luke Monk, Alice Monk or the other men attending this session?"

"My job is to model to Matt's instructions, not to check who booked us. That's Jenny, Jenny Mason and her husband Andrew Smith."

"Two of the men on Monday evening you'd seen during an earlier photographic session."

"That's right. Matt said one of those men admired me and he would have wanted me for their shoot. That made sense."

"Do you really think they admired you?"

"What are you asking? Do I think I'm pretty? Do I think I'm beautiful? I'm beautiful and I'm sure those men would have wanted me to pose in their pictures."

He went red and swallowed while Asha smiled at his reaction. "Why do you think you're beautiful?" he then asked.

Asha knew well enough. "Men, white men, First Nations men, have been admiring me since – I was about 14. There's no shame in knowing you're being admired."

"Does Matt Taylor think you're beautiful?"

"I know he thinks more of me than that."

"Matt Taylor seemed upset when he left the shoot. You kissed him. Did he tell you why?"

"Matt didn't tell me. During the shoot he told me about young men my age in bombers with shrapnel and bullets ready to kill them in a moment, and canvas aircraft, and the other machinery of death there. I thought he knows too much. No, when you think about it, that hall is full of death and tragedy. So I kissed him to make him feel better."

"The two men who saw you earlier, went away from watching you for a time. Did you see where they went?"

"I was too busy to notice who was watching us."

"Is there anything else?"

"I was there to pose, I posed. Matt takes good pictures so I'm sure, if that shoot was legitimate, it would have been good. I know it wasn't legitimate, only because I'm now speaking with you from ASIO."

"Thank you Asha." He opened the door. "You can go."

The guard waited to escort Asha but to a different building. She was taken to a single room.

"What's this for?" Asha asked.

"I was told to detain you in solitary confinement."

"Alright, fine," Asha said. That guard had no choice so there was no point in getting upset. Asha would have much rather shared with Jenny, who might end up on her own too. Asha hoped this ASIO interview thing wouldn't take too long.

* * *

Adam waited alone. There was something magnetic about Matt Taylor and Asha Reid. Talent, potential, beauty, admiration. She wasn't naive, far from it. Passionate too. Adam couldn't get visions of them together out of his head, even as Jenny Mason was escorted into the room. He needed to interview Jenny Mason for the sake of it.

"Jenny Mason, I'm Agent C11, ASIO. Please sit."

Mason sat in the other chair.

"The purpose of this interview is to gain information in relation to a recent terrorist attack at the Australian War Memorial. Under the ASIO Legislation Amendment Act of 2003 you are required to answer all questions. Failure to do so carries a penalty of five years imprisonment. Do you understand?'

"Yeah, alright," she sighed.

"In addition, under the terms of the ASIO Legislation Amendment Act, you do not have access to legal representation."

"Okay."

"How did the photography session at the War Memorial on the evening of Monday December the seventh come about?"

"Luke Monk contacted Gemini Modelling Agency to use Asha Reid in his shoot. Gemini put Monk onto my husband Andrew who booked it with the Memorial. Andrew told me so I could arrange costumes, makeup and hair styling, while I told Matt and Asha."

"Matt Taylor is your regular photographer for models."

"Matt's got a good eye especially for the female form, and he gets on well with models which is essential."

"He's had relationships with a few models, including Asha Reid."

"Yes he has, but that's never gotten in the way of his work."

"Including Asha Reid?"

"Matt trained Asha in freestyle posing which expands her repertoire. This makes their relationship an advantage to us.

What they do when a shoot is over is down to two consenting adults."

"Asha Reid is 18."

"Asha is an adult."

"Thank you Jenny Mason?"

"Is that it?" she asked while frowning.

"For now. Your detention will be finalised when we've gotten to the bottom of a few facts."

"How long can this go on for?"

"A detention and questioning warrant is issued for seven days, but we have the option to extend your warrant for further blocks of seven days if we think that's necessary."

"Get this over as soon as possible, please," she said with her jaw firm.

Adam opened the door.

"You can leave now, Jenny Mason."

She left to be put in solitary confinement too. Adam switched off the camera, done.

Chapter Twenty Six

Adam eased his Lexus into the garage while the door rattled closed behind. Soon he was upstairs where Susan had a glass of white wine while lazing on the couch. She looked up.

"I ordered Indian to be delivered. Get a glass and join me."

Matt poured a glass to sit on the couch with Susan in jeans almost wrapped around him. Jeans didn't totally suit her but they highlighted her long legs.

"You look delicious," he said.

"It's been a long day."

That was 'no'. Adam sipped his wine: *pity*.

Chapter Twenty Seven

Kasir didn't want a state funeral for Yaseera, who was a daughter, wife and mother before she was a Prime Minister. But it was expected that the departed leader of government would have a state funeral, and as the days passed Kasir sensed the nation needed this funeral. In a Covid-19 size-restricted ceremony, Kasir couldn't bring himself to give a speech, but fortunately Sajia and Najam wrote and delivered their speeches, as well as representatives from major political parties.

The three hours of the ceremony and internment went like a blur. Only when Kasir returned home to suburban Notting Hill with his daughters, did the reality of what happened really hit him. Yaseera's motivation for entering politics was to do good for her country, and also to be one of the first minority members of parliament, and certainly the highest ranking. Sadly Yaseera was killed because she wanted to do the right thing for the country of her birth, although Kasir knew only a few were involved with that hate crime and the majority of Australians didn't care about race or religion. Yet Kasir's thoughts of good Australians didn't help when his home was lonely and his future was bleak. Even when those terrorists were caught, Kasir knew that wouldn't help him either. When alone in their room which never gave Yaseera the creeps like The Lodge, Kasir didn't know what to do. He felt terrible, lost and alone. He'd lost his soul mate.

Chapter Twenty Eight

The days dragged in his cell. Matt finished Hammond Innes to be given an old John Grisham paperback, The Firm, which was dreary but passed the time. It was a relief to be called to another interview. Same room, same man, Agent C11, same suit, video camera on a tripod. This time Agent C11 simply gestured for Matt to sit, which he did.

"You seem to be attracted to models," Agent C11 said.

Matt was startled by that. "What has this to do with terrorist attacks?"

"You're required to answer my questions or face five years imprisonment."

Matt sighed. This ASIO agent had accessed Matt's Centrelink records. "I happen to be a photographer who works with models, and workplace romances do happen."

"You've had relationships with three models in four years."

"I made the same mistake twice. This time I haven't made that mistake."

"Asha Reid is only 18."

"Asha's from a loving family with a great attitude towards life."

Matt watched Agent C11 frown. "You're turned-on by her brown skin."

Matt thought. "Because Asha is First Nations, she has The Dreaming which gives her a calm acceptance of life and her place in it. This seems to percolate through many aspects of her personality which I find especially attractive."

"I still find this age difference – unusual."

Matt suspected Agent C11 in his dark suit, obsessed with models and relationships, had a few relationship problems of his own. He wore a wedding band which meant unhappily married. Matt pondered. "Age and looks don't interest me," he said. "I've been searching for that special woman where we compliment each other in all ways. With Asha we do. What's more, I'm learning from her and she's learning from me."

"What are you learning?"

"I need to discover the reason for my existence." Matt paused while he thought of something sarcastic. "Do you have any other questions of a personal nature, Agent C11?" he asked. "If not, I would much rather be in my cell. I'm sure you understand."

Agent C11 opened the door where the guard waited to escort Matt.

* * *

Asha entered that room: same Agent C11, same two chairs, video camera on a tripod but no red light this time. He gestured, she sat.

"Asha Reid, we're here to talk about Matt Taylor," Agent C11 said.

Matt had nothing to do with terrorism while this wasn't being recorded. "I refuse to answer," Asha said.

"Refusing to answer my questions is punishable by up to five years imprisonment."

"You can't prove I refused to answer unless you record this interview, can you?"

"Ah." He went to the camera while Asha turned her head to make sure the red light was on. He sat.

"Now Asha Reid, are you aware of other models Matt Taylor has had relationships with?"

"I am."

"Do you think in time you'll be like those other models? Used and discarded?"

"No I don't."

"Why not?"

"What Matt and I have is strong."

"Those other models would have thought the same. Have you ever thought of them? Young, naive, preyed upon?"

Asha hadn't but there was an element of truth in that. "No, I haven't thought of them."

"Are you being preyed upon by someone older and more experienced?"

"No," she said. They already shared a deeper connection, like Matt's fascination with The Dreaming. That led to his search for spirituality which actually didn't go very far. Asha then wondered. *Did Matt pretend fascination with The Dreaming just to keep her in his life?*

"Do you ever think about those other models, young like you?" Agent C11 asked.

"I told you I don't think about them," Asha said, while thinking very much.

"If I was you I would."

Asha didn't know what to say.

"You can go now, Asha Reid," he said.

Asha left to be escorted to her cell. There she lay on her bed thinking about two girls her age, who thought they had something but were discarded after a time. Were Asha's beliefs just an illusion? She wondered.

Chapter Twenty Nine

Erin looked up as Adam passed her cubicle to go into his office, where through partly-opened vertical blinds on the glass wall separating him from them, she saw Adam put the video camera on his desk. Erin wondered what Adam was up to. Special Powers Detention and Questioning Warrants were rarely issued, rarely they needed to be, and were intended for hard-core witnesses who were terrorists or potential terrorists themselves. Not Jenny Mason, Matt Taylor or Asha Reid, who Erin was certain weren't directly involved in the attack. Erin wondered why they were being detained and questioned under the Special Powers regime. She then wondered why Adam questioned them alone, and multiple times too. With Adam on his phone, Erin searched for Adam's interviews from four days ago. Once found she took headphones from the second drawer of her desk, plugged them into her laptop to first watch to a relatively short interview with Matt Taylor, an equally short interview with Asha Reid, and a very short interview of a personal nature with Jenny Mason. Those interviews proved the connection between the photographic session and the assassination of Prime Minister Devi, while Matt Taylor observed two men leaving the session for a while, of course to plant the IED. Those two pieces of information could have been obtained by routine questioning. Erin looked up to notice Adam's office empty. She grabbed a USB to plug into the camera, scrolled the camera menu to download which didn't take long, to quickly return to her desk. There she watched Asha Reid being interviewed quite explicitly about her relationship with Matt Taylor and what she thought of Taylor's previous relationships. That was weird – no. Erin understood. Adam had gone off the deep end which was jeopardising their investigation. There was one possible, no the only solution to this. Erin unplugged and folded her laptop before, as casually as possible, strolling to Rebecca staring at her computer screen.

"Excuse me Rebecca," Erin asked as pleasantly as she could manage. "Is Nicole free?"

"Is this important?" Rebecca snapped.

"This is important."

Rebecca went to Nicole's door, asked, where Erin overheard she had three minutes. Erin sat opposite Nicole with her laptop on her lap. She pressed 'enter' for the clip on the USB to play. While sound of the video clip played though the laptop speakers, Erin looked to Nicole frowning.

"Who knows about this?" Nicole asked.

"Only me. I believe I know the reason why Adam asked those questions," Erin said as she returned to the case file. There she found the catalogued version of the clip Lachlan filmed. "Can I show you this?"

Nicole nodded so Erin stood beside Nicole's chair to place her laptop on Nicole's desk. Erin pressed 'enter' to play.

"This is Matt Taylor and Asha Reid. Our surveillance team thought they were having a covert meeting but clearly it's not."

"Alright, that's enough," Nicole said. "I get the picture. You think these two are connected."

"Adam saw this clip and now we have Mason, Taylor and Reid in detention, with Asha Reid being asked personal questions. I listened to their earlier interviews, where what was obtained would have been obtained during normal questioning. In their interview, Adam asked Jenny Mason questions about models and about Asha Reid. Adam then asked Jenny Mason quite specific questions about Matt Taylor and his relationships. We know Taylor has had relationships with three models including Asha Reid."

"I understand. Erin, keep this secret for now."

"I've got no agenda against Adam, other than this jeopardises our investigation which has stalled."

"I understand."

Erin returned to plug her laptop back into her cubicle, and put her head down to work, as little as there was. Shortly after she sensed people approaching. She looked up to see two Nicole and two young guys go into Adam's office, to escort Adam out with one young guy holding Adam's satchel.

"Erin?"

Erin looked up to Rebecca.

"Nicole wants to see you."

Erin went to Nicole's office to be shown to the meeting table, while Nicole closed the door before sitting opposite.

"Adam Winter has been suspended pending a review. In the meantime I'm promoting you to Acting Director of Intelligence, and I'm promoting Mia Watson to Acting Surveillance Team Leader. Your first task is to resolve the detention of Jenny Mason, Matt Taylor and Asha Reid while stating nothing about the circumstances of their detention or questioning."

"I understand," Erin said. She thought. "I'll get Leon to speak with the police superintendent he dealt with."

"I don't need to say this might be awkward for you."

That was for sure. Some team members might blame Erin for what happened to Adam. Erin gained, after all.

"I'll get this matter underway," Erin said before leaving. While she walked she thought, until she got to her cubicle where she went to her laptop. Meeting Room One was free; Erin booked it for five minutes time, while sending a meeting invite to members of teams formerly reporting to Adam. There, Erin waited for 21 to assemble, with her laptop on the edge of the meeting table.

"Thank you all for coming at short notice. I have something I want you all to see."

Erin played the so-called interview with Asha Reid to absolute silence when it finished.

"Adam Winter has been suspended for a review, while Nicole has appointed me as Acting Director. Leon, can you contact Superintendent Robson to get Mason, Taylor and Reid released as soon as possible, and for all three to be taken home? No mention is to be made of what happened and why they're being released."

"Yes Erin."

"Mia; Nicole has appointed you to the position of Acting Surveillance Team Leader. We won't be putting either of Mason, Taylor or Reid under surveillance. For all of you, thank you for your time."

Erin carried her laptop to the office, her office, where she paused at the doorway before placing it on her desk and sitting in the big, leather chair.

"Congratulations mate," Leon said from the doorway.

"Thanks Leon but I'm only acting."

"Regardless, this won't do your career any harm, especially if we get somewhere."

Erin thought. "Please sit, Leon. Luke and Alice Monk planned this to the finest degree and I wouldn't be surprised if we have extreme difficulties locating them. This leaves us with John Connell. Once you've resolved those detentions I want your team to search for any possible clue pointing to where, and possibly with who, John Connell might be."

"Alright mate."

Leon left while Erin rotated her chair to look out the window. Now she had a view.

* * *

Adam sat in the living room with his thoughts wandering from place to place. *How stupid?* He should have deleted that interview of Asha Reid. For a simple mistake his career was ruined. ASIO would dismiss him although he could fight that and possibly get compensation. Adam couldn't tell Susan he conducted those interviews to break up Matt Taylor and Asha Reid, but for sure he'd broken their relationship which was something positive. Then Adam remembered a conversation about Susan's subordinate making things up if Susan reported her bullying. That would work. Adam reported Erin, calling her his team leader, for unsatisfactory work, only his team leader made things up about Adam. Susan would never get to the truth of that, especially in ASIO. That would work for sure. Now feeling calmer, Adam waited.

After a while Adam heard Susan climbing the stairs from the house. He heard her keys rattle as she put them on the granite bench top in the kitchen, and then footsteps as she approached the living room. There she stood, in black slacks and a blue blouse with arms crossed.

"I'm surprised to see you home with all that's going on," Susan said with her jaw clenched. "Never mind this is an opportunity. What can you tell me about a teen girl about two weeks ago in Red Brick Espresso at Curtin? A bit shorter than average, a little plump but attractive, I was told puppy fat, in a blue floral dress? Let's say she's about James's age."

"Ah...," Adam said while trying to think of an answer.

"Let me make it easier for you, Adam. Did you fuck her?"

"No I didn't."

"But you met her with that intention?"

"Why would I?"

"Why would you meet a teenage girl? A mid-life crisis, of course."

"Nothing happened," Adam said.

"I remember you brought me flowers that afternoon while never really saying what you'd been up to. The problem is Canberra's a bit like a country town."

"Yes, well, nothing happened."

"You were intending for something to happen."

Adam looked into Susan's eyes. "I couldn't," he said.

Susan tilted her head. "Regardless, you intended to cheat on me with a schoolgirl and I'm not going to be cheated on! Do you understand?"

"She wasn't a schoolgirl. She's 20 and in university."

"Well you emotionally cheated on me despite what I do for you! Working full-time, cooking most nights, looking after this house; while you fantasise about university-aged girls!" Susan stepped closer. "I want you to pack your bags and get out of my sight! Maybe one day I'll forgive you but I'm not in the forgiving mood at the moment!" Susan pointed at the kitchen beyond which was the stairs to the garage. "Do it now Adam!"

Adam almost sneaked past Susan to go to their bedroom with Susan now standing in the doorway, watching. He took his usual backpack and grabbed shirts, trousers and underwear. Bathroom next, electric shaver, deodorant and other things, still with Susan watching. There were hotels in Woden, he'd checked before he met Sarah. He eased past Susan to go down to the garage where he pressed the door release on his Lexus. Adam looked across to see Susan in the doorway, arms crossed and still glaring. He'd never seen her so angry. Adam tossed the backpack onto the backseat before getting into his SUV. *What a fucked-up day? What a fucked-up mess?* Maybe Susan would have him back once she calmed down, but those things she said were right. Even their once a week sex, more than many men his age seemed to get; Adam was sure he'd done his dash with that. Adam pressed the remote to open the garage door with Susan still glaring with her arms crossed. It was only when he reversed onto the driveway and the door rattled closed did her anger disappear from view. How stupid could Adam have been; not only this but with Matt Taylor and his girlfriend? In just a few weeks by blowing that one issue in their relationship out of proportion, he'd ruined everything. There were lessons to be learned but those lessons had come too late. Adam drove away furious with himself.

Chapter Thirty

Erin felt somewhat out of her depth; not only as Acting Director but that she was more a surveillance agent than intelligence. She could do both but had more experience with surveillance. Yet she was where she was, where this investigation was going nowhere. The two unknown males were now being investigated by Nate, which left John Connell hanging. Erin began by reading documentation from Nate's team which catalogued all documents relating to John Connell's security clearance, his family, parents and a younger sister in Arunda where Connell previously resided, but hadn't been seen since the day of the assassination, and where surveillance was posted. Three close male friends going back to high school; also interviewed and documented by Nate's team. With these friends there were no suspicions although none of them admitted to being close. Finally interviews with a department manager, Connell's supervisor, and a total of 21 work colleagues, some who know Connell better than others although none seemed to know him well. John Connell seemed a loner.

Erin turned away from her computer screen while feeling something was missing but not knowing what it was. She'd been at her computer for a couple of hours and needed a break, where perhaps things would come clearer. In the tea room Leon had just filled the coffee percolator which was bubbling. That smelled delicious.

"How are you going, mate?" Leon asked.

"I'm getting my head around things," Erin said. "Luke and Alice Monk have false identities, they knew to keep their car out of CCTV view so we wouldn't get their rego, while using a photo shoot as cover was elaborate. I don't think we'll find them easily so I'm concentrating on John Connell, who's gone to ground." Erin frowned. "There's something missing."

"This will help," Leon said as he filled Erin's mug.

Erin added milk and sugar and stirred. She sipped, nice, especially freshly brewed. At home Daniel liked fresh coffee, and often tossed out over-stewed coffee to make a new jug, and then it hit Erin.

"There's no girlfriend," she said. "We've found his parents, his sister, three friends, a whole bunch of co-workers, and even though they were all asked about a girlfriend, there was none." Erin sipped her coffee. "For a 24 year old that doesn't seem right." Erin wondered where there was one possibility. "Leon, bring Issy and James to my office."

"Yeah mate."

Erin sat at her desk as Leon and James sat with Issy standing.

"I'm looking for John Connell's girlfriend," Erin said. "Contact Canberra University, find all his tutors and talk with them. Don't frighten them; we're just after their help. I'm after a girlfriend he might have had at university, and any other male friends at that time too. If his tutors don't know about a girlfriend his university friends might. Any questions?" No questions. "Thanks."

They headed out. Erin decided to email Nicole about her investigation, copy Nate.

Chapter Thirty One

Matt was pleased to be home. No, amazed. First things first.

"Do you want to shower, Asha?"

"Yeah, no. You shower Matt."

"Are you sure?"

She nodded her head, so Matt went to the bathroom, stripped off, and showered quickly. He emerged from the bathroom with his dirty underwear left on the floor.

"Your turn."

Asha went to the bathroom to undress before stepping into hot water. She started by washing her now greasy hair while thinking. That guy, Agent C11, might be right. But then, Matt might feel different about her than the other girls. Even so, thinking about those girls gave Asha a chill despite hot water. They started with the bikini shoot and then they picked up momentum like it had a life of its own. Maybe that was real or maybe that was experience against naivety. *What was the answer?* Asha didn't know. She needed to get home anyway and that would give her time to think. Under magic hot water, Asha worked out a plan.

Asha stepped out to dry her body, and with the towel wrapped around her hair she left her dirty underwear beside Matt's dirty underwear. She went to their bedroom to grab panties and a matching bra.

"Feeling better?" Matt asked from the doorway.

"I am, and you?"

"Sort-of."

Asha looked to the floor in front of Matt's socks. "I would like to go home for a while. When I'm ready I'll call you."

"That ASIO agent spoke about you, and about my past girlfriends which I've told you about. If he spoke to you about that, don't let that get you down."

Still staring at the floor. "I just need time at home."

"How many times did he interview you?"

"Twice."

"Me too. His second interview went too far."

"Me too," Asha admitted.

Matt stayed where he was. "I just want you to know I love you," he said.

Asha thought he'd said that to a few girls. "I know," Asha said. "The bus for Cootamundra leaves Jolimont at eight. I'll get up early to catch the light rail."

"If that's what you want."

"It's more what I need, which is different."

"Yes it is."

She pondered Matt and what he said. She wouldn't burn her bridges, instead sleep in their bed tonight as normal. Then go home, spend time with family, and think.

* * *

The front door was never locked during the day. Asha went inside.

"Asha, you're home," Mum observed.

"I've come home to reconnect," Asha said, as she rehearsed on the bus.

"We've seen you on television."

"I know. That was a good day. I'll go to my room."

Sue was cross-legged on her bed with a textbook and the old laptop, as Asha dumped her backpack on her bed. They greeted each other.

"How's school?" Asha asked.

"Fine; the usual. How's modelling?"

Asha shrugged her shoulders. "I'm taking a break for a while. Do you want to go to Wagga on Saturday like we used to?"

"That'll be great!"

"I'll speak with the rest and we'll have a special day out."

"Cool!"

Asha wondered what to do until it was obvious. "What's that assignment for?" she asked.

"This is English. Can you help me?"

"I'll try but remember I didn't get top marks."

"You did alright. Can you read what I've written and tell me what you think?"

Asha sat on Sue's bed to be handed the laptop. She frowned as she read the assignment question. Year 12 was a long time ago.

Chapter Thirty Two

Matt parked outside his parent's house, his old home, to tilt the sunroof before leaving and locking his car. It was a quiet street in Belconnen, a 1970s part of Canberra, with well established gardens, native shrubs and many gum trees. Matt rang the buzzer to be greeted by Dad, who expected him.

"Hello Matt, come in."

Mum was in the background.

"Hi Mum."

"Hello Matt."

Dad went into the living room where Matt was invited to sit. Nothing had changed, right down to pale green walls, slightly deeper green carpet, darker green trim, and a burgundy-coloured, leather lounge suite, regularly cleaned and conditioned.

"You texted you were detained by ASIO," Dad said.

"We were detained as witnesses and forced to give evidence: that's Jenny, the model and me. We were kept for five days in solitary confinement in Canberra Prison."

"That's terrible. When you texted me I looked into it, and found the act that ASIO used against you was passed in 2003, to expire in September this year, but has been extended to March next year. At the time, Labor watered it down and put in a sunset clause before passing it."

"Piss-weak," Matt grumbled.

"That wasn't long after the World Trade Centre bombing where the threat of terrorist attacks seemed more dangerous than they turned out to be. In 2003, to deny this legislation would have seen Labor painted as soft on terrorists, but if there had been a terrorist attack here, Labor would have worn not only political fallout but would have been moral culpable."

"Yeah, I understand. Do other countries have anything similar?"

"Not in terms of forcibly detaining and questioning witnesses effectively indefinitely, with the possibility of denying legal representation. How did you get involved?"

"We innocently crossed paths with the terrorists behind the assassination of Prime Minister Devi. ASIO could have interviewed us and we would have told them what we knew, but one of their spies was obsessed with the model."

"That's wrong!" Dad exclaimed.

"I know. My real problem is these powers shouldn't be there."

"I agree. The odd thing is a Labor government used these Special Powers against you. By rights these should be done away with."

Matt remembered something. "When ASIO released us they told us it's a criminal offence to talk about what happened. Be careful of that, Dad."

"I understand. That means you can't talk to the media about that agent's misuse of these powers."

"We can make a complaint which I will be doing in writing. I want that agent to suffer the consequences of what he did."

"That's something."

"Have you heard from Jenny?" Matt asked.

"I'm seeing Andrew and Jenny on Monday," Dad said.

"Tell Jenny I'm alright, but Asha, that's the model and I, were fucked-up by that ASIO agent."

"You're not having much luck there."

Matt shrugged his shoulders. "Maybe one day I'll have luck, but this girl Asha was looking good. You've probably seen her."

"Ah yes!" Dad exclaimed.

"Great model, lovely personality, really interesting; everything."

"Attractive."

"That too," Matt said. "The one good thing is we helped put First Nations out there by using her. I particularly like the shot at the cafe. If anyone saw that and didn't think First Nations are equal to us, different in some ways but as capable, I would be surprised."

"She looks like she belongs seeing the sights of Canberra and buying a new wardrobe."

"I know she belongs, and I spent a few hours with her immediate family and they belong too. In remote Australia things are more complex, but that could be fixed because under the surface they're the same as Asha."

"Frank!" Mum called.

"We have a barbeque to cook," Dad said.

What else?

"Come with me Matt," Dad said.

That late December day, warm and sunny, was a good day to cook a barbeque. Beyond fine weather, some things never changed, as t-bone steaks and sausages were on a plate by the barbeque under the rear plexiglass veranda. Dad cooked, Matt pretended to, to later bring too much meat inside to be accompanied by roast potatoes and a green salad.

"At least the new government has done away with the previous government's university funding cuts," Mum said.

"I haven't been following that," Matt admitted.

"They proposed an overall cut in funding to universities when we really needed more funding, and a cut in fees to some courses like science and nursing, and a near-doubling of fees for arts."

"Accounting was going to be half as expensive again," Dad said.

"That's your qualification," Matt said. "To cut university funding in a recession didn't make sense. Besides, university doesn't teach you narrow-focussed, job-related skills. It takes an hour to master the basics of a digital SLR camera, but that was only the start of what I learned. The end result is a broadening of your knowledge and the ability to shoot something big-scale, like what the Canberra Chamber of Commerce needed to help our economy. Really, what conservative politicians like the previous government don't want are university graduates who can critically think and analyse, because that will be the end of their fascist authoritarianism. For them, the less university graduates, the better, because misuses of power like the forcible detention and questioning of witnesses, will go unchallenged."

"Or growing inequality will go unchallenged," Mum said.

"Give them a donation and you get special treatment, while the rest have their living standards dragged-down, but voters didn't critically think about what was really happening until their corruption became too much."

"Even now the majority don't understand that university isn't vocational education."

"Where would we be without creative individuals like artists, musicians and other performers? Asha the model liked Roxy Music; arts graduates who developed quite unique music, but not so far off-tangent to be non-commercially viable. Their music has brought joy to millions. What economic value is there in that? Not so much, but the cultural value of their music is incalculable."

"Bikini calendars?" Mum asked.

Matt smiled at that insinuation. "Anyone can shoot a model in a bikini, but I try to make the theme of my shoots and the posing of my models as far from run of the mill as I can get away with."

"Different to the usual but commercially viable."

"That's right."

"By being an artist with a broader view of the world, you're part of a culture war."

"I've heard that term too many times in the recent past," Matt said.

Things went silent. Matt thought that was time.

"I better go, Mum and Dad. Thanks for lunch and I'll keep in touch."

"I'll let Jenny know you're alright."

"Recovering is a better description. Being tossed into solitary confinement and intrusively questioned takes some getting over." Matt stood. "Thank you Mum and Dad and maybe next time I'll have better news."

Matt headed out to his car to drive home, which didn't take long. Home felt empty. Matt sat in one of his armchairs where he remembered he had unfinished business. He pulled out his smartphone and scrolled contacts to compose a text.

'hello emma i wouldnt mind talking with you about your beliefs matt'. Send.

'hi matt let me know a day and time'

It was about a two hour drive to Young. Matt thought then composed. *'is tomorrow morning about 11 alright'*. Send.

'tomorrow morning 11 is good unit 1 82 edward street'.

'see you then'. Send.

'kk'.

Something good might come from that.

Chapter Thirty Three

Erin looked up to see Issy at her door.

"Erin?"

"Come in."

Issy came in and sat. "I found a girlfriend; her name's Syeda Niazi. Once I got her name I double-checked her licence photo with Connell's Project Management tutor at the university, which confirmed her address. I rang and she's working from home."

"That's an Indian name, isn't it?"

"I checked and it's Urdu, which is Indian or Pakistani."

"She could be Muslim."

"Yes."

Erin was surprised a guy associated with a far-right terrorist plot had an Indian or Pakistani, possibly Muslim girlfriend.

"How old is Syeda Niazi?"

"She's 24 like John Connell. She has the same degree as John Connell and was in many of the same tutorials. She's a contractor at the Department of Finance and Administration."

"Let's pay a visit on Syeda Niazi."

"I'll let Leon and James know and book a car."

"Great Issy."

Soon they were on their way to Ngunnawal near Gungahlin with Issy driving, which was one advantage of Erin being Acting Director.

"How are you feeling, Erin?" Issy asked.

"I'm good. I think there are two rules we need to work by: do our best and do the right thing. It doesn't matter if you're Acting Director or Intelligence Officer Grade...."

"Grade Three. I'll remember that."

"Our work can be complex at times but the wrong thing usually stands out."

"Like that interview!"

Ngunnawal, named after the First Nations people who originally inhabited the Canberra region and still lived there in some numbers, was about a quarter-century old. A planned development with higher density units near the shopping centre and along access roads, and stand-alone houses away from those zones, all brick veneer with colourbond windows and facia, and colourbond garage doors because Canberra's many sub-zero winter mornings really needed proper garages. Syeda Niazi lived in a unit on Jabbanungga Avenue where Issy parked the Camry just around the corner in a quiet side-street. They walked to number 10 which was part of a development of units opposite a local shopping centre. Issy pressed the buzzer for the door to be opened by a woman somewhat younger than Erin's 31, tall and startlingly

325

attractive with medium-dark skin, big dark eyes that Indians often have, and long, black hair. If she wasn't an information technology contractor she could have been a photographic model and the face of Canberra. Erin showed her ID card as did Issy, while noticing Niazi's wide-eyed look of shock.

"I'm Agent B87 of ASIO and with me is Agent B98," Erin said. "I'm sorry for the subterfuge but I would like to talk with you."

"What's this about?"

"It's best if we talk privately. Is anyone else at home?"

"No."

"If we can talk inside...?"

Syeda Niazi stepped back to allow Erin and Issy to enter. Issy closed and locked the front door before doing a quick check of the unit and returning to the living room to nod her head.

Erin took out her notebook. "We're here about a current or former boyfriend, John Connell."

"Ah yes, John. He's a former boyfriend."

"When was the last time you saw John?"

"About two weeks ago."

"Were there reasons for you breaking-up?"

"There are always reasons for a break-up. John changed, I can't quite understand why, but he became more and more concerned about immigration, which was awkward with my parents being immigrants."

"Did he meet your family?"

"Seeing as he lived here, yes he met them many times."

"He lived here?" Erin asked.

"He lived here until I asked him to leave about two weeks ago."

Erin wrote that. "Have you met his family?"

"No, never. That was another issue. There was always an excuse, especially at Christmas. Christmas isn't a religious event for me, but here it's time to meet family. His excuse was his family visited his grandparents in Sydney and stayed with relatives there, then the next year he wanted just us, and then the year after his family was in Sydney again. I thought he was hiding me, and then when he got involved with a deep web forum and started talking about immigration, that was the last straw."

"Have you met John's friends?"

"I've met a few of his friends when we went out, but to be honest the only person he was close to was me. I didn't mind, he was a nice guy when we met and we had things in common, but less as time went by."

Erin took out her smartphone to find Luke Monk's picture cropped from CCTV.

"Have you ever seen this man?" as she handed it across.

"No."

Erin scrolled to Alice Monk. "Have you ever seen this woman?"

"No."

Erin scrolled to the first unidentified male. "Have you ever seen this man?"

"No."

Erin scrolled to the other unidentified male. "Have you ever seen this man?"

"No."

Erin thought. "Do you know where his parents stayed in Sydney?"

Syeda Niazi frowned. "They stayed with John's uncle and aunt in Sydney. Ah, Parramatta, no, Prospect. There must be a suburb in Sydney called Prospect."

"Did he talk about his uncle and aunt?"

"He visited them once or twice."

"Would you have an address?"

"No, I'm sorry."

"That's good, Syeda; we can work with Prospect."

"Alright."

"I'll ask you two personal questions pertinent to our enquiries on John Connell. What is your ethnic ancestry and what is your religious background?"

"My parents are Pakistani and I'm Muslim, but I don't really practice."

Erin wrote that before looking up. "Thank you for your time, Syeda. Now I must get official. It's critical you don't tell anyone the content of this interview, because you may face the prospect of five years imprisonment if you do. Thank you for your assistance."

Syeda Niazi now had her mouth literally hanging open. Erin and Issy left to walk to the Camry, where Issy pulled out onto quiet suburban streets.

"We need to find this uncle and aunt," Issy said. "Do you want me to look into that when we get back?"

"Yes please."

"I'll start with births, deaths and marriages to find his parents and grandparents, then siblings of his parents. From there the driver's licence database will give me their current addresses. Given Connell's a loner and given what's he's been involved with, he might be staying with those relatives."

"If he's staying with his relatives in Sydney, we'll find him."

With the car left behind in the car pool, Erin went to her office to wait for Issy's investigation. Maybe, with luck, they would find John Connell. With more luck they might find the names of those two unknown males. Erin hoped so.

Chapter Thirty Four

Facebook had its uses when it came to arranging a day trip to Wagga Wagga. On Saturday just before 10, the bus for Wagga Wagga waited outside Cootamundra Railway Station as Asha and Sue went inside the station building. There in perpetually near-still, near-quietness, Asha's other girl cousins Emily and Chloe, and her school friends: Jessica, Hannah and Georgia, waited with backpacks strewn everywhere. They greeted; Asha was hugged by Emily and Chloe and Georgia too, before she and Sue bought concession return tickets, Asha still being on the Covid-19 job benefit. Once that was done, they went to the bus to show their tickets to the driver before six sitting abreast and one in the row ahead.

"We've seen you everywhere!" Chloe exclaimed.

Asha was expecting that. "I went to Canberra to be photographed and I enjoyed that day very much."

"Such lovely clothes! I love the picture of you drinking coffee."

That was Asha's favourite too. "That was at a place called Kingston. Canberra is really nice."

"We can see that. I'm sure many from here will visit Canberra now."

"Before then, Asha was photographed in a bikini," Sue said.

"No!" Chloe exclaimed even louder.

"I was photographed in different bikinis with two other models, for a 2022 calendar to be released in the middle of next year: Australian Country, Australian Girls."

"Were you embarrassed?"

"Models often pose in bikinis and lingerie, while some runway fashions are mesh and see-through."

"Would you do that?"

Asha thought they might see the calendar picture kissing Sophie or they might see 'Reconciliation'. "During the bikini shoot I posed topless with a white girl who was topless."

"White and First Nations together."

The bus pulled away.

"That's right," Asha said. "There are other pictures of us together which you might see." She didn't want to say more than that!

"You've had a real adventure," Emily said.

"Now I'm home."

Asha gazed out of the window. The corner of Australia she called home never changed. After one hour and 25 minutes the bus eased into Wagga Wagga Railway Station with the main shopping street, Baylis Street, opposite.

"What do you want to do?" Sue asked.

Asha had it planned. "First we'll window shop like we used to. Then we'll have lunch at the usual cafe, and later we'll visit the elders."

"Some things never change."

They headed off as a group along the main shopping street of one of the biggest inland cities in New South Wales, but Wagga had changed. No, it hadn't changed but after living in Gungahlin for a few weeks, Baylis Street seemed small and pokey."

"You don't need to window shop after your shopping expedition," Chloe said.

"That was pretend. They knew my size and borrowed clothes for the day."

"And jewellery."

"Jewellery too."

"People are looking at you."

Asha noticed that.

"I need underwear," Asha said.

"Matching, as always."

"Let's see what Target's got."

Ladies underwear was towards the rear where most were size 14 and above. Asha rummaged through racks until she found a burgundy lace size 8B bra and matching burgundy lace size 8 panties. She held them up.

"What do you think?"

"Do you have a boyfriend?" Emily asked.

"No, not yet. I think these look nice."

"They do."

"Let's see if they have other colours in the same style."

They rummaged through the size eights until a black lace bra and black lace panties were eventually found. Pleased with her purchases and cheap too, and who would know once Asha cut the Target labels off as she always did? After purchase at the registers, they headed to the Bayleaf Cafe which literally hadn't changed, except for Covid-19 distancing restrictions. They used their backpacks to take possession of the biggest table before queuing to order, with all ordering burgers or wraps, except Asha with a chicken and avocado salad and a skinny flat white.

"Salad?" Chloe asked.

"You know I'm a model."

"What's a flat white?"

"That's the coffee I drank when they took my picture."

"Ah. I might order one."

"It's nice but make sure it's got skim milk."

"You know I'm not a model."

"Skim milk is healthier."

"I know."

Back at the table.

"What's it like after — how long?" Sue asked.

Asha thought. "It's been fourteen or fifteen months since I last came here. Nothing has changed except for me."

"What was Boggabilla like?"

"There are many problems in places like Boggabilla."

Their meals were brought by two waitresses. The salad was decent enough but not as good as Asha made. Coffee was nice though.

"What can we do about places like Boggabilla?" Chloe asked.

With distance, time and a few discussions, Asha now knew the answer. "If not jobs like my Dad making pallets, they need something to keep them employed with dignity. Train them to paint traditional pictures or something like that, and they need alcohol and drug addiction programs to make that possible. There wasn't anything to help our people except the medical clinic where I worked, also dealing with health problems like heart disease and diabetes."

"You've made me feel guilty about my burger," Chloe said.

"Sorry," Asha apologised. "Maybe we don't process white food the same as whites do."

"There are many whites with diabetes and heart problems."

Asha ate the last of her salad. "Our people used to eat mostly yams and other roots, in white terms like carrots and potatoes, with protein from a bit of meat which we need for iron and energy. They ate other protein like grubs and moths but not that much."

"In modern terms, a chicken and avocado salad."

"Plant-based with a little protein."

Chloe laughed. "I'll remember that for next time."

"We need nutrition classes in remote communities like Boggabilla, but there's nothing beyond the medical clinic. A doctor and a nurse can only do so much."

"Chronic disease, alcohol and drug addiction, and nutrition issues."

"Yes." Asha wanted perspective. "The world isn't bad, though. Look at us here as welcomed customers. How much of a change since our parents' times?"

"That's right."

"You've learned so much, Asha, with your time away and modelling in Canberra."

"Now I can share my experiences with my family and friends," Asha said. "I won't recommend Boggabilla, and maybe the opportunities for modelling are limited, but that doesn't mean other places aren't possible."

"Would Canberra be a good place to live for a while?"

"Canberra's great." They'd finished eating and distancing meant limited tables and limited customers for that cafe. "Let's visit the elders."

Their home was about 10 minutes away from Baylis Street where Asha knocked on the door before heading inside.

"Auntie? Uncle?"

"Is that Asha?" Auntie Margaret said.

"It's all of us," Asha said.

"It's been a long time but I know you've been away," Auntie said. "I won't ask because you must be tired of telling the same story."

That was true. "I learned we need a few changes to turn remote towns around, which won't happen without money and effort."

"State or Commonwealth money and effort?"

"It's mostly State Government issues, but the Commonwealth has to step up with training programs and job creation programs."

"There are many remote communities."

"Now there's acknowledgement that what happened to us was wrong," Asha said. "Who knows in time?"

"Is that Asha?" Uncle Stephen asked.

"Yes, it's me with my friends."

"Have you been painting?"

"I've been quite busy."

Then silence where Asha realised that they didn't have as much in common now. They talked for a while, Auntie made tea, before it was time to return to the station. The journey home was quiet while Asha knew she'd outgrown Saturdays in Wagga as the highlight of her week. When she got home with Sue, Asha knew what she should do. She had one piece of masonite left. Under the back veranda with the masonite propped upright on an old sheet on the plastic outdoor table, Asha remembered an evening north of Canberra; the best evening of her life. She took a brush to start on Baiame and the emu fallen, just as the stars showed that special evening.

Chapter Thirty Five

Emma's unit was in a block of six, some decades old as was that part of Young. Nearby was a shady gum tree where Matt parked; grabbed the tablet and locked his car before pushing the buzzer beside her door. Moments later Emma opened that door, dressed in jeans, a white t-shirt, white runners, and her hair in a ponytail like on the bikini shoot.

"Hi Matt, come in," Emma offered. "Can I get you something?"

"Hi Emma," Matt greeted. "A glass of water would be nice."

"Come with me."

Matt followed Emma into a combined living room, dining room and kitchen, which had a brown, fabric-covered lounge suite, a budget table and six matching chairs, and the kitchen immaculate without a thing out of place. Emma went to her fridge to fill two old-fashioned glasses from a jug. She took them to the lounge suite where Matt sat on the couch, tablet by his side, and Emma sat opposite in one of two armchairs.

"It's good to see you again, Emma."

"I've seen Asha – everywhere!" Emma exclaimed before laughing heartily.

Matt had to smile at that comment.

"That must have been an amazing day for her," Emma said. "I can't wait to see the bikini calendar but I know I have to be patient."

Matt powered up the tablet. "I have the 12 calendar pictures here."

"Oh I must see!" as Emma sat alongside.

Matt opened the folder to select the January picture of Asha on the tree.

"Classy."

Matt swiped.

"That's me. That doesn't leave much to the imagination!"

"Are you alright with that?"

Big smile. "I'm fine."

Next shot was Asha in white, leaving less to the imagination than on the tree, then Sophie with Emma, then Sophie leaving little to the imagination, until the picture for December with the best of the kissing shots.

"That's incredible!" Emma exclaimed.

"This is a calendar so we can't show nipples. Fortunately this picture does that by fluke."

"They really got into each other."

Matt had thought about that. "Men would never have done that," he said.

"Men wouldn't. Women – well, it takes emotional connection to generate attraction. We were together all day,

339

we talked over lunch; Asha's totally lovely and Sophie's totally lovely too. That's the result: attraction leading to passion."

"If you kissed Asha instead of Sophie?" Matt asked.

"Yeah, the same could have happened. I made friends with Sophie when we danced together at a party. I don't know how long we danced for; a long time. I forgave her for dating my ex and kind-of loved her a bit. You know that lovely, warm glow you can't ignore. I suppose I still love Sophie and maybe I always will."

"If you think about First Nations, they set up a camp and then the men went off hunting or fishing, leaving women to dig for food and look after their children together, talking and socialising for most of the day. Then the men returned to the camp with whatever they caught, and maybe women cooked that for their evening meal."

"For 60,000 years in this case, women spent most of their days with other women, platonically. You think this feminine connection is what sometimes spills over into more?"

"Perhaps," Matt suggested.

"That might be right," Emma said, and laughed.

Matt swiped the calendar pictures away to open Reconciliation.

"Amazing!" Emma gasped. She stared at it. "That's a great pose, Matt."

"Thanks. Now, as you know the reason I wanted to see you is to speak about Buddhism."

"Ah, yes. I've been practicing for a while now. My boyfriend of the time, Sophie's boyfriend now, bought me my tattoo for my birthday. That was a lovely thought."

Matt was quite shocked. *Sophie's boyfriend now and they were friends?* Pulling himself together. "What sort of road do you travel?" he asked.

Emma sipped her water while frowning a bit. "I started with meditation. I did six lessons in Wagga which isn't that far from here, and now I meditate for half an hour each morning. That sets me up for the rest of my day. What other things? What matters after my morning meditation is treating people decently, regardless of how they might treat me, treating the world as decently as I can, like driving an economical car or not buying things that have too much packaging. I've not gone as far as vegetarianism but I have more vegetarian meals now, which means less environmental damage like methane from cattle. These things must add up to a good life now and a better life next time."

"How do you worship?"

"We have a group of mostly Chinese Buddhists here where we have a calendar of worship in people's houses, including my place here. In Canberra you won't have that problem. There are a couple of temples there."

"Has this helped you, Emma?"

"The two big things are meditation and our worship. Worshipping with followers of the same path is something I can't really explain until you do it. That's when you'll know."

"Like trying to explain love?"

"Yeah, like that! When you worship together you sense the love of the infinity more than ignoring someone who's rude, or cooking pasta and a tomato sauce, not a steak. I hope that makes sense."

"It does, Emma, especially talking with you here. I sense your calmness and your enthusiasm for the path you've chosen."

She laughed.

"And your laughter," Matt added.

"I might laugh more now than before. That's a good thing, too. Seeing as it's close to midday and a fair drive for you to get home, do you want to stay for lunch?"

"If that's no bother."

"It's no bother because I'm prepared! I have an appointment at one but you're welcome to share lunch with me now. You sit there and I'll prepare."

Matt watched Emma in her kitchen. Asha's beliefs were about care of the land and its creatures, and traditions like respecting elders. When Asha left this world, her spirit would take a journey, but not conditionally on her behaviour.

Emma's beliefs weren't that much different, broadly care and respect, to be reborn into a better life. In Emma's case, not to care and respect would mean to be reborn worse, but Buddhism didn't have the rules and silly folktales of Western religions. Matt thought Emma's way wasn't too far different from Asha's way, with Asha being the most complete young woman he'd ever met, apart from Emma who was just as together. As Emma put a cheese and tomato multi-grain sandwich in her sandwich press, Matt was sure this was what he'd been searching for.

Chapter Thirty Six

Erin sat beside Nate while Nicole was late. Erin poured a cup of coffee from the jug. There was an awkward silence as Erin expected.

Nicole swept in to sit opposite.

"Erin, how's your investigation going?"

Erin looked to her notepad. "Our team has located John Connell's uncle Joseph Connell, his aunt Christine Connell, with two daughters: Jemma aged 15, and Natalie aged 17, living at 39 Heath Street, Prospect in the western suburbs of Sydney. Connell's grandparents on his father's side are in a nursing home in Sydney. There are relatives on his mother's side in Melbourne where it's less likely he would seek refuge. Connell's ex-girlfriend mentioned he'd visited his relatives in Prospect a few times."

Nicole finished writing a note in her compendium before looking to Erin. "This now becomes a police matter. Australian Federal Police should take all who occupy that premises in for questioning. If John Connell is there, they should apprehend him as a suspected terrorist."

"I sent two surveillance teams to discreetly observe over the weekend," Erin said. "Unfortunately Heath Street is perfectly flat and has no trees or shrubs, or any landscape beyond blocks of land with houses and grass, like much of western Sydney. This makes unobtrusive visual surveillance difficult. Despite that, our teams have observed the four known inhabitants of that premises coming and going at different times, once together as a family group, but not John Connell."

"At least we know his family lives there. Erin, contact Superintendent Robson of the Australian Federal Police to brief him on what your team has discovered. You'll be our representative on any raids the AFP conduct, and you will be our observer to police interviews. If John Connell is apprehended, you and I will question him using Special Powers, with a prescribed officer in attendance as is protocol."

"Yes Nicole. If we apprehend John Connell now or in the near future, that might not lead us to Luke and Alice Monk."

"I'm aware of that. However, the Monks could never have achieved what they did without the assistance of John Connell."

That was true.

"Now it's time to take your good work to its next step," Nicole said.

Erin left to contact Superintendent Robson, who would need access to relevant records from her investigation, which she would copy to the police Crimtrak computer system. After that, it was down to the Australian Federal Police.

Chapter Thirty Seven

Parramatta in Western Sydney was like a city within a city. Parramatta Police Headquarters was a modern, multi-storey building in the centre of the busy Parramatta retail precinct, where traffic was gridlocked all day. On the first floor outside Interview Room One, Erin waited with a folder under her arm, standing beside Nicole and Magistrate Keenan. The door opened where a middle-aged male Australian Federal Police officer in uniform beckoned them inside the windowless room, except for a large mirror which was really a one-way window.

John Connell was at the table with what looked like a legal aid lawyer in a suit. Nicole and Erin took seats opposite while Magistrate Keenan sat at the head of the table. Hanging from the ceiling, the video camera had a red light on, recording.

"For the record I'm Magistrate Gordon Keenan of the New South Wales District Court. I'm acting as the prescribed officer in this interview, conducted by Agent A15 and Agent B87 of the Australian Security and Intelligence Authority, or ASIO. John Connell, under the ASIO Legislation Amendment Act of 2003 you are required to answer all questions. Failure to do so carries a penalty of five years imprisonment."

"For the record," the likely legal aid lawyer said. "My name's Kyle Prince and I'm acting as lawyer for the accused, John Connell."

"Noted," Magistrate Keenan said.

Erin opened her folder to slide the first page across the table.

"John Connell, the attached is a screen shot from Parliament House security cameras taken 15 days before the assassination of the Prime Minister of Australia, Yaseera Devi. This screen shot shows you in company of a middle-aged male. Can you name this male?"

"Luke Monk."

"Do you recognise the surroundings of this screen shot?"

"That's the public gallery of the House of Representatives."

Erin slid the next page across.

"This is a screen shot taken from security cameras at the Australian War Memorial on Monday December seven, which shows Luke Monk, one middle-aged woman and two younger male individuals. Can you name this woman?"

"Alice Monk."

"Can you name the two, younger males?"

"Mike Thomas and Jake Tanner."

"How did you first come into contact with Luke and Alice Monk?"

"Luke had set up a message board on 8 Chan."

That was the message board Erin's team was monitoring until it went quiet.

"Then what happened?" Erin asked.

"We corresponded by Gmail where Luke invited me to show him Parliament House and the Prime Minister's Lodge. Later we drove to his flat in Hawker which is where I met Alice Monk, Mike Thomas and Jake Tanner.

"Where in Hawker was this?"

"It was flat 13, three Bonrook Street."

"Then what happened?"

"We discussed the troubling issue of a female, Muslim Prime Minister. We all agreed this wasn't acceptable for Anglo-Australia."

"Wasn't your girlfriend Muslim of Pakistani descent, like our late Prime Minister?"

"Syeda was a friend who knew how to look after me."

"Look after you in what way?"

"Syeda cooked, cleaned, washed, ironed, and Syeda looked after me sexually." Connell leaned forward. "Syeda didn't know the meaning of the word no."

"Unlike an Australian woman?"

"Not all Anglo-Australian women are like that. Look at Alice."

"What about Alice?"

"She knew a woman's place."

Erin sensed an implication there. "A woman's place sexually?" she asked.

"Alice knew a woman's place is submission to her husband."

Erin wasn't surprised that Alice Monk was a Tradwife.

"Going back a step," Erin said, "you lived with Syeda Niazi until she told you to leave."

"I had bigger issues happening by then."

"Did you discuss other things at the Monk's flat in Hawker?"

"I offered to provide Luke with entries from the Prime Minister's diary, which I did in relation to her press conference at the War Memorial."

"Is that all?"

"Yes."

"Were you aware of the plans of the attack at the War Memorial?"

"I was aware that Luke and Alice discovered where to plant explosives at the War Memorial."

"What explosives were involved with these attacks?"

"PETN but I didn't know what that was."

"Did you later look up PETN on the internet?"

"I found an attack in Germany in 1983 where a building was partly destroyed using PETN. I hoped Luke and Alice didn't do more damage to the War Memorial than what was necessary to eliminate the Prime Minister."

"What lasting impact will result from this attack, do you think?"

"We merely sought to eliminate a female, Muslim Prime Minister of Australia."

"Did Luke Monk give you instructions on how to avoid arrest after these attacks?"

"He said I should get out of Canberra so I arranged to stay with my family in Sydney."

"Did Luke and Alice Monk tell you how they were avoiding arrest?"

"They were getting out of Canberra too."

"Do you know where they came from?"

"They come from Sydney."

"We'll take a break for ten minutes," Magistrate Keenan said.

Nicole and Erin left the room. In the secure area they could talk. Erin filled a plastic cup from a water cooler near where New South Wales police officers were busy at work.

"Connell wants to confess all details so his trial will be publicity for his cause," Nicole said.

"That's right," Erin agreed.

"We've convicted him of terrorism based on his confession. He's looking at life imprisonment."

Erin knew John Connell was aware of life imprisonment and didn't care. As the years ticked by his enthusiasm would wane and never tasting freedom again would matter, but that didn't bring back the many lives lost.

"I can't get over John Connells opinion of his ex-girlfriend," Nicole said.

"Worse that she's a university graduate and an IT contractor like him."

"Indian and Pakistani women are possibly more submissive than Western women."

"Which Connell took advantage of, until she had enough of being used."

"Erin, we need to explore members of this group more deeply."

"I'll do that."

"We better get back," Nicole said.

Erin tossed her cup into the bin near the cooler, to follow her superior to continue their questioning.

"John Connell," Erin said. "What can you tell me about Luke Monk?"

"Not much other than he and Alice come from Sydney, he was laid off because of Covid-19 but he didn't say from where. Luke regarded that as an opportunity, because he was able to devote his time to bringing Yaseera Devi down."

"Assassinating Yaseera Devi?"

"Killing Yaseera Devi."

"Anything else?"

John Connell frowned. "He spoke with a pommy accent, as did Alice."

"What about Alice Monk?"

"Alice was laid off because of Covid-19, which gave her time to kill Yaseera Devi. Even when the economy recovers she's not going to return to work, instead she's going to remain traditionally feminine."

"A Tradwife?"

"Yes. One thing, Alice has a nice body."

That much was obvious from CCTV of her at the War Memorial. One odd thing. "Why did you mention Alice Monk's body?" Erin asked.

"Once Luke made her stand in the corner of the room in a see-through nightie of some sort, and a couple of times she was told to take her clothes off so he could beat her."

"In front of you?"

"Yes."

Erin swallowed and felt flushed. "What was Alice Monk's reaction to this?"

"I think she provoked him to beat her."

Erin nodded her head. In the USA, there was a right-wing movement called CDD for Christian Domestic Discipline, which was husbands beating their wives and their wives submitting to being beaten, or as often as not wives initiating this lifestyle and then provoking their beatings. Erin wondered.

"Did Luke or Alice Monk mention religion at all?"

"No never."

"Anything else about Luke and Alice Monk?"

"No."

None of that was strictly relevant to the assassination of the Prime Minister of Australia, other than Luke and Alice Monk might have blended primarily alt-right beliefs, pro-white, anti Islam, anti-feminist, with this other American conservative practice of female submission. Either that or Alice Monk was turned-on by the intersection of sexual pleasure with pain. Erin focussed.

"What about Mike Thomas?" she asked.

"Mike comes from Sydney where has a partner but I don't know her name. He's a mechanic only the Toyota dealership where he worked was taken over by an Indian who made his brother-in-law the workshop manager. Before he knew it, he was dismissed."

"Next, Jake Tanner?" Erin asked.

"He came from Sydney too. He said he lived at home where he had a food delivery job. Jake and Mike stayed with Luke and Alice in Hawker."

A household of alt-right radicals keeping under the radar.

"How did Mike Thomas and Jake Tanner connect with Luke Monk?" Erin asked.

"Through the message board on 8 Chan."

"Do you know any addresses, which suburbs in Sydney, which food delivery company, which Toyota dealership?"

"Luke said we shouldn't talk about details."

Erin couldn't think of anything else. "They're all the questions I have," she said. Agent A15?"

"John Connell, as per your bail hearing you will be held in custody in the Amber Laurel Centre in Penrith," Nicole said. "In the meantime the Australian Federal Police will apply for your extradition to Canberra for a bail hearing there. I expect bail will be denied. Your trial will proceed in due course."

"My client intends to plead guilty," Kyle Prince stated.

"I understand," Nicole said before standing. "This interview is concluded."

Erin and Nicole left the room.

"Please come this way," Erin said as she headed to the secure area. "I'll email Leon to search for Jake Tanner and Mike Thomas. If they're real names he'll find them in no time."

Erin leaned against a partition to compose her email; then sent it.

"That's done," she said. "This might flush out Luke and Alice Monk."

"It might," Nicole said. "Now while we're secure, let's talk. Adam's dismissal will take some time. When that's finalised we'll advertise his former position internally and maybe externally, and form a panel to evaluate selection criteria responses. Those who are successful will go onto be interviewed by this panel, which I will head."

"I understand," Erin said, and she understood well. Nicole was going to guide that process and may stack the selection panel with her supporters. "We should go," Erin said. "It's a long drive but thank heavens for cruise control!"

"I don't use cruise control."

"At first it's a bit freaky when the car seems to have a mind of its own, but after a while you get used to it. Next time you're driving on the motorway, give it a go."

"I will; thanks."

They headed to the lifts nearby where Nicole pressed 'down'. Inside, Nicole pressed 'B1' where their car waited. Erin got behind the wheel for the near-three hour drive to The Ben Chifley Building or Lubyanka by the Lake.

* * *

Erin went to the fridge, took out the half-empty bottle of white wine and poured a glass. She sipped, nice, then went outside to the table and chairs on their balcony while thinking she would get their meal delivered, until remembering delivery riders and drivers had shit lives and might end up being radicalised alt-right. But what could a girl do about that? Shortly after she heard Daniel before he came to the balcony. He bent down to kiss her cheek.

"Hi darling," he greeted. "Busy day?"

"Yes, today was busy," Erin said. "John Connell confessed while we've now got names for the two previously unknown males."

Daniel sat while Erin pondered. She could talk with Daniel about a case he had access to as part of Nate's team, but other things had to remain secret. Her future would reveal in time.

"Did you drive to Sydney and back?" Daniel asked.

"I did."

"Are you feeling weary?"

"Yes, a bit."

"Do you want me to fill the spa?"

Erin sipped her wine while knowing what Daniel really wanted. But unlike John Connell their relationship was multi-dimensional, including loving sex. "Fill the spa and join me there," she said.

Daniel headed inside where soon water was running. Erin wasn't that much fussed but a few hours of not thinking about alt-right terrorists and Tradwives never hurt a girl. In fact that might do a girl some good. She put her empty glass down before going inside their apartment.

Chapter Thirty Eight

Erin's work phone rang from Superintendent Robson.

"Acting Director of Intelligence, Agent B87," Erin answered.

"Agent B87, we have a lead from a security guard at Port Botany who'd seen pictures of Luke and Alice Monk in the Daily Telegraph and contacted New South Wales police. This guard confirmed they were at Port Botany on the afternoon of Thursday, December 10."

"Have your people undertaken any investigations on this?"

"We compiled a list of outbound ships which I can email to you."

"My email address is B87@asio.gov.au."

"Our list will be on its way shortly."

"Thank you Superintendent Robson."

Erin ended the call to think. John Connell mentioned pommy accents, which might mean they caught a freighter to the UK. Freighters sometimes took paying passengers as a commercial venture although Erin wondered if that was the case during Covid-19. Besides, getting official permission to leave Australia would have been difficult. The email arrived showing four ships total: one arriving from Singapore, one arriving from Melbourne, one departing to Italy and one departing to the UK.

'Leon, the attached is a list of ships at Port Botany on 10 December. Please contact shipping companies of the two outbound ships to confirm any paying passengers. Thanks, Erin.' Send.

Erin re-read the list where the APL Phoenix was bound for Felixstow, UK, with a stop in Brisbane then a stop in Singapore for refuelling due in two days time, and the Ital Laguna was bound for Genoa with a stop at Brisbane and a refuelling stop in Singapore as well. Erin thought through what they needed to do.

Email arriving. *'Erin, no passengers booked on either of those ships. Leon.'*

Erin picked up her phone to call Superintendent Robson.

"Agent B87," Erin greeted.

"Yes Agent B87."

"Superintendent Robson, I'm going to issue an Interpol Red Notice on Luke Monk and Alice Monk. Can you issue a warrant for Singapore Police to board and search both the APL Phoenix and the Ital Laguna when they arrive there for refuelling?"

"I'll ring our contact in Singapore Police and brief him now."

"Thanks Superintendent Robson."

He ended the call. Erin was almost certain the Monks, whoever they really were, were on the APL Phoenix. Almost certainly in two days time, she would have them. But for now, coffee time.

In the tea room she poured a mug, and added milk and sugar.

"Hi mate."

"Hi Leon." She turned to him with her finger and thumb one centimetre apart. "This close."

"I know. You're doing a good job, mate."

"Are you alright with me as Acting Director?"

"I'm fine." He looked around. "You've shown Nicole made the right call."

"Thanks Leon.'

Erin sipped her coffee just as her phone rang. Superintendent Robson. Mug on the bench to answer the call.

"Agent B87."

"My contact in Singapore told me police there might be reluctant to board any freighter due to Covid-19. Police could be exposed and at the very least will have to quarantine for two weeks."

"Do they know this is a major crime?"

"Yes."

Erin thought of one possibility. "Can you advise your contact that if their boarding officers are correctly kitted in hospital-grade PPE, they should be safe?"

"I'll advise that and let you know."

"Thank you Superintendent."

Erin ended the call, frowning, while Leon had left the tea room. Coffee mug in hand, Erin headed to her office where she decided to brainstorm strategies if Singapore police didn't cooperate. She opened the top drawer of the desk, really she had to do something about Adam's matched pens and clutch pencils. He was too anal! Erin took a clutch pencil to write option one and then another before pausing, mind blank. Surely there were other options? But as much as she tried there was nothing there.

Erin's phone rang with a call from Superintendent Robson.

"Agent B87," Erin answered.

"I'm sorry Agent B87 but my contact stated Singapore Police won't act on our warrant given it's based on flimsy evidence, being a security guard seeing alleged terrorists at the largest port in Australia. They want actual evidence that suspects are on those ships before they'll board them."

"I understand. Thank you Superintendent Robson."

Erin ended the call before turning to her computer.

'Nicole, A security guard at Port Botany recognised Luke and Alice Monk on the afternoon of Thursday December 10, where there were two outbound freighters, the APL Phoenix and the Ital Laguna, both due to refuel in Singapore in two day's time. Singapore police are reluctant to

board either of these ships, one of which I believe is carrying the Monks. Singapore cites Covid-19 risks boarding these ships and our lack of direct evidence. I'm reasonably sure if it wasn't for Covid-19 this wouldn't be a problem. I don't have contacts but I felt either the Department of Foreign Affairs or our High Commissioner in Singapore might be able to help in this matter. Erin.' Send.

About five minutes later a simple response: *'Agreed suspects could be on one of these ships, leave this with me, Nicole.'*

When it came to the upper echelons of government a Director of Intelligence could only do so much, Erin knew that, but that didn't stop her thoughts going around and around and around. Erin felt the tension in her arms and hands on the steering wheel of her car driving home, but tried to relax when she kissed Daniel.

"My turn to cook," he said.

"What? Ah, yes."

Daniel set to preparing mince with parsley and eggs, while Erin poured a mineral water from the fridge to sit at the counter while he made home-made hamburgers on multi-grain buns.

"You're not with me tonight," Daniel said.

"Pardon?" Erin asked before realising. "Oh, sorry. It's just that we're this close to getting Luke and Alice Monk," Erin indicated with thumb and forefinger a centimetre apart, "but Singapore isn't helping, or at least it's down to what Nicole can conjure up."

"Acting Director of Intelligence, and I've noticed this with other women; sometimes women try to fix and solve everything without realising this isn't always possible. Remember, shit can happen."

"Have you noticed a difference with women at work?"

"We men seem to be a bit more accepting of situations, which isn't necessarily good but isn't always bad."

Erin sipped her mineral water. "I haven't noticed a difference but maybe you're right. There's a time to pull out all stops and there's a time to say I've done the best I can."

"Something like that."

"But we're this close," Erin showed with thumb and forefinger.

Daniel threw a tea-towel at her. Erin pulled it off and grinned.

"I would hate them to get away," she said.

"Me too."

Erin hoped they wouldn't get away. That would be tragic, but on the other hand, shit can happen.

Chapter Thirty Nine

Asha was pleased with her painting just finished.

"Asha," Mum called. "There's someone to see you."

Asha put her brush into the glass of turpentine before she went to the front door. "Hello Jenny," she greeted while surprised. "Come in."

"Hello Asha," Jenny replied. "I hope I'm not intruding."

"No, it's good to see you. Asha led Jenny to the living room which was a bit crowded. "Do you want to go outside?"

"Outside looks good."

They sat under the back veranda, on the two plastic chairs near the table and painting.

"How are you?" Jenny asked.

Asha thought. "Not good and not bad. I'm recovering. How are you?"

"Recovering is a good way of describing it. That's why I came. We have something three of us can share. The other reason I came is to tell you know how Matt is."

Asha felt a twinge of guilt. "How is he?"

"I haven't seen Matt but his father said he's recovering too. He's always been close to his family and I'm sure they know what really happened. Matt's father also told me about you." Jenny looked to Asha. "I don't want to intrude but I hope there's a chance. We worked together a few times where photographers and models are often close, Matt certainly is, but you two were more. It was the day of the tragedy when I really saw your magic together, after you came home from shopping. Do you remember?"

Asha remembered that well.

"I would like to see that magic rekindled if there's a chance," Jenny said.

"Is it magic?" Asha asked.

"How many men would eat salad for lunch because their girlfriend's a model, and tell me that you make great salads? But then I said something silly. Is what I said a problem?"

Asha thought this was an opportunity. "Can you tell me about the models Matt dated?"

"Jade was a mistake but they were both to blame. Jade was 21 and had just broken up with her boyfriend. Matt had just broken up with Linda after many years together so I'm sure he was vulnerable. I think they saw each other for several months, going out for dinner and picnics and things like that."

Asha was surprised. That age and a past boyfriend was quite different to what she imagined. Even more they didn't live together. Just friends. Adult friends but that didn't matter. Matt was probably 23 at the time so only two years difference in their ages.

"Rachel was," and Jenny frowned. "Rachel was 20, and she was light-hearted and had a good sense of humour. They were together for almost two years. Matt's relaxed and easy-going but he's not frivolous, and as time went by you could see them drifting apart, Matt more than Rachel."

That made Matt 23 or 24 when he dated Rachel, 20; not a big difference in ages.

"Rachel didn't connect here as much," Asha said as she touched her forehead.

"I think so, yes. Do you think there's a chance you could?"

Asha wondered. "I sometimes wonder if he picked me for the Canberra shoot because he wanted me."

"Matt would never do that," Jenny said firmly. "I won't say he didn't want you but he would never pick a model who wasn't suitable. You were great on our two shoots and great with the bikini shots too. Can you tell me how the bikini shoot went?"

Asha remembered. "Sophie Weaver sensed Matt and I had something."

"Sparks."

Asha smiled with the memory. "Yes, sparks."

"Do you know anything about Sophie other than she's 17 and has just finished year 12?"

"Sophie lives with her mother, her step-father and her boyfriend. She plans to move to Wagga, where she wants to study something and model for spending money."

"Living with her boyfriend at that age is unusual."

"She said she felt sparks with her boyfriend and didn't want to miss out. She and Emma told me to go with my feelings."

"I saw the order that Matt took his shots, with you on the tree where we're going to use the shot of your arms around your leg. You have lovely legs which that pose highlights. Then he did a shot of Sophie sitting on a stone wall which was more adult."

Asha remembered.

"I think Matt sensed Sophie was more comfortable posing like that," Jenny said, "which she probably was given she lives with her boyfriend."

"Would Matt have sensed that?"

"Yes he would. But later he asked you two to kiss."

"Matt wanted Sophie and Emma to kiss, but Sophie wanted to kiss me to show reconciliation."

"Ah. Sophie recommended Emma for the shoot so they're friends, while Emma's older and she was posed more adult too. That's why Matt asked them to kiss."

Asha thought that made sense.

"I've seen all of the kissing shots which are remarkable," Jenny said. "After that, Matt knew Sophie and you would be comfortable with the final reconciliation shots on the fallen tree, topless holding hands and looking at each other with – love. It was love."

Asha felt flushed but couldn't deny what Jenny had seen. "It was love; no, it was lust. Our kissing was real."

"I saw that Asha!" Jenny exclaimed. "Matt saw it too. Still waters sometimes run deep."

Asha wondered if Matt was attracted to her sexiness kissing Sophie; then remembered they were attracted before then. She wondered.

"Matt told me you went away for a year and had some challenging experiences," Jenny said. "Surely that shaped you?"

Asha had challenging experiences for sure, and that turned into a new goal for her life. "Yes, it shaped me."

"Matt knew you did well at the bikini shoot so he knew you'd be right for the Canberra shoot, and even though you're young you've been shaped by experience."

"Sophie could have done the Canberra shoot, but on the day I did it well, didn't I? Matt knew I would. And from the beginning we felt sparks."

"So what do you think?" Jenny asked.

Asha wondered, no, was certain. "There's room for sparks and magic."

"I came here to see how you are and I came here to give you good news. Reconciliation won the APP award for portraiture."

Asha couldn't believe it. "That's awesome!"

"This is up to you, Asha," Jenny said. "Now that Covid-19 restrictions are easing, Matt can accept this award in Sydney in person. I'm sure he won't mind if you accompany him and give a speech too."

Asha's heart really did skip a few beats.

"Don't worry about public speaking," Jenny said. "Write down what you want to say, practice it with friends or relatives, and on the night it's easy. Beyond that, supermodels give speeches and especially interviews, as you probably know."

Asha knew. She wouldn't know about Samantha Harris except through many interviews. "You're right; this is good experience."

"You won't regret this," Jenny said. "Now I need to make a call. Do you mind?"

"No, I don't mind."

"I'll put it on speaker." Asha watched Jenny dial and then heard a familiar voice, Sophie Weaver.

"Hello Sophie, it's Jenny Mason again. Asha has agreed to give a speech so we're good to go."

"That's fantastic!"

"Hello Sophie," Asha greeted.

"Hi Asha. I've seen your shoot in Canberra everywhere! You're great!"

"Thanks Sophie, but that shoot was down to Jenny and Matt."

"How is Matt?"

Asha knew what to say. "We're almost boyfriend and girlfriend but we need to tell my family first."

"Good for you both."

"I'll text you the date, time and address in Sydney," Jenny said.

"Cool," Sophie said.

"See you."

Jenny ended the call.

"Sophie will give a speech too," Jenny said.

Asha wondered and there was one other thing she wanted to know. "Whose idea was it to do the bikini calendar of Australian country girls in the Australian bush, no makeup or stilettos or anything like that?"

"That was Matt," Jenny said. "He's proud of how as a nation we've controlled Covid-19, especially compared to most of the world. So for this year's shoot he wanted to highlight the real Australia, our bush and our country girls with their natural beauty, not city girls with all their pretensions. First Nations was part of his concept."

That sounded like Matt. Asha checked the time on Jenny's phone resting on the arm of her chair. "Jenny, do you want to stay for lunch?" Asha asked.

"If that's no trouble."

"It won't be trouble. Come with me and I'll introduce you to some of my family." Asha then realised. "I'll need an evening dress for this award," she said.

"I'll borrow a dress for you for the night," Jenny said. "I'll borrow a dress for Sophie too. Do you have stilettos?"

"I bought a pair to practice for the Canberra shoot. They're patent black."

"Matt was right choosing you; you're a professional. Keep practicing because there might be coverage of your award."

Asha would go back to her YouTube clips showing how to walk, then - *coverage of the award?*

"Have you arranged something for this award, Jenny?" she asked.

"I called in a favour or two. I'm looking forward to meeting your family."

That was a hint. Asha got up from her chair feeling – light. Unburdened. Free. There was room for sparks and magic. More, she looked forward to introducing Jenny, one of the nicest women she'd ever met, to her family.

* * *

It was a shame to escort Jenny to the front door to say goodbye, but Jenny had to get home to Canberra where driving at dusk was dangerous with kangaroos. Asha watched Jenny drive away before going to her room. There Sue lay on her bed listening to music with earbuds plugged into her phone. Asha sighed, at that moment she wanted privacy, or what she had with Matt. She sat on her bed cross-legged and took her phone from her pocket, with no real thought in mind except to compose a text.

'jenny called around told me ur better im better too'. Send.

Moments later. *'im glad to hear it i miss you'.*

Sparks and magic. *'i miss you too'.* Send. Asha thought. *'come here and rescue me'.* Send.

'i can come tomorrow'.

'pack to stay the night my boyfriend has lots of family to meet'. Send.

'will do girlfriend'.

'kk'. Send.

Asha reread those messages before pressing her phone to her heart, smiling gently. Peace and calm.

"What is it?" Sue asked.

"It's a little thing called love. Have you heard of it?"

"Is it like loving our family?"

Asha's bright sparkle from thinking about Matt was impossible to explain. "It's a bit the same but you feel it deeper – more," she said. "When you find love you'll understand it."

Asha lay on her back on her bed, still with her phone pressed to her heart.

Chapter Forty

Matt eased up to 30 Sutton Street as he pushed the sunroof control open to let heat out after he parked his car. Leaving his backpack behind he strolled towards the front door when it burst open and Asha, in denim shorts and a red halter top, raced down front steps seemingly in one leap, to throw herself at him, which thankfully he caught, to have her arms and legs wrapped around him, holding her while she kissed him.

"I missed you," she said.

"I missed you too."

"Bad things happened and I guess I blew things out of proportion."

"We were psychologically tortured."

She kissed him again. "I'm better now."

"Me too."

Matt gently let Asha go. She took his hand.

"Come with me," she said.

Instead to taking Matt inside, she led him to a pair of white plastic chairs on the veranda. They sat.

"We need time to talk before we meet my family and things go out of control." Asha reached down to pick up a piece of masonite, to turn it around to show a traditional indigenous painting of a type Matt had seen online.

"These past weeks have been kind-of empty, until I painted this. This is the story of Baiame and the emu."

"That's incredible, Asha," Matt said, but that didn't do such art justice. "I love this style of painting and what it represents."

"How's your quest going?"

Matt pondered the pine slat flooring of the veranda. "In a way being apart for a while has done me good. I spent time with my family where my father told me the history of the powers ASIO used against us. I also visited Emma in Young. You were right when you said Emma was calm and good, which is down to her beliefs. I've already begun my spiritual journey." Matt knew there was something else but wondered what it was, until it came to him. "Oh yeah, we won the portraiture prize with Reconciliation."

"Jenny invited Sophie and me to give speeches when you accept your award."

"Oh has she?" Matt asked almost in shock.

"Is that alright?" Asha asked.

Matt caught her dark eyes. "I wanted Sophie and you to gain publicity for your careers, and I want the concept of reconciliation to be front and centre. Who better than the two models who brought our picture to life, to tell the story of what happened and why?"

"Have you spoken in public before?"

"It's all down to preparation. Write a script, practice it, and it'll be good."

"Jenny said that." Asha stood to put her hand out. "Come with me to meet the closest part of my family again. Later this evening we're having a barbeque with more uncles, aunts and cousins."

Matt knew what to ask. "How many?"

"Lots! There's always some sort of drama or problem but when I have dramas and problems, like these past weeks, I have support too. And support for my successes."

"Like being the face of Canberra? Giving speeches too?"

"To be reported in the media."

"Jenny has been busy."

Matt stood to take Asha's slim hand, dark against his white, as she opened the front door of her house. He was sure this was going to be an interesting few days.

Chapter Forty One

Jason got as comfortable as possible in the too-small blue chair while he shuffled the cards. Opposite on her bed, Belinda sat cross-legged.

"What do you want if you win?" she asked.

"I want to fuck your arse," Jason said as he shuffled.

"That's original."

They'd done a bit of that over past weeks.

"What do you want if you win?" Jason asked.

"Tie my hands behind my back, no foreplay, fuck me hard, slap me, call me names and come on my face."

"Fine," Jason said while thinking that was just as original as fucking Belinda's arse, given they'd done that script quite a few times too.

"If there's a God he got it wrong," Belinda said. "Men are obsessed about sex but they only get one shot, two if they're lucky, and then they're done. I could have satisfied all of those guys in Canberra, no problems, and been ready for more."

Jason had been curious about that. "Why didn't you?" he asked.

"The young guy Jake was a loser especially with women, Mike too, while I didn't trust John. He was sleazy."

"They would have fucked you in a moment."

"Like most men, but that was reducing me to my vagina. Besides, being naughty is as much fun."

Jason smiled at that comment while he dealt one card each, face-up, second card to Belinda face-up, his second card face-down. Already Belinda had 17.

"I'll have one more," she said.

Jason dealt a five of hearts. He turned his cards over: 19:

"That's a bad start," as Belinda removed her blouse.

"Maybe next time you'll get your fantasy," as Jason shuffled and dealt. This time Belinda had 14.

"One more."

An ace of spades. Jason turned his cards over to reach 18. Belinda removed her bra.

Jason shuffled and dealt, for Belinda to get 18.

"I'll stand."

Jason turned his cards over where he had 14. He took one more, a seven of diamonds.

"You're having all the luck," as Belinda stood to remove her jeans with some difficulty given they were quite tight.

As Belinda peeled those jeans off, Jason shuffled before dealing. She got 15.

"One more."

Jason took the top card and turned it over to place on Belinda's pile. A king of diamonds.

"No!" she exclaimed as Jason turned his cards over. They reached 12.

Belinda removed her panties.

"Looks like you fuck my arse," she said. "Pity."

Jason thought. "I'll tie your arms behind your back; I'll fuck your arse hard, and slap you about and call you names."

Belinda smiled. "I like anal, actually, and being slapped with anal might be good."

"My pleasure."

"And mine."

"Ha!"

Suddenly the door handle turned and a flood of Chinese in blue uniforms, three actually, burst into the cabin. One gestured to Belinda naked.

"You, get dressed."

"What's this about?" Jason asked, even though he knew.

"You are known as Luke Monk and Alice Monk or have other identities, and we are here to arrest you on terrorism related offences. You are to come with us."

"My name's Jason Rogers and this is my wife, Belinda Rogers."

"Regardless of what you call yourselves, we have your pictures and you are to come with us."

"Jason...," Belinda called.

"It's alright darling."

But Jason knew it wasn't alright. He took a look at Belinda now dressing. For what they did they would get life imprisonment with no chance of parole. Belinda cowering in the corner of that cabin might be the last time he ever saw her. This wasn't what Jason planned.

* * *

The job of Acting Director of Intelligence wasn't all excitement and glamour. Erin set aside that day to report on last month's budgeted expenses against actual. She wasn't an accounting person, until an email arrived from Superintendent Robson to rescue her from repetitious, almost terminal boredom.

'Agent B87, Singapore Police have taken Jason and Belinda Rogers AKA Luke and Alice Monk into custody pending extradition which our people are working on now. They were signed-on as crew for the APL Phoenix. Regards.'

Erin punched the air with delight before forwarding that email to Nicole. Moment's later: *'Congratulations. My office now.'*

Rebecca gestured for Erin to go straight in where Nicole was at her meeting table. Erin sat opposite.

"Congratulations," Nicole offered again.

"This is down to you, Nicole."

"This is down to you, Erin. You knew when to act, like putting John Connell's family under surveillance, and you knew when to ask for help."

"Did you have contacts?"

"Personally no, but I knew someone in the firm who was able to help. Have you heard about Adam?" Nicole then asked.

"No."

"Apparently he had a date with a girl from university only his wife got wind of it and threw him out. He's renting an apartment while looking for work in Sydney."

Erin understood. "A male, mid-life crisis."

"This explains his thing about the model and her boyfriend."

"I hope Adam didn't cause damage there."

Nicole frowned. "Aged 18 and 26 was an odd relationship."

Erin didn't think so. "Women grow-up faster than men and maybe she's a mature 18. The CCTV showed they worked well together." Erin remembered. "Did you see them talking before she kissed him and took his hand?"

"I remember that. You're right; there's something there."

"Love is love, after all."

"Unless you're a middle-aged man in the same job for several years, and it seems unsatisfied."

Nicole meant sexually. Erin wasn't going to do that to Daniel, because it took two to nurture a relationship and it took two to break it.

"Now important things," Nicole said. "The panel's been formed, the selection criteria we already have, applications will be invited and the rest you know about. The other outstanding issue is the apprehension of Mike Thomas and Jake Tanner."

"We have both under surveillance. Now that Jason and Belinda Rogers are in custody, I can hand Thomas and Tanner over to the AFP."

"Are they in Sydney?"

"Both are in Sydney, Tanner is living with his parents and Thomas is living with his partner. I'll ask Superintendent Robson to plan a raid."

"Tomorrow morning would be preferable."

"I'll suggest tomorrow, because they're under surveillance which makes it easier."

"Given there's no further intelligence to be gathered and given Connell's statement already convicts Thomas and Tanner, the AFP can interview them."

"I'll let Superintendent Robson know."

Nicole sighed. "This has been tragic and heads will roll. Islamic terrorism is still a threat; recent events in France show that, while right-wing terrorism has been overlooked until recently and we're playing catch-up."

"Jason and Belinda Rogers benefited from our campaign against Islamic terrorism, such as knowing to keep their plot offline and also their use of PETN."

"Islamic State's explosive of choice."

Erin shrugged her shoulders. "Is there anything else, Nicole?"

"We should have been looking at the alt-right and nationalists years ago. We're just starting to penetrate their structures and forums now."

"Will you be okay, Nicole?"

"That inaction wasn't my level of delegation."

"I'm glad. Now, I have a superintendent to brief and a budget to report on."

Erin headed to her office to ring Superintendent Robson with good news: the last two arrests to wrap up the assassination of the Prime Minister of Australia.

Chapter Forty Two

They stood side-by side, Asha in a sleeveless tight, white evening dress, plunging between her breasts, virtually backless with the upper of the dress tied around her neck, and slit up the left side to somewhere below her hips, showing her left leg and sandal in a classy way. Sophie was in shimmering blue, like Asha sleeveless and tight although this dress, even though cut low, was not as revealing of Sophie's breasts, and it was slit to show left leg and sandal but not too much. Matt closed wearing a black suit, white shirt, red tie and a relaxed smile.

"It's easy for men," Sophie said. "Suit and tie and you're done."

"You two look beautiful," he said. "You never think that about a man, no matter how he's dressed."

"Men don't know what women think," Asha said. Tall was manly, she loved the colour of his hair and the way he wore it longer, she loved his eyes: big and pale blue, and she loved his kissable lips.

"Alright ladies," Matt said. "Now it's time. Our award is first but after you have to listen to the other awards. There's only one way we can enter."

Matt slipped his hand inside Asha's arm, and his other hand inside Sophie's arm. Through the doors into a semi-darkened hall not that big, with about 50 men and women on chairs at a distance from each other. At the far end of the hall bathed in light was a timber rostrum with a microphone. Out of the corner of her eyes Asha noticed a photographer, well the room was full of photographers, but this female photographer was standing with her camera ready and another woman standing by her side. Matt, Asha and Sophie sat in their allocated chairs which were three abreast but distanced from the other chairs. An older man in a dark suit went to the rostrum; even though he had silver hair he was handsome in his suit. Men didn't know what women thought.

John Watson introduced himself before welcoming all to the 52nd APP Awards, early in a new year that was sure to be better than the year just passed. The first award was for portraiture, which Matt Taylor won with his portrait 'Reconciliation'.

As Matt stood, Asha looked up and gasped. 'Reconciliation' showed on a big screen behind the rostrum, almost larger than life. She followed Sophie to the far end of the room where Matt went to the rostrum while Asha and Sophie stood to one side of their picture.

"I would like to thank Australian Professional Photographers for hosting these awards each year," Matt said. "These awards give us something to strive for. I'm honoured to receive the 2020 portraiture award for 'Reconciliation', which I took during a routine shoot when one of my models, Sophie Weaver, came up with the idea. My role was easy; I posed two models using Sophie's idea and I took the picture you can see behind us. Sophie is a young model from Wagga Wagga and I would like her to tell you how this picture came about, and also Asha Reid, who is Wiradjuri from Cootamundra and is currently the face of Canberra. Sophie."

Sophie strode forward. "I would like to thank Matt Taylor for his guidance during our shoot and for listening to my idea, and I would like to thank Jenny Mason for her help for this evening. I know Australia is trying hard to heal and this is why I asked to pose with Asha. I felt that if one person who hasn't yet realised the need for reconciliation, but sees our picture of white and indigenous together and that makes them think; we will have done a service to Australia. Thank you and now Asha Reid will speak."

Asha went forward to look to many pairs of eyes watching her. "Like Sophie, I would like to thank Matt Taylor and Jenny Mason for all they have done for me in the short time I've been modelling. To me, 'Reconciliation' tells the story of what was once our land, shared with people who have come to our shores in more recent times, and with who I sense a genuine striving for equality between us who are First Nations and those whose ancestry is more recent. Thank you."

Asha stepped back for silver-haired John Watson to go to the rostrum.

"Do any of you have questions for Matt, Sophie or Asha?" he asked.

The woman standing beside the photographer with the camera put her hand up.

"Asha, did you have problems posing topless?"

Asha went to the microphone. "First Nations women were topless for many tens of thousands of years."

"Sophie, did you have problems posing topless?"

Sophie went to the microphone. "Reconciliation is white meeting indigenous part-way. By posing topless, I'm meeting First Nations in the way they dress."

"You thought it was symbolic?"

"Yes I did."

"Asha, not all First Nations people would sense equality."

Asha removed the political comments from her speech but that question was political. She remembered what she originally wrote as she went to the microphone. "In the distant past our people loved their families, they sought love as we do now, and they had purpose in their lives, being custodians of the land and taking from the land only what was necessary to survive. Since then many of our people have lost access to the land they once nurtured, and instead congregate in towns or settlements near to their former homelands, where there's little or even no purpose in their lives. Simply, there are too few jobs or other forms of gainful employment in these towns and settlements. This lack of purpose has led to decades of self-destructive behaviour resulting in many gaps that need to be closed. If Australia wants to close these gaps, you now know what needs to be done."

"What makes you different?"

Asha thought through an answer while realising 50 or more waited. "Unlike remote towns and settlements in the outback, my hometown of Cootamundra has provided opportunities for my family. My personal opportunity is my career as a model."

"I understand. Thank you Asha."

"Are there any other questions for Matt, Sophie or Asha? No? The next award is for landscape...."

While that was announced, Matt escorted Sophie and Asha to their chairs. Asha noticed the photographer with the camera, and the woman who asked the questions, leaving the room, which was the coverage Jenny promised. Asha wondered where pictures taken and speeches recorded, and especially their answers to those questions which were like models being interviewed, would be published. Vogue Australia of course.

"Why are you smiling so brightly?" Matt whispered.

"I'm happy," Asha whispered back as someone gave their acceptance speech for the best landscape; outback desert now shown on the big screen.

Asha took Matt's hand and held it tight. She loved him, every part of him. How he loved her, how he respected her differences, his talent like the pose he designed for 'Reconciliation', how he made her feel calm and settled just by holding his hand; everything. Life was unpredictable and at times even tough, but for Asha, life was sweet.

Chapter Forty Three

That downhill path was challenging enough, let alone with trees and shrubs making it single file. Erin trailed last but one of the paying customers, with Daniel behind and Mick, the second guide, at the rear. There was an art to horse riding even on docile horses, especially on challenging, narrow, downhill paths. Erin hoped Daniel was enjoying this part of their holiday; a special treat after a good start to the year. It was brighter ahead where forest changed to alpine grasslands. Daniel rode alongside.

"How are you?" Erin asked.

"I'm fine," Daniel said. "I'm enjoying your part of our holiday. I know you are."

"When we're young, we girls have a thing about horses."

"And to be models when you get older."

"That too. I'm 167 centimetres which I thought was close enough, but 170 was the minimum, and better if you're taller."

"Like the model at the War Memorial."

"You know Adam tried to break them up. I hope they're alright."

"They're alright," Daniel said. "The photographer, Matt Taylor, won an award for a picture he took of the indigenous model and a white model, topless straddling a fallen tree, facing each other and holding hands. They had pictures of

Matt Taylor, his girlfriend and model Asha Reid, and the white model Sophie Weaver."

"That's good," Erin said. "That's a remarkable concept," she realised.

"Asha Reid and Sophie Weaver gave speeches and were interviewed, which was interesting."

"You can see why a girl would want to be a model."

"Newspaper and magazine articles at that age, while dressed in hideously expensive evening gowns, free of charge it seems. Not to mention that picture, amazing!"

"You're a man."

"Yes I am."

Silly. "Would a 26 year old guy be okay with an 18 year old girlfriend?"

Daniel frowned. "There's 18 and there's 18, so if she's grown-up 18 and willing to stretch herself, I think so."

As they rode across that pasture of scrubby grass, Erin felt nicely satisfied for some reason.

"Do you think we'll ever forget 2020?" Daniel asked.

"Never! Catastrophic fires, terrible loss of life, blanketed in toxic smoke for weeks and weeks, and then a pandemic! We were getting over that, unlike many countries, when Prime Minister Devi was assassinated. I feel terrible that happened, especially for her husband and children, and for the press and others senselessly slaughtered, and their families and loved-ones too."

"At least we caught and charged the perpetrators."

"This year 2021 has started well, with all perpetrators charged and me interviewing well enough to be appointed permanent Director of Intelligence."

"What's it like reporting directly to Nicole."

"In a word, Nicole's magic. She doesn't waste time on meetings that go on and on, just a once a week catch-up to plan the coming week. She lets you get on with things, expects to be kept in the loop of course, and she's always available for help when you need her. Once I asked her for help and later she thanked me."

"That sounds like magic."

"I'm really comfortable with the way things turned out."

"Happy?"

"Yeah."

Happy didn't begin to describe it. Horseback riding across alpine grasslands on their first day of three days and four nights, followed by five nights in a luxury villa in Jindabyne, which was Daniel's treat. Promotion beyond her expectations but which Erin felt more than comfortable with, and love. Daniel by her side, agreeing with her horseback safari idea, showed how much he loved her. For sure life was good, as they rode their horses across the roof of Australia on a cool, fine, summer's day.